SUNS OF THE ARANOL

OBSIDIAR FLEET BOOK 5

ANTHONY JAMES

IX-GASTIOL

The Vraxar capital ship *Ix-Gastiol* was like nothing seen before in Confederation space. In terms of size alone it was incredible - larger even than *Ix-Gorghal*. It measured seven hundred kilometres from end to end. The distance from its underside to the top part of the upper section was nearly three hundred kilometres and almost the same again from portside to starboard.

Where *Ix-Gorghal* had been ovoid, *Ix-Gastiol* was not. Its outline was cuboid in the very loosest sense, yet in reality, there was no single word capable of describing it accurately. It flew through space, the blackness of its hull rendering it near-invisible against the background. Here and there, dark sparks of energy jagged from place to place, appearing and disappearing with an infuriating randomness which hinted at an underlying pattern, though one which defied the eye to identify it.

The spaceship wasn't travelling at lightspeed. Instead, it relied on gravity engines to complete this final section of its journey. A sun lay directly ahead and the Vraxar ship forged on, entering the searing heat of the corona. Any spaceship without an energy shield would have burned up in moments and even the most powerful energy shield on a Space Corps vessel would have been drained by the million-degree temperatures. Not *Ix-Gastiol*'s. It sped ever closer to the sun's chromosphere, where the heat was a rather more amenable six thousand degrees Centigrade.

There was no sign the mighty vessel was troubled by the roiling gasses and it maintained an exact speed, appearing as a pin-prick speck of darkness against the majesty of light. Just when it appeared as though *Ix-Gastiol* would plunge into the surface of the sun, it levelled out at an altitude of five hundred kilometres, where the photosphere and chromosphere met.

For a few hours, the Vraxar ship coasted at the same altitude and speed, with an occasional variance in its trajectory, as though it were searching for something. After completing three full orbits of the sun, *Ix-Gastiol* came to an abrupt halt. It waited in place for several hours, moving not at all.

After a time, a solar flare formed on the surface directly below, producing a huge area of even greater brightness. Then, a fountain of white-hot plasma ejected, blossoming upwards and outwards for fifty thousand kilometres, with *Ix-Gastiol* in the centre and making no effort to move away.

Slowly, the ejected matter dispersed, leaving the Vraxar spaceship unharmed in the centre. The vessel rotated on the spot and accelerated off on a new course, keeping to the same altitude as before. Something had changed – where previously *Ix-Gastiol*'s outer hull had been marked by dark energy, now there were flashes of dirty blues and greens which played across a series of domes and spheres. These tendrils of energy were weak and sporadic, reaching for only a few hundred metres. Soon, they faded to nothingness, as though something within the vessel was greedily sucking the energy into the centre.

Ix-Gastiol's hunt continued.

CHAPTER ONE

WITH A VIOLENT, shuddering thump, the damaged Hadron battleship *Ulterior-2* entered high lightspeed, leaving New Earth and its people far behind. The spaceship's crew were pensive, each a prisoner to their thoughts.

The Vraxar had arrived into human Confederation space, unwelcome and despised. Every time this hostile species of aliens made an appearance, it was with the intention of bringing endless death and misery. The Vraxar hadn't been given an easy ride and, in fact, had suffered a string of defeats to the combined human and Ghast forces, the most recent being the loss of the immense capital ship *Ix-Gorghal*. None of it seemed to matter and the Vraxar just kept on coming. For the crew of the battleship it was a constant plague on their minds.

"Three days until we rendezvous with the *Maximilian*, sir," said Captain Charlie Blake.

Fleet Admiral Duggan raised his head and nodded in acknowledgement. He was a passenger on this journey and he kept himself to one side of the bridge in order to minimise the distraction to the crew. It would have been better if he remained in his quarters, but he had a need to be here. He rubbed his eyes – it was only seventy-two hours since the destruction of *Ix-Gorghal* and his body was far from recovered. The battlefield adrenaline was a harsh mistress and every boost left the host with days of relentless, debilitating exhaustion and any soldier who pretended it was easily ignored was a liar.

Naturally, there were other drugs to combat the side effects of the battlefield adrenaline, some of which had side effects of their own, which in turn could be countered by more drugs. Duggan was pumped full of so much crap he felt like a stranger in his own body.

"Damn, I feel like shit," he said with a bitter laugh.

"That is because you are far too old to be taking Trygion-893D," said Doctor Flossie Templeton, a member of his personal medical team. They insisted he have someone in attendance at all times.

Templeton was one of the more agreeable doctors, with the kind of dry sense of humour Duggan appreciated. In addition, there was something about her name which he couldn't get over, no matter how often he told himself it wasn't a cause for amusement. Not that he felt like laughing at this particular moment in time.

"I've got another forty-five years left, assuming I hit the average expected lifespan for a Confederation male."

"The standard deviation is nine years, sir," Templeton replied. "And the long-term effects of Trygion-893D are not entirely understood. The battlefield adrenaline is known to affect a number of areas in the human body."

"The last study I was made aware of suggested the adrenaline might actually *extend* life."

"I am familiar with that study, sir."

"Maybe I should take *more* battlefield adrenaline, rather than less?"

Templeton smiled, looking ten years younger. "I'm not going to fall for your games, sir. I'm fully aware of your reluctance when it comes to boosters."

"Or any kind of medical assistance," chimed in Lieutenant Caz Pointer. "I read that in a book."

Duggan scratched his head, wondering if his wife had been having a word with the crew. "If there was time to sleep, I would gladly rely on it as my sole method of recovery. You'll be aware, Doctor Templeton, that I require at least four days of bed rest and you'll be equally aware that I can't permit myself to be unavailable for so long."

Templeton was distinctly unabashed. "I am giving you my professional opinion."

"I understand," said Duggan, still unsure exactly what she was trying to tell him.

"What happens when we rendezvous with the *Maximilian*, sir?" asked Blake.

"That entirely depends on what happens during the next three days it takes us to reach them. I hope to make some decisions before we arrive." Duggan did his best to suppress a heavy sigh. "In reality, we're at the mercy of events. *Ix-Gastiol* could appear anywhere and at any time."

"Do you think the Vraxar know how we defeated *Ix-Gorghal*?"

"I doubt they have more than guesswork, and I'm sure they'd be very interested in the truth."

"Interested enough to come to New Earth for a second time?" asked Blake.

Duggan felt his stomach clench at this unintentional reminder of his flight. He felt like the most abject sort of coward to be leaving the people of New Earth behind, effectively unde-fended from whatever the Vraxar might send.

For all his comparative youth, Blake wasn't lacking in percep-tion. "Sorry. I didn't mean it that way."

"I can see no alternative," said Duggan. "The people of New Earth are best served if the Space Corps' officers are able to operate without risk of being easily killed by an unexpected orbital attack."

The words sounded glib and he felt dirty saying them. His wife was rather less emotional than he was when it came to making the hard choices and she'd tried her best to make Duggan understand he was doing the right thing. In reality, the decision wasn't entirely his to make – the Confederation Council had made it quite clear what they expected from him.

"There's no such thing as a lose-lose situation," said Lieu-tenant Dixie Hawkins, as if she'd been reading his mind.

"If I'm so obvious to my officers, perhaps I should try harder to keep my thoughts hidden," said Duggan.

"You've made the best choice, sir, if you don't mind me saying it," said Hawkins. She ploughed on. "The Vraxar could have shown up anywhere – it simply happened that they turned up at New Earth. If they'd arrived at Overtide or Prime and you'd been safe and sound on Tucson, it would have still been the right thing for you to go to the *Maximilian*."

Duggan had no argument to present and he wasn't a man to get angry at advice honestly offered from his officers. He'd come to terms with the fact that no amount of words were going to assuage his guilt. The next step was to achieve a state of accep-tance so that he could get on with business free from the chains. He looked at his wrist for the watch that wasn't there, before checking the bridge clock.

"I have a meeting with my staff," he said, pushing himself upright with a wince.

With Templeton following at an indiscreet distance, Duggan exited the bridge and made his way towards one of the few open spaces on the *Ulterior-2*. The mess hall was a popular gathering place for a warship's soldiers and it was busy with men and women. They laughed and joked as if they didn't have a single worry. The carefree chatter made Duggan feel a pang of jealousy that he couldn't take part in the camaraderie, even for a short while.

The few members of his staff were at a table in one corner. The space around them was empty as though an exclusion zone had formed naturally to afford them some privacy to speak.

Lieutenant Charissa Paz was the first to see Duggan and she stood, waving with exaggerated enthusiasm.

"We got you a coffee, sir."

Templeton tutted loudly at this revelation. Duggan pretended he hadn't heard and made his way across the room, through the narrow aisles between the fixed metal seats. Secretly, he was grateful Paz had got him the forbidden drink, since it saved him from the guilt of having to make the decision himself.

"Good afternoon," he said, taking a seat. Templeton remained standing a few paces away and watched disapprovingly as Duggan took a sip from the steaming metal cup.

"Are you sure it's wise to meet here?" asked Lieutenant Joe Doyle, looking around the room as if he expected each and every soldier to be taking notes.

"No one is listening, Lieutenant. They have better things to do with their time."

Doyle wasn't convinced – he'd always been the suspicious one on the team and he continued watching out for eavesdroppers. Duggan wasn't in the least bit concerned – there was far too much background noise for anyone to listen in. He got started.

"As you're aware, I'm relocating to the ES *Maximilian* and will remain onboard until our conflict with the Vraxar is resolved for better or worse. I have ordered a number of my admirals onto fleet warships, where they are to stay until told otherwise. We've already lost Admirals Judd and Caskey on Tucson – I can't risk losing any more of my top officers."

"What about the Confederation Council, sir?" asked Lieutenant Allison Jacobs.

Duggan gave a half-smile. "They are keeping their feet on the ground." He let that one hang in the air.

"What?" asked Jacobs. "All of them?"

"Yes, all of them. There wasn't a dissenting voice to be heard. Or so I've been told."

"When did they suddenly get brave?" asked Doyle.

The Confederation Council had their failings – numerous failings – but for once they were getting their act together and Duggan had no intention of criticising them for it. "They want the best for the Confederation," he said simply.

"Yet they've ordered you to run into space, sir."

"It's not running, Lieutenant," said Duggan sharply. "You know I don't like this and I'd be grateful if you didn't bring it up again. If I'd wanted to, I could have defied their recommendations, yet I chose otherwise."

The realisation he'd suggested his superior officer was taking the coward's route sank into Doyle. "I didn't mean it that way..."

"Enough! What's done is done and I won't change my mind. The Vraxar wage a mobile war and it's time we adapted our own strategies to match. Now let us get on with the business at hand!"

"I'm not exactly sure what we can accomplish until we reach the *Maximilian*, sir," said Paz quietly.

"You're amongst the finest minds in the Confederation! What we need are ideas!" Duggan's voice climbed and he reined it in with an effort. "*Ix-Gorghal* is defeated, yet victory eludes us. We do not even know if *Ix-Gastiol* represents the last threat from the Vraxar!" He fixed his gaze on one member of the group who had remained silent so far. "Research Lead Norris? Have you anything to divulge?"

RL Marion Norris was a member of the Projections Team and with a brain which could divine likelihoods from pure, random chaos. She smiled nervously at Duggan. "*Ix-Gastiol* is the key, sir. The longer it remains active, the greater the chance humanity will fall to the Vraxar."

Doyle snorted, not unkindly. "It doesn't take much to realise the truth of that, RL Norris."

Duggan identified a subtlety in Norris's words. "There's more to it than the simple destruction of *Ix-Gastiol*?" he asked.

Norris shrugged. "I can't be sure, sir. I see a series of numbers in my head which suggest an ever-increasing chance we will fall to the enemy."

"Are these numbers consistent with a one-by-one attack on our planets?" asked Paz.

"Maybe. I just don't get that feeling," said Norris. "It's the key," she repeated.

Duggan sat back in thought. He was quickly learning that Marion Norris was one of his most valuable assets when it came to obtaining insights on the Vraxar. The fact of her uncertainty made him concerned that the enemy were doing something completely unforeseen – something entirely off his radar. He didn't like the idea one little bit.

"We're in the same position as we were before *Ix-Gorghal* came to New Earth," he said. "There's an inevitability about everything, yet no way to predict where they will strike next."

"I can't be any help this time," said Norris. "I haven't seen anything that tells me what the Vraxar intend."

"If we relied on prescience alone, then the magnitude of our failure to prepare would be a shame to the Space Corps," said

Duggan. "In this we must rely on our scouts and our monitoring stations to give us advance warning." He thumped the solid table top in irritation. "The failure is also mine! I could have prepared us better for different kinds of warfare. I fought the Ghasts for so long it has left me blinkered."

"What else could you have done?" asked Paz. "You are human, the same as the rest of us. We need places to live and we call our planets home."

"I am meant to see beyond the usual, Lieutenant. We could have built more interstellar craft, pushed our frontiers outwards until we were as numerous as the Estral!"

"None of which we did, sir," said Paz.

"And the Estral did not destroy *Ix-Gorghal* – it was the Confederation which pulled that one off," added Doyle. "When our backs are to the wall, there's no species fights harder than us."

There was truth in the man's words and fire in his eyes. Duggan took heart from Doyle's fervour and asked himself how much the cocktail of drugs in his body was dragging down his outlook. He'd always considered himself a realist rather than a pessimist.

"Well, Lieutenant, our backs are most definitely hard against the wall, so let's see if we can surprise those Vraxar bastards for a second time. I will learn to accept that I can only react to *Ix-Gastiol* and I will do everything I can to guess at every likely eventuality in order to give us a fighting chance."

Duggan steepled his fingers in front of his face, realising too late it was the same mannerism used by Malachi Teron, a figure from his dim and distant past.

"Tell us your thoughts, sir, and we'll see what we can do to refine them into something we can act upon," said Jacobs.

"Admiral Morey could be a problem," said Duggan. "I've replaced her with Admiral Henry Talley as my second-in-command, but this isn't the best time to deal with her properly. She has friends and I don't wish to be undermined."

"Not so many friends, sir," said Jacobs. She was Duggan's chief intelligence officer and it was her job to know.

"Enough to keep her shielded from the fallout. I am not a vindictive man. However, what Morey did deserves punishment and I will see that she gets it in due course. For the moment, I don't wish to go through the process when there's a war to fight."

"You could suspend her from duties, pending investigation," said Paz. "You have the authority."

"It will eventually come to a suspension, I'm sure. As it stands, she is no longer in a position where she can jeopardise so many people so easily. Lieutenant Jacobs is having her watched closely."

"Using good people who would be better placed elsewhere," confirmed Jacobs.

"Which brings us to Last Stand," said Duggan.

"There's news on the protocols?" asked Doyle.

"Councillors Stahl, Ellerson, Newport and Watanabe have agreed to share the burden, along with myself. A trigger event requires the codes from four of us, and the bombs are currently being reprogrammed to prevent an unintended detonation."

"How long until the new receivers are retrofitted?" asked Paz.

"There are only three factories capable of producing the new comms units and it's not as if we have a production line set up yet. It'll require ten days for the final units to be made, taken to their destinations and installed."

"And after that we can initiate a detonation via any of the deep space monitoring stations," said Jacobs.

"Does Admiral Talley have the codes, sir? If something were to happen to you, there would be no Space Corps involvement in the final decision."

"Henry has the codes," said Duggan. Talley was a good man

and, in many ways, Duggan was relieved to be given this opportunity to promote him to second-in-command.

"You'll both be on the *Maximilian*," said Paz flatly. "That's not how redundancy works."

Duggan chuckled inwardly at the blunt words. "I'm aware of the conflict, Lieutenant Paz. You remember I'm leaving New Earth precisely because I wish to stay out of trouble. The *Maximilian* will act as mobile command and control – nothing more."

"I'm not sure that choice will always be yours to make, sir," she said.

"Nevertheless, we will not pursue this topic any further. On the subject of Last Stand, I am content that the ultimate decision is in the right hands."

"If – when – *Ix-Gastiol* shows up in planetary orbit, is that a trigger moment?" asked Jacobs.

"We will see, Lieutenant. There are times when it's wise not to think about the worst possible outcome until it's unavoidable. I am aware the choice may well be forced upon me, as are the four councillors. Let us leave it at that."

None of the others pressed the matter, grateful they weren't holding the codes for the Obsidiar bombs hidden on each Confederation world.

Paz sighed noisily. "Give us three years and our fleet, combined with that of the Ghasts, would have enough new warships to give *Ix-Gastiol* a run for its money. In five years, we'd blow the crap out of whatever else the Vraxar have left."

"We believe the enemy still possesses thousands of warships," said Norris. "They are simply not in Confederation Space."

"In the forty years it would take them to get here by light-speed travel, we could be facing them with a fleet five times bigger and with ten times the motivation."

"Let's not play at what ifs," said Duggan. "In the here and

now we have *Ix-Gastiol*. If we manage to pull off another victory I can begin planning for the future."

The meeting continued for another hour, during which the mess hall filled up, emptied and then filled up again. Duggan got something to eat from the replicator and couldn't remember what it was once his tray was clear. With the *Ulterior-2* at lightspeed, he was cut off from the rest of the fleet and reliant on these few members of his team to help his thought processes. There were numerous breaks planned for the journey, during which he'd have the opportunity to speak to his senior officers throughout the Space Corps. For a man who was used to having immediate access to everything, it was frustrating.

When the meeting ended, with little accomplished, Duggan headed to his suite of two rooms. His wife was elsewhere. *McGlashan,* he thought. It was decades ago they'd been married, yet he still sometimes thought of her as Commander McGlashan.

"I'm getting sentimental," he muttered. It was an increasingly familiar refrain.

He picked up a book, lay back on the pristine white sheets covering the meagre foam mattress and tried to calm himself by reading. It was no good – the pleasures of the written word had always eluded him. He tossed the book to one side and closed his eyes to rest them. He woke up some hours later, feeling not at all refreshed, and headed off towards the bridge, where he found everything more or less as it had been when he left it, with the exception of the two ensigns who were away on their scheduled break.

"Welcome back, sir," said Blake.

"Sixty-two hours until rendezvous," added Lieutenant Quinn helpfully. "Including three scheduled entries into local space of fifteen minutes each."

"Another long trip," said Duggan.

"They're all long when you're in the middle of them," said

Hawkins. "When you look back upon this one, you'll wonder where the time went."

"The passing of time is both a blessing and a curse, Lieutenant."

He knew the truth of Hawkins' words through many years of experience and he settled himself in for the longest sixty-two hours of his life.

CHAPTER TWO

"THERE'S THE *MAXIMILIAN*, SIR," said Lieutenant Maria Cruz. "It's just coming up on the bulkhead screen."

"It's a beautiful ship," said Blake.

"Always has been and always will be," said Duggan.

The Hadron *Maximilian* had been in service for as long as Duggan had been in the Space Corps. He remembered it from the Ghast wars, and from each exercise it had taken part in since. It was a fraction shorter than the *Ulterior-2* and more of a wedge shape. The *Maximilian* didn't so much look intimidating, rather there was something timeless about it, as if it could feasibly be in active service a thousand years from now and still be capable of inspiring awe.

The original Hadron Ulterior had been destroyed long ago, along with the *Precept* and the *Lancer*. There were other Hadrons in the fleet to replace them, yet these new models lacked the pure, clean lines of their predecessors. Duggan couldn't quite put his finger on why he felt this way; all he knew was that the sight of the *Maximilian* still had the power to fill him with wonder at the feats of humanity. Admiral Talley's usual ship

Devastator was another warship built from the same plans and the two battleships remained the pride of the fleet, even if their hulls were far from the newest. Talley was no longer onboard the *Devastator*...

"They're hailing us," said Cruz. "Admiral Talley sends his greetings and advises there is nothing new to report."

Duggan laughed. "Henry knows me too well. That would have been my first question."

"The *Maximilian* will hold position until we're within shuttle range."

"I'm bringing us around," said Blake. "Shouldn't take long until we're close enough."

Under Blake's control, the *Ulterior-2* accelerated hard. The second Hadron wavered on the sensor feed, still a long way distant. The crew kept their eyes fixed on it, taking in the details as the *Ulterior-2*'s sensors gradually sharpened the image.

"What did the *Archimedes* look like?" asked Pointer suddenly. "In the flesh, I mean."

"A bigger version of the same thing," said Duggan. "For some reason it wasn't so kind on the eye. Or maybe that's because of the memories."

"Memories?" asked Pointer.

"A man who hated me." He didn't elaborate.

"It would be good to have the *Archimedes* in the fleet again," said Blake. "It would have made an excellent platform for every new weapon we could come up with."

Duggan's voice was distant. "We should never have broken it up and we should have finished work on the *Aristotle*. I didn't have a say in the matter and by the time I did, they were gone for good."

"Could they be rebuilt?"

"Now, perhaps. Back then, the Confederation Council would never have approved the replacement hulls, given that they were the ones who applied the pressure to have the originals dismantled. They would have looked foolish in the extreme."

"Politics," said Blake.

"It's a part of life, Captain. I accept that in normal circumstances there is more to humanity's existence than war."

"This is the second time we've been pushed to the brink, sir."

"Keep that thought in your head, Captain Blake. If you ever find yourself in a position where you hold some sway over the direction of the Space Corps, remember it when you're asked to justify your budget. Don't give anyone an easy ride. I have every reason to believe that if we beat the Vraxar, there will be other wars to fight and I also believe that each of these wars will have the potential to bring us to the same position again."

"I won't forget. This means everything to me."

"That's the attitude we need in order to win, Captain. I include your crew in this as well."

"Thank you, sir."

"Don't thank me," said Duggan sadly.

Blake looked puzzled.

"He means we're going to be given all the shit jobs, sir," said Lieutenant Hawkins. "We're the best, so we get to dance with the Vraxar wherever they pop up."

"Lieutenant Hawkins, you remind me of a comms officer I once worked with," said Duggan.

"I'll assume that's a compliment."

"It is." Duggan rolled his shoulders, pleased to discover his body almost recovered from the beating it had taken in the aftermath of the attack on New Earth. "I'll be leaving in Shuttle One as soon as we close to within twenty thousand klicks of the *Maximilian*."

"You should go there now, sir," said Blake.

"Very well. Do I need to repeat your orders?"

"No, sir. The *Ulterior-2* is to remain with the *Maximilian* until we receive instructions to head towards Pioneer where we will undergo an emergency refit and repair."

The *Ulterior-2* was badly damaged from its engagement with *Ix-Gorghal*. The Tucson base had been almost wiped out by the Vraxar, but there were enough personnel and equipment remaining to complete some basic patching up. If the Hadron was to be any use in the future, it would need a more comprehensive programme of repairs. Luckily, its twin Obsidiar cores were still operational, so the battleship's energy shield would be enough to protect it against most smaller vessels. There wasn't time for spit and polish – the Hadron would spend ten days in the dock and be fixed up as much as possible.

With Duggan and his medical officer gone from the bridge, Pointer used the internal comms to ensure the remainder of his staff got the message it was time to depart. Admiral Colton Gillespie was still in the medical bay, having been brought up from Retulon base – he would need a large team to get him off the *Ulterior-2*.

With the death or incapacitation of the three admirals stationed on New Earth, Duggan was left to rely almost entirely on his personal team until he could get settled on the *Maximilian*. The Vraxar had done a good job of killing off the majority of the most senior officers in their recent attack, seemingly through luck rather than intention.

"That's twenty thousand klicks between us and the *Maximilian*, sir," said Lieutenant Quinn.

"I'm bringing us to a stop," said Blake. "Nineteen thousand klicks it is. Lieutenant Pointer, please advise Fleet Admiral Duggan that he is free to go when ready."

"Will do, sir. The internal sensors indicate he's still a few minutes from the shuttle bay. They're already moving Admiral Gillespie."

Thirty minutes later, Shuttle One left the docking bay and

sailed out into space towards the *Maximilian*. The closer it came to the Hadron, the smaller it appeared, until it was eventually little more than a moving dot against the silver-grey flank of the battleship. Pointer zoomed the sensors in and the crew watched the shuttle enter the docking bay of the distant spaceship.

"Please confirm success," said Blake.

"Shuttle One is safely docked," said Cruz.

"Bring it back on autopilot when the passengers have disembarked."

"Yes, sir. I've sent the instruction and the shuttle will return as soon as ready."

The minutes ticked by and Blake clenched his jaw, wishing to be on his way.

"What're we expected to do for the ten days the *Ulterior-2* is in the dock?" asked Hawkins. "I'm getting frustrated just waiting for a shuttle."

"I think it's getting to us all," said Cruz. "There's no break from the pressure."

"I don't mind the pressure," Blake replied. "I don't know exactly why I'm feeling so pissed off. We pulled off a good victory against *Ix-Gorghal* and I still feel like we lost. If we manage to blow the crap out of *Ix-Gastiol*, I worry that I might feel the same."

Hawkins gave one of her husky laughs. "If we destroy *Ix-Gastiol*, that leaves the rest of the Vraxar fleet stranded in Estral space. It buys us a lot of time and they may not bother with us in future.

"Yeah, they could go straight for the Antaron," said Pointer.

"Except we could have left them so weakened they have no choice but to come for us. They were after bodies on New Earth and if those satellites had remained operational for another few hours, there would have been plenty of corpses to choose from."

Cruz interrupted. "Shuttle One is starting its return flight."

"Contact the *Maximilian* and check for an update to our orders, please."

"On it."

Cruz had a short conversation with one of her opposite numbers.

"Admiral Duggan thanks us for the lift and asks that we make fastest speed for Pioneer."

"That's what I wanted to hear."

The *Ulterior-2* couldn't depart until its shuttle returned. Shuttle One was amongst the faster models in the Corps, yet it crossed the intervening space with agonising slowness.

"Come on," said Blake softly.

In spite of his perception to the contrary, the returning craft took only a few minutes to dock in the *Ulterior-2*'s bay. As soon as green lights came up on the gravity clamps, Blake gave the order.

"Take us to Pioneer, Lieutenant Quinn."

"Aye, sir. Pioneer it is."

The *Ulterior-2* was equipped with a cluster of latest-gen Obsidiar processing units and they made short work of the light-speed calculations. With a shuddering indicative of the unre-paired damage, the battleship's engines fired it away from the *Maximilian*. Usually, things would have smoothed out after the transition, but the floor and walls continued to judder faintly.

"Twenty hours to Pioneer," said Quinn. "Ten days isn't nearly enough to finish the repairs."

"Don't be too sure," said Blake.

"I know they've got the experience, but..."

"My grandfather worked in the shipyards of Miol-3 during the Ghast wars," said Blake, his eyes faraway. "He was part of the team working on the new Hadrons. I remember he told me how one of the yards on Prime laid down an Anderlecht hull on exactly the same day as Miol-3 began work on the *Precept*."

"They finished the *Precept* first?" asked Quinn, his eyes wide.

"Not quite, Lieutenant, but there was only a week in it. Imagine that – they finished a thirty billion tonne battleship in almost the same amount of time as it took the yard on Prime to build a light cruiser. The shipyards on Pioneer have always been the best."

"Which yard is dealing with our repairs?" asked Pointer.

Blake smiled. "We'll be docking at Miol-3, Lieutenant, so we'll be in the most capable of hands."

They completed the journey with only a single entry into local space. There was no significant news, so Blake ordered the battleship into lightspeed once more. To his surprise, the journey passed quickly, which he put down to his distraction. The Vraxar were proving to be difficult to outguess, though it didn't stop him trying whenever he found himself with a spare moment. The crew noticed, but didn't comment.

"We'll enter Pioneer local space in two minutes," said Quinn.

"I want full alert when we arrive, everyone. Assume we're arriving into a combat situation."

No one asked for confirmation. *Ix-Gastiol* could be anywhere and they didn't want to stumble into it without warning. The *Ulterior-2*'s fission drive grumbled and the switchover to the gravity drive wasn't smooth.

"We are now in the Laspan solar system," said Quinn. "Activating stealth modules. Energy shield online."

"Commencing scans," said Pointer. "Nothing on the nears. Beginning the fars and supers."

"I've got inbound comms from the surface," said Cruz, breathing a sigh of relief. "Colonel Maurice Watson wishes us a good morning and asks to speak to the captain of the battleship *Ulterior-2*."

"Bring him through," said Blake. The tone of the greeting indicated all was well on Pioneer and he felt the tension drain from his shoulders and neck.

"Captain Blake," drawled Colonel Watson. "Welcome to Pioneer."

"Me or the ship, Colonel?"

Watson gave a gravelly laugh. "A bit of both. You've got clearance for an emergency landing – you can come in as quick as the autopilot will allow, without concern you're going to run into anything taking off."

"Glad to hear it. Are the repair teams ready?"

"I've got eight thousand men, women and machines waiting to bust a gut. I've told them I want the *Ulterior*-2 at 98% inside ten days. I've bet a week's wages with a man I know on Old Earth we can do it."

"Thank you, Colonel. I appreciate your efforts and your confidence."

"You can buy me a drink when we're done."

The conversation finished and Blake closed the connection.

"I think I like Colonel Watson," he said.

"The man sounds driven," said Pointer. "Like he has something to prove."

"That's fine by me, Lieutenant. Activating autopilot, emergency landing routine."

It required high-level clearance for an emergency landing, since it could bring an entire base to a standstill and potentially interrupt critical work. Blake was happy to find Colonel Watson was proactive enough to have put the wheels in motion.

With the emergency routine activated, the *Ulterior*-2 accelerated to the highest speed its onboard computers believed the damaged engines were capable of, which in this case was hardly diminished from its maximum. The battleship took a dead-straight line, aiming directly at the second of Pioneer's three major land masses.

"Not a bad view," said Cruz. "Check out the screen."

Blake raised his head to see. The battleship's angle of approach showed the most perfect view of Pioneer. The planet itself was fairly arid, and the almost pastel yellows of its sands contrasted against the solid greens and blues of sea, forest and cultivated land. To the upper left of the display, the planet's two moons were visible, one a deep red and the other an ethereal white. The far sun Laspan shone directly between them, its beams of light refracting through the scant atmospheres of the moons and showing up on the Hadron's sensors as shards of many colours.

The view didn't last. The battleship's punishing speed carried it onwards, until the further of the two moons was hidden behind the closer, and Laspan itself no longer shone so beautifully.

"There's a total of twenty-six fleet warships in close proximity to Pioneer or one of its moons," said Cruz. "It's the heavy stuff as well – only five of them are destroyers."

"It's still too few."

"I can see Miol-3," said Pointer. "All by itself in the desert."

"The base used to be home to a monitoring array," said Blake. "The clear air makes it a good place."

Quinn was busy checking out a triangular arrangement of three dome-shaped buildings. "It looks as if they're still operational."

"I'm not sure what they're used for, Lieutenant. Everything important is up in space these days."

"Except our people."

"Maybe in a hundred years we'll be living on interstellars, safe from aggressors. Until then, we shouldn't worry about the things we can't change."

"Eight docking trenches," said Cruz. "I'm impressed."

"What've they got in them?"

"One Hadron, three Galactics and two other hulls which

look a bit like the Earth's Fury. They don't even have the barrels in place."

"I guess they don't build the little stuff in places like Miol-3, huh?" asked Quinn.

"They've cut back on production of the Crimson class, Lieutenant. The Space Corps wants warships it can fit out with every new weapon currently in development, and that means bigger hulls with Obsidiar cores."

"Any hints as to what those weapons are, sir?" asked Hawkins innocently.

"If I knew, I would tell you. I believe incendiaries and shield disruptors are the current priorities, though I don't know what's coming first. I should imagine weapons research is an interesting line of work at this current point in time."

The *Ulterior-2*'s autopilot slowed the vessel to prevent burn up in Pioneer's oxygen-rich atmosphere. At an altitude of one hundred kilometres, it began the final rotation to orient the battleship with the assigned repair trench on the base. The Hadron's advanced sensors showed work at a standstill on the directly adjacent docks, whilst everything continued apace on the others.

"So much for stopping construction," said Pointer.

"The risks are small, Lieutenant. Sometimes it's best to sidestep procedure."

The battleship descended at a tremendous rate, pushing through the air above the Miol-3 base. On the ground, thousands of faces looked upwards to the sky, watching the dark dot grow larger against the clear desert skies. To an inexperienced crew member, a crash would have seemed inevitable. At the last possible moment, the *Ulterior-2*'s autopilot system slowed the colossally heavy spaceship and placed it precisely in the centre of Trench Five.

"Well, folks, that's another safe landing," said Blake.

Cruz had her eyes fixed to the external feeds. "Here come the repair robots. These guys don't stick around."

The space surrounding the Hadron was soon crowded with heavy lifter shuttles and alloy-cutter robots. Mobile gravity cranes moved in from every direction, and Blake could also make out two of the largest gravity crawlers he'd ever seen, each carrying a premade section of engine and plating, ready to drop into place.

"I think Colonel Watson's wages are safe," said Quinn. "We'll be at 98% in eight days if this is anything to go by."

Blake didn't respond – in spite of Quinn's sudden confidence, he knew it was going to be a tall order for Watson to win his bet.

"What now?" asked Cruz.

"Grab yourself a coffee, Lieutenant. The *Ulterior-2* is on the ground and its crew will be way down on the priorities list."

Pointer blinked. "We're going to be left here?"

"Don't be surprised if we are. I checked the Space Corps database and there isn't a single warship nearby that needs a captain or crew. Fleet Admiral Duggan wants us on the *Ulterior-2* and I reckon this is where we're staying."

"For ten whole days?" asked Hawkins. "I was hoping to stretch my legs."

"I thought we were going to get falling-down drunk," said Cruz.

"Not anymore, I'm afraid."

In truth, not one of the crew had any particular ties to Pioneer except for Blake. They weren't required to stay aboard, but there was nothing to disembark for other than to take a look around. The *Ulterior-2* was carrying far more than its usual complement of troops and Blake arranged for the soldiers to exit the ship in small groups, with the understanding they didn't do anything stupid that might prevent their immediate return if required.

As he settled down for several days of tedium, Blake was

struck by an inescapable sense that something bad was going to happen. He didn't try to shrug the feeling off and he didn't speak of it to the others. With each passing minute, his disquiet grew.

The other members of the crew felt his unspoken tension and it started getting to them. They kept to their stations as if they expected *Ix-Gastiol* to emerge into a low orbit at any moment.

"Permission to stand down, sir?" asked Hawkins in exasperation.

"What do you mean? We're docked."

"You're like a coiled spring. Something's getting to you."

Blake sighed. "Correct as ever, Lieutenant. I'm damned if I know what it is. There's something gnawing at me and I'm worried."

He didn't have to wait long to find out the answer.

"Sir?" said Cruz, her dark hair shading her eyes and disguising the extent of her fear. "You need to see this."

Blake was absolutely certain that in this instance he absolutely did *not* want to see whatever it was his comms lieutenant had found. He had no choice in the matter and his feet carried him over.

"See this?" asked Cruz, one slender finger indicating an area of the upper sensor feed.

Blake squinted. "Oh, crap," he said.

CHAPTER THREE

IN SPITE of his fond memories, Fleet Admiral Duggan had never spent an extended period on the *ES Maximilian*. Even so, it felt like a homecoming when he made his way from the shuttle bay to the bridge. Everything about the battleship felt familiar to him, down to the lights, the background noise of the engines and the smell of charged metal.

The Hadron had been rapidly staffed and equipped to act as the Space Corps' mobile command and control station. Such had been the suddenness of the warship's change of use, there was an unmistakeable air of uncertainty and confusion. Personnel walked rapidly in groups along the wide corridors, talking in hushed tones amongst themselves. So focused where they, that many failed to identify Duggan or his staff and they brushed past, not rudely, yet as if they were just other faccs in the crowd. Duggan didn't mind – he knew how important discipline was, but it became tiresome having to return a thousand different salutes and make countless polite responses to countless polite greetings. He liked getting down to business efficiently, without the bells and whistles.

One of the mess areas had been converted into a makeshift secondary control room and it was packed with a haphazard array of advanced consoles, staff, chairs, tables and a huge number crunching robot which looked too big to have been brought here in one piece. The place hummed with activity and Duggan saw and heard the reason for the high level of motivation.

Admiral Gary Hamer strode amongst the two hundred people, shouting orders and waving his arms furiously. He was renowned as a man who could break up one expletive with a second and he brooked no nonsense amongst his staff. Nevertheless, he was exceptionally competent when it came to logistics and he treated others with respect where it was due. Hamer saw Duggan at once and broke off from what he was doing.

"Fleet Admiral Duggan," he said, offering a salute. Hamer was a broad man, with short hair and hands big enough to strangle an elephant.

Duggan returned the salute. "Admiral Hamer. What is the status of operations here?"

Hamer growled and lowered his brow. "It's not good, John. These people are out of their comfort zones – back on Pioneer I thought I had them whipped into shape. Up here on the *Maximilian* it's like they don't know their arses from their elbows."

"They look as if they know what they're doing," said Duggan.

Hamer grinned. "They do now that I've spelled out my expectations."

"What's the latest?"

The grin faded. "We're tied in with the Space Corps network and also the three main civilian networks. In terms of comms, I can link you to anyone and anywhere."

"How is the testing on the *Maximilian*'s new comms array?"

"They got it fitted, John. There was a unit already built, specifically for installation on this warship. It was only waiting for testing on the *Ulterior-2* to finish and we can safely say that went to plan."

"The new kit is working better than I could have hoped. Knowing it's on the *Maximilian* makes me feel a whole lot better."

"It's not fully integrated yet. We're working on it, but suffice to say, if the Vraxar try and lock out this vessel's comms, they're going to be surprised at the outcome."

Duggan reached across and clapped Hamer on the upper arm. "I'm going to the bridge to see how Henry is getting along. Keep me informed – *Ix-Gastiol* is coming and we need everything running smoothly if we're to have any hope of countering that particular threat."

The sound of someone timidly clearing their throat made Duggan turn. RL Norris was standing nearby and the expression on her face told him what he needed to know. "It's here?"

"There is a seventy percent chance *Ix-Gastiol* is in the Hyptron sector. That's all I know."

Duggan felt cold at the news. "Why didn't you tell me earlier?"

"I just worked it out now, sir. While you were talking."

Hamer wasn't slow to act on the information. In several quick paces he was next to one of the three large comms consoles which had been recently brought onboard. Duggan joined him while a team of ten comms officers frantically checked the status of every Confederation planet and each Space Corps asset. The personnel were under pressure but came up with a quick response.

"No known issues," said Hamer, breathing out. "Good work," he said to the officers. "I want someone permanently assigned to doing this exact thing until I say otherwise. Am I clear?"

The comms team were definitely clear.

Duggan returned to his team and spoke to Norris again. "You

ANTHONY JAMES

said there was a seventy percent chance *Ix-Gastiol* is in Hyptron.
What of the other thirty percent? Could the enemy have gone
straight for the Origin Sector?"

"I need access to a processing cluster, sir. And I'm cut off
from my team – without collaboration I can't give you much more
than guesses. I don't have complete control over what comes into
my head and I usually fill in the gaps by using a computer."

"Don't try to guess, RL Norris." Duggan turned back to
Hamer. "I asked for the Miol-3 Projections Team to be brought
onboard."

"They're over there." Hamer lifted an arm and pointed a
thick finger towards a fixed table against the far wall. "All two
of them."

Duggan grunted. "I thought we had more on Pioneer."

Norris tried to smile. "No, sir. We lost several on New Earth
and there were two on Pioneer. The rest are spread elsewhere."

"Hopefully you'll be able to perform your duties from here.
Gary, I want the Projections Team to have access to the comms
and sole use of a main console. Plug them into a number cruncher
if you can. If there's no spare unit, assign ten percent of the *Maximilian*'s core cycles for their use."

The Projections Team's modelling needed as much
processing grunt as they could lay their hands on. Ten percent of
a Hadron's core cluster was as fast as anything they'd see on a
military base.

"Yes, sir," said Hamer. "I'll get on with that right away."

Duggan took his leave and continued towards the bridge,
whilst Norris left to join the others of her team. He walked
quickly and the other members of his staff hurried to keep up.

"Do you believe *Ix-Gastiol* is in Hyptron, sir?" asked Lieutenant Paz.

"In a way it doesn't matter whether it's in Hyptron, Origin or
Garon. I think it's coming and I think it's coming soon. I will

speak to Admiral Talley and then I need to decide on the best way to counter what's about to happen."

"Last Stand?"

"Don't press me on it, Lieutenant."

"That wasn't my intention, sir," Paz replied stiffly. "I am not in the least bit excited by the prospect."

"No, I don't think you are. The time is nearly upon us, Lieutenant and I may soon be required to agree the sacrifice of billions for a notional greater good, and with no guarantee the sacrifice will achieve its aims."

Any sign of Paz's usual dry humour was gone. "Whatever you decide, you can't falter. Hesitation will guarantee failure. Whilst I hate the saying, if you're going to shoot, shoot."

"I am not known as a procrastinator, Lieutenant," he said with a wry smile. "Anyway, here is the bridge."

Duggan climbed up the wide, solid steps and the blast door dutifully rolled aside to let him pass. The *Maximilian*'s bridge had undergone a few modifications, but nothing could take away the *feel* of it. During a normal patrol, there would be anything from twelve to fifteen officers on the bridge. With the Hadron's new role, nearly every seat was occupied on a rotating shift to ensure it was fully-staffed at all times. There were fifty officers in the room and they filled it with a low hubbub of conversation.

Admiral Talley was waiting and he shook Duggan's hand firmly. "I'm glad to see you, John. When I heard about your death..."

"I've got a few more years left in me yet, Henry. We've come this far and I won't let the Vraxar kill me – not until I've shown them what the Confederation is capable of."

Talley lowered his voice. "The fires haven't dimmed, I see."

"Sometimes they flicker and just when I think they might go out, they come back, as bright as before." Duggan felt his voice crack and he took a deep breath. "Every time it's a little harder than the last."

Talley met his eyes. "You won't break, John. You never have and you never will. Once you accept that, every burden will feel light as a feather."

"I'll accept the wisdom of your words."

"Whilst not believing them for a moment."

Duggan laughed. "We still haven't had those catch-up drinks."

"Once this is over, John. We'll make time."

The two of them would have talked longer in other circumstances. With the situation as it was, they got on with business. Talley introduced Duggan to the crew. There were a few familiar faces – men and women brought from the *Devastator*. In addition, there were others whom Duggan didn't recognize and he did his best to commit their names to memory. He had yet to meet a person who didn't respond better to the use of their name.

With the greetings over, Duggan spent time both with his staff and with Admiral Talley, familiarising himself with the movement of the Space Corps' fleet, as well as every other resource at his disposal. It was surprising how much everything had changed in the short time since the Vraxar's arrival at New Earth and he was reminded how his position consumed almost the entirety of his life. The pangs of guilt he felt at the thought of how much he and his family had to give up for this were painful to bear, and he resolved to give serious thought to his future once this was over.

We're all making sacrifices and this one is mine.

Duggan found a place to sit and he got himself comfortable, ready for hard work and planning. There wasn't much privacy on the bridge, but it was well-enough spaced that he didn't feel overlooked. He worked on a few ideas and sent off messages to his most senior staff, requesting their input. With the Confederation

Council seemingly onside, he kept a number of its senior members in the loop.

After a time, he concluded that all the preparations in the world wouldn't be of anything other limited use when the Vraxar decided to strike. He didn't care – he'd never given up at anything difficult in his life and he wasn't about to start.

"You're up to something," said his wife quietly. "What is it?"

Duggan looked around, startled. "Who let you on the bridge?" She didn't answer and he caught the wistful expression. "You feel it too?" he asked.

"It never left me. I hide it better than you."

"I always knew, Lucy. I'm many things, but blind isn't one of them."

"There's definitely no cure." She leaned away and studied one of the weapons consoles nearby. "Same as it ever was."

"And same as it always will be."

"You haven't answered my question, John."

The words spilled out in a rush, before he could stop them. "Once this war is over, I'm going to retire. For good."

His wife studied him. "You mean it."

"Yes. I really mean it."

"Now you simply have to engineer the destruction of an enemy warship which is approximately seven hundred klicks long and then finish off whatever Vraxar forces remain. After that, you can get to know your grandchildren a bit better. Maybe they'll stop referring to you as a curmudgeon."

Duggan didn't rise to the bait. "I'm making you a promise, Lucy. Once this is over, I'll have played my part."

"There'll be no regrets?"

"I'm not stupid enough to say there'll be none. I'll have more regrets about what I'm missing outside the Space Corps."

"I'm glad you've seen sense."

The words struck home and the guilt thundered into him

again. He should have retired a decade ago and Lucy had given up so much in order to allow him the time to come to the realisation himself. He took hold of her hand and pulled it to his heart. "Thank you," he whispered.

Lucy Duggan squeezed his hand and, when she thought no one was looking, ruffled his short hair. Then, she walked away across the bridge, leaving him alone. He turned his head and saw her stop to watch Commander George Adams for a few seconds before she finally exited the bridge.

Without his realising it, the guilt had vanished utterly in those few seconds. In its place was the vigour of his youth. With his decision to retire made and confessed so easily, he was determined to keep to his word.

"I've never broken a promise," he said under his breath. "And the Vraxar aren't going to make it happen."

The only thing standing in his way was the largest spaceship known in Confederation history. For once, he didn't worry about the strength of his enemies. There was nothing going to stop him seeing this through to the end.

When news came of the sighting, he felt neither shock nor surprise.

CHAPTER FOUR

ON THE BRIDGE of the *Ulterior-2*, Captain Charlie Blake found himself holding his breath as he watched the replay of the sensor feed. A tiny, insignificant anomaly made its way across the surface of Pioneer's sun, obscured by a mixture of heat, light and radiation.

"There's no chance it's a mis-read?" he asked. His knuckles were white from gripping the back of Lieutenant Cruz's chair so tightly.

"No, sir."

"How the hell did you see that from here?"

"I was just bored and looking, sir."

"There are twenty-six fleet warships in the Laspan system. Why they hell haven't they noticed?"

"Without the *Ulterior-2*'s new sensor arrays I wouldn't have had a hope of spotting it, sir. We have new filters and about three times the processing power of the *ES Grant* and the *ES Railer* combined."

The *Grant* was an old model Galactic, updated with the

latest gear and currently in orbit around Pioneer, while the *Railer* was a fresh off the production line heavy cruiser.

"This object is absolutely not one of ours and neither is it Ghast?"

"No, sir."

"Are you able to estimate the size and speed of the object?"

"It's big and it's travelling at about two thousand klicks per second."

"*Ix-Gastiol* big?"

Cruz shifted, uncomfortable with what she was about to set in motion. "Definitely."

Lieutenant Pointer did her best to corroborate. "The object will be out of sight in approximately eight minutes, assuming we don't lose it amongst the solar activity."

"Can you confirm Lieutenant Cruz's findings?"

"Yes, sir. We have a Vraxar spaceship – most likely *Ix-Gastiol* - in orbit around Laspan."

"Please inform Fleet Admiral Duggan immediately. Lieutenant Cruz, I want you to keep a close eye on the enemy craft."

The Vraxar ship continued on the same course and speed. Cruz worked hard on the sensor arrays, adjusting the focus and the filters to try and keep *Ix-Gastiol* in view. It was difficult work and a less experienced officer would have failed. However, try as she might, Cruz was unable to obtain anything like a clear image of the huge spaceship and it remained as an amorphous, dark speck.

"We're too far away," she muttered. "Too much going on."

"Keep trying."

Instead of fear, Blake felt a rising excitement at the discovery. "For once, we've found them before they've found us," he said. "This gives us a chance to strike first!"

Outside, the Miol-3 alarms started up and the base mainframe triggered the *Ulterior-2*'s bridge alarms. The sound wasn't excessively loud, but it was piercing and uncomfortable to listen to for any length of time.

"That's a Priority 1 alert," said Hawkins, raising her voice to be heard over the siren.

"Shut the alarm off, Lieutenant. I can't hear myself think."

"Roger that."

Hawkins overrode the alarm and the noise on the bridge returned to normal. It was a great relief.

"What's going on outside?" asked Quinn. He had access to the sensor feeds and was doing his best to help Pointer and Cruz.

"It's busy," said Hawkins. "And no one's running for the bunkers."

Blake expected the shipyard activity to decrease after the Priority 1 alert and for the personnel to head for their bunkers. Instead, the movement outside increased until it was a frenetic ballet of automated plant and personnel.

"Seems like we're past the point of hiding," said Quinn. "Colonel Watson must have received direct orders to keep the base running flat out."

"Why bother trying to keep out of sight anymore?" asked Hawkins. "We know what the Vraxar want from us and staying underground won't stop them."

"I've got Fleet Admiral Duggan on the comms," said Pointer.

"Good, bring him through."

When Duggan spoke, there was something different in his voice. Blake couldn't claim to know the other man well, but he detected a serenity which wasn't usually present. *He's no longer caught in the current.*

"Captain Blake, I would like to congratulate your comms team on their skill. Can you provide me with a one hundred percent certainty that you have located *Ix-Gastiol*?"

"There is nothing else it can be, sir. It's too far away to make out the details – in truth, we're lucky to be onboard the only warship with the new sensor arrays. There's too much interference for the other craft at Pioneer to see clearly through Laspan's corona."

"Do you have any guesses as to the Vraxar's intent? Are they waiting for something?"

Duggan didn't need to spell out the reasons for his concern. If *Ix-Gastiol* was waiting, that meant there was an as-yet unknown Vraxar threat inbound.

"I don't know, sir. If they are waiting for something, we may be too far away to detect it."

"I'm sure you realise this gives us a chance to launch a surprise attack. I have a total of fifteen fleet warships I can call upon in addition to those already at Pioneer. The furthest is eight hours away."

"What of the Ghasts, sir?"

"I will speak to Subjos Kion-Tur shortly to confirm. I believe the Ghasts could contribute as many as twelve of their fleet at short notice, by which I mean hours instead of days."

"A total of fifty-three."

"Plus the *Ulterior-2*."

"Fifty-four."

"I know what you're thinking, Captain Blake – it isn't enough."

"No, sir. I don't imagine it will be enough."

From the corner of his eye, Blake caught sight of Lieutenant Cruz waving frantically to get his attention.

"One moment, sir." He hurried over to see what was so important. "What is it?"

"*Ix-Gastiol* has stopped, sir. Look here."

Blake leaned over and saw the now-motionless shape of the enemy ship, still at the same altitude above Laspan. "Any idea what they're up to?"

Cruz shrugged. "There are no visible clues."

The comms channel was still open to the *Maximilian* and Duggan was able to hear the exchange. "I don't like it."

"There's no indication of hostile activity," said Hawkins. "No weapons launch – nothing."

Duggan made an audible rumbling sound. "The Vraxar don't usually hang around – everything so far has been a case of them attacking without hesitation."

"They've come to Pioneer to kill us, sir. Whatever they're doing at Laspan can only be to enable that goal."

"I agree. Unfortunately, it puts me in an even more difficult position. I can either launch an immediate all-out attack, or I can wait for the reinforcements to arrive and hope the Vraxar don't decide it's time to attack Pioneer."

"Is that a problem, sir?" asked Blake. "If we sit back and wait, the warships at Pioneer can still mount an offensive if necessary. We know the Vraxar are here, so they can't take us by surprise."

"It's not quite so straightforward, Captain. What if this is a sign of weakness from the Vraxar? What if they are orbiting Laspan because they are missing something they require to guarantee success?"

"*Ix-Gastiol* is massive and surely it's completely self-sufficient." Blake tried to keep the doubt from his voice. "What weakness could it possibly have? *Ix-Gastiol* must have presided over the destruction of a thousand worlds – Pioneer and a few dozen warships can't be a challenge."

"That's what I would like to know – if there is an opening to exploit, I would not like to miss it through hesitation."

"Will you order an immediate assault?"

Duggan didn't answer the question directly. "One of the inbound warships is the *ES Devastator* and it is carrying Falsehood in its shuttle bay. Bomb 000016 lacks the design improvements of Benediction; however, the theoretical blast modelling suggests it will have the second largest explosive force amongst our entire stock."

"Was Falsehood part of Last Stand?"

"That was its initial intention. Once we realised it had far more destructive potential than was necessary to annihilate Zircon and its three moons, we replaced it with a different bomb – Star Taker - and added Falsehood to our arsenal."

Blake couldn't stop himself from asking. "How large is this arsenal?"

"A single bomb is too many. We have more than one."

It was clear Duggan wasn't going to be drawn further, so Blake moved onto his next question. "When will the *Devastator* arrive, sir?"

"Eight hours, which is far longer than I'd hoped."

Blake fell silent for a moment, conscious that Duggan had countless other things to get on with. "We have to act as normal, sir, else the Vraxar might be driven to bring forward the inevitable attack on Pioneer. If they detect the fission signatures of our reinforcements, it might be the catalyst and take the choice out of our hands. An engagement at Laspan would be preferable to one above Pioneer."

With a loud exhalation, Duggan made his decision. "I'll order a halt on the *Ulterior-2*'s repairs. You are to stay on the ground for the time being and do your best to figure out what *Ix-Gastiol* is doing. I must speak with the Space Corps high command and make arrangements."

"Does this mean we are waiting for the *Devastator*?"

"That's exactly what it means. I will ensure the reinforcements stay a short lightspeed distance away from Pioneer and synchronise their arrival with the *Devastator*. After that, we will launch an Obsidiar bomb attack on *Ix-Gastiol*. If the enemy should force a change upon us, then the existing fleet at Pioneer will meet them head-on."

"Who will coordinate, sir?"

"Main orders will come direct from the *Maximilian*. However, I am putting you in personal charge of local fleet operations. Admiral Willard Harvey commands the *Devastator* – as soon as he arrives he will take over from you."

"Yes, sir."

"Understand that anything may change at a moment's notice and I trust you to follow your instincts on this one. They've served the Space Corps well so far."

"I don't know any other way, sir."

"That's what I thought. I have much to do, Captain Blake, but please ensure you contact me the moment you unearth anything new." Hints of anger and excitement crept into Duggan's voice. "This could be the moment we've been waiting for. If we play it right, this could spell the end of the Vraxar in Confederation Space. If we destroy *Ix-Gastiol* I won't care if they have ten thousand ships in Estral space – by the time they reach us, we will have twenty thousand of our own to meet them and this time it will be the Vraxar who fear extinction."

With those words, Duggan was gone, leaving Blake lost in thought.

––––––––

WHERE PREVIOUSLY THE *Maximilian* had been a hive of activity, now it was hectic. With Duggan, Talley and Hamer running on full throttle, the personnel onboard were given no opportunity to relax and they dashed from place to place, console to console and team to team.

In the centre of it all, Duggan did his best to deal with the hundreds of requests coming his way, whilst also trying to find the time to refine his plan for the destruction of *Ix-Gastiol*. Whichever way he looked at it, there was nothing sophisticated about his intentions. If the Vraxar remained near to Laspan, he'd send the *Devastator* in and detonate Falsehood on top of the enemy shields. There was no launch mechanism for the bomb, so the existing crew would have to evacuate first, but that was a detail to be handled closer to the time.

An hour after he first heard about *Ix-Gastiol*'s appearance, Duggan summoned a number of his senior staff to a progress meeting. There wasn't much in the way of unclaimed space within the battleship and since he didn't want to interrupt the ongoing efforts of the other personnel, he held the meeting in a corridor leading to one of the maintenance passages. There was no need for anyone to come along this way and it was nearly quiet.

He cast his eye over the assembled people. Lieutenants Doyle and Gallant leaned against the same wall, with cups of steaming coffee in their hands. Lieutenants Paz and Jacobs, alongside Admirals Talley and Hamer made more of an effort to stand straight, but the overall effect was one of distinct informality, in spite of everything which was at stake.

"In seven hours, the *Devastator* will arrive. I will instruct Admiral Harvey to evacuate using the battleship's four shuttles, leaving the battle computer in charge. It will execute a short-range transit towards *Ix-Gastiol*, leaving the Obsidiar bomb to detonate inside the hold."

"Will it require codes from the Confederation Council's appointed members?" asked Jacobs.

"Not for this one. Falsehood is no longer part of Last Stand and is therefore under the direct control of the Space Corps."

"Can the battle computer detonate the bomb?" asked Paz. "It will be far less risky than relying on human reactions."

"Negative, Lieutenant. We'll need to use Falsehood's inbuilt timer."

"Shame."

"We'll have to work with it," snapped Hamer.

"What if it fails?" asked Doyle. "What if *Ix-Gastiol*'s shield are so damned tough, even an Obsidiar bomb can't break them open?"

"In that case, we will launch a full assault on the bastards. We have three Ghast Oblivions due within two hours, and an additional six of their Cadaveron heavy cruisers."

Doyle gave a low whistle. The Ghast fleet was smaller than that of the Space Corps, but marginally newer overall and with a slight technological edge. None of this stopped the alien warships achieving something of a mystical status in the Space Corps, particularly amongst those who lacked direct experience of the Ghast forces. There was a truth to it and somehow the Oblivions in particular always seemed to punch far above their weight. It caused Duggan to feel both admiration and irritation in more or less equal measures. Irrespective of this unspoken rivalry, he was ecstatic to have the Ghasts as allies.

"I have spoken with Subjos Kion-Tur and he advises me that two of the Oblivions are fitted with Particle Disruptors, whilst the third has earlier-model incendiaries. If Falsehood isn't enough, we must hope it weakens the enemy shields sufficiently that an outright attack will punch through."

"Fingers crossed the bomb works," said Lieutenant Gallant.

Duggan looked from face to face and saw the uncertainty. There was more to it besides, and he realised what it was. The war against the Vraxar had reached a pivotal moment and the Confederation had been granted what appeared to be the perfect opportunity to gain a huge advantage. None of them quite dared to believe it.

"We can't fail because we're scared to take the initiative - we've got too many people relying on us to succeed." He took a deep breath. "In all my years fighting, I never dared to expect victory. I just did my damnedest and threw myself at each opportunity with everything I had. I trusted my crew, I trusted myself and I gave thanks when it worked." He met their eyes, one-by-one. "We need to do the same right now. If our efforts aren't enough, then we were destined to fail, but we have to do everything we can to spit in the eye of fate and make our own future."

Talley nodded. "We've been served up a game-changing opportunity on a plate, folks. We should be invigorated rather than lethargic."

The Space Corps generally only accepted applicants with an underlying positive outlook and Duggan was pleased to see his officers make a visible effort to become enthused.

"Let's get these bastards, sir," said Doyle. "And if the bomb fails, we'll shoot them to pieces. If that's not good enough, then we'll..." He faltered as his brain followed the path to its logical conclusion.

"Then I'll request the activation of Last Stand," said Duggan. "Whatever happens, I will not allow the Vraxar to escape from Pioneer."

The positive mood evaporated before it had taken hold, with each member of the group reflecting upon the grim reality of Duggan's words. It didn't get any better. There was a flurry of activity towards the end of the corridor and the sound of a voice raised.

"Where is Fleet Admiral Duggan? Where is he? Anybody?"

Duggan recognized the voice and he took several paces towards the sound. Research Lead Marion Norris came around the corner, her hair as wild as ever and her achingly pretty face distraught. There was a much older, grey-haired man behind her, whom Duggan recognized yet without being able to identify.

"What can I do for you, RL Norris?"

"We've been working on the modelling you requested." She looked over her shoulder. "Along with RL Page here and his team."

"I take it you have reached a conclusion?"

"Not exactly, sir. We have reached an impasse."

"I don't have time to deal with team disagreements," said Duggan impatiently. "Tell me you have interrupted my meeting for something more important than this?"

The older man stepped forward. He was average build and his eyes betrayed a mind unbowed by his physical years. His voice was clear when he spoke. "Our apologies for a lack of clarity, Fleet Admiral. There is an impasse of sorts – interpretation of the same data often produces different conclusions, especially when we are dealing with..." he cleared his throat, "things we don't fully understand. I work with the men and women responsible for calculating the theoretical performance of our Obsidiar bombs."

The man's name clicked in Duggan's head. "I saw your signature on the design documents for Benediction, RL Page."

The man nodded his head once. "I have studied the potential of the Falsehood bomb during the last hour and revisited a few of the original calculations." He lifted up a sheaf of papers which Duggan hadn't seen him carrying until now. There were hundreds of calculations on each page, written out in incredibly small, neat characters.

"What have you found?"

"It was as we expected – the median diameter blast sphere will be absorbed by Laspan without lasting effects to the sun itself or the planets in orbit."

"What about a larger than median blast?"

Page grimaced. "There's a fifteen percent chance the reaction within the bomb casing will significantly exceed our expectations and..."

Duggan raised a hand. "Just tell me."

The words tumbled out. "There is a chance Falsehood will inflict so much damage to Laspan that the sun's output will reduce sufficiently to turn Pioneer and every other planet in the solar system into spheres of ice. It should recover in due course, but by then everyone will be dead."

"RL Norris, does this differ from your findings?"

"Yes, sir. RL Page deals with a branch of absolute mathematics. He takes the theoretical and forces it to give him an answer."

"That's not precisely accurate..." began Page.

"Quiet! Let RL Norris speak!"

Norris continued. "You know how the Projections Team works, sir. We assume every possible unknown is a certainty and we derive an infinite model from which we can extract..."

Duggan was familiar with the theory and it had been explained to him in great detail on more than one occasion. He knew what his skills and his limitations were and the Projections Team's methods were beyond him. The little brown folders they produced contained the closest thing to magic he could think of and he valued the work of Norris and her team mates as much as he valued anything in the Space Corps.

"Let me have your alternative conclusion, please."

"If you detonate Falsehood anywhere close to Laspan, the resulting chain reaction will destroy the sun."

Duggan was stunned. "We might destroy an entire star?"

"That wasn't what I said, sir," said Norris. "I said it *will* destroy the sun."

Admiral Hamer was standing nearby, having heard the exchange. "Shit," he said.

When he considered the ramifications, Duggan also swore. If Norris was correct, this was a real spanner in the works. He recalled the blast radius of the Inferno Sphere – 180,000 kilometres and that bomb had exceeded its expectations by more than one hundred percent. Laspan had a radius of more than a million kilometres...

"I should have realised sooner," said Duggan bitterly. "I was a fool to think we could let off an explosive of such magnitude without it having catastrophic effects, even on something as large as a sun."

"What next?" asked Paz.

"What next is that I'm going to have to come up with something different. This meeting is done."

With those words, Duggan sent the others to their stations. He took himself back to the bridge where he sat, lost in contemplation of what he needed to do.

CHAPTER FIVE

FOR A PERIOD of several hours *Ix-Gastiol* remained stationary, close to the surface of Laspan. On the *Ulterior-2*'s bridge, Blake watched and waited, unsure how events would play out. The inbound reinforcements gathered a short lightspeed hop from the Laspan system and they began work on coordinating attack formations and other tactics. Blake took charge and did his best to make provision for every possible eventuality. He quickly learned that each additional ship in a fleet made the job of command exponentially harder and he developed a healthy respect for those with the knack.

The biggest single issue was the comms. Assuming it came down to a fight, the Vraxar would be able to disable the comms on all warships bar the *Ulterior-2*. The days of hand signals were past and a ship without its comms was often a liability. A whole fleet without comms would be something else entirely and Blake wasn't able to come up with a way to make things better. Part of him longed for the *Devastator*'s arrival, so he could hand off to Admiral Harvey.

Then, news came in that there was to be no Obsidiar bomb

attack on the Vraxar while *Ix-Gastiol* was anywhere within a million kilometres of Laspan. Other than that, there was little guidance and Blake became concerned that the Space Corps high command didn't know how to handle the situation.

"So, if this Obsidiar bomb is powerful enough to destroy Laspan and is also the most likely way we have to destroy *Ix-Gastiol*'s shield…" began Hawkins.

"We'll have to pull the enemy ship away from the sun," finished Blake. "It's going to get messy."

"As soon as we begin the engagement, there's no way to tell what the Vraxar will do," said Pointer.

"Yup. Their destruction of Atlantis shows them to be capable of punitive action that doesn't benefit their overall war effort."

"There'll be no choice, will there?" asked Cruz. "*Ix-Gastiol* is here and the Space Corps will take whatever action is necessary."

"Like I said, it's going to get messy."

"How long until the *Devastator* arrives?"

"Two hours and it's right on schedule."

"I feel vulnerable on the ground," said Hawkins.

Her words made Blake perform another check on the Hadron's status. The damage inflicted by *Ix-Gorghal* hadn't gone away, but the ship itself was ready to lift off without notice.

"I'd prefer to be in the air," he admitted. "We don't want to give the game away, though. It's as if we're holding our collective breaths and scared that anything we do will bring the enemy to Pioneer when we aren't ready for it."

"There's something going on," said Pointer. "Activity on Laspan."

"*Ix-Gastiol* is moving again?"

"No, I mean there's a change in surface emissions on the sun, consistent with an imminent flare."

The viewscreen image of the enemy vessel didn't immediately show anything new. It cast its attenuated near-white over the bridge equipment, while the darker spot of *Ix-Gastiol* remained in place.

"Nothing," said Hawkins.

Then, the flare came. It erupted from the surface, appearing as little more than a lighter-coloured smear. The flare enveloped the Vraxar ship, hiding it completely from sensor view.

"That's a big one," said Pointer.

"It might destroy them," said Quinn. "That's enough to put tremendous stress on their shields."

Blake wasn't convinced. "Somehow I don't think it's a problem for them."

"Yeah."

The flare lasted for a few minutes and eventually the *Ulterior-2*'s sensors were able to adapt and get a lock onto the enemy spaceship again. It was still there, unmoved and apparently untroubled.

"What the hell are they playing at?" asked Blake.

Quinn was on to something. "A big energy spike," he muttered, scanning through the raw sensor data. "Not coming from Laspan."

Blake turned. "You read a spike from *Ix-Gastiol*?"

"I believe so. I'm double-checking it now." It didn't take long. "I was right – the energy readings from the enemy ship climbed for a period of seventy-four seconds and then dropped away to normal."

"Do you have a theory?

"Well, it was definitely not coincidence that they were in the exact spot where that flare appeared." Quinn paused, thinking. "They must be extracting something from the expelled matter." He shrugged. "There's a lot of energy in a sun."

Blake grimaced, sure his engine man was onto something. "Which might be useful if you have a way of tapping into it."

"Fleet Admiral Duggan mentioned a weakness," said Pointer. "That's why he was torn between waiting and attacking."

"I don't think this will change anything. Not now," said Blake.

"The enemy spaceship is moving again, sir. Same speed and altitude as before, this time on a new heading."

"Looking for another flare," said Quinn.

"At least it means they aren't ready to attack. It gives the *Devastator* time to get here."

"And then the fun and games start."

"Lieutenant Pointer, please inform the *Maximilian* about our latest observations and theory."

Pointer sent over the details and Blake wasn't surprised when she received no updated instructions from command and control. It was tempting to try and speak directly with Fleet Admiral Duggan, but then Blake realised he couldn't offer any new insights. Whichever way he looked at it, a brutal confrontation with a vastly superior enemy spaceship loomed and it was inevitable there would be a huge number of casualties. The risks were about as high as they could go.

The minutes went by. The *ES Devastator* was the final piece in the puzzle and it was also the last to arrive. Blake drummed his fingers, waiting for confirmation that the fleet was to attack. The comms remained silent, no matter how hard he stared at his console, daring it to light up with notification of an incoming message.

"The *Devastator* has arrived, sir," said Pointer. "I've received a standard greeting from Admiral Harvey's comms team informing us they are in the middle of final preparations and that local orders will now be issued from the *Devastator*."

Blake had expected these words would make him feel better. They didn't, and he felt a tugging regret that he hadn't been able to command the coming action. "Any indication he's in possession of more recent orders than ours?"

"I can't tell you one way or the other."

"Fleet Admiral Duggan is kind of leaving everything until the last possible minute, isn't he?" said Hawkins.

"As much as I wish it was otherwise, I don't think he has a choice." Blake thumped the arm of his seat. "Get me a link to the *Maximilian*. I need to know what the hell it is we're meant to be doing."

His words were spoken a fraction late.

"Incoming comms from Fleet Admiral Duggan."

"Bring him through."

Blake expected Duggan to sound tired, or weighed down by the choices before him. His voice betrayed neither.

"Captain Blake, thank you for your patience. I believe you have handed over to Admiral Harvey."

"Just this minute, sir."

"Admiral Harvey has his orders and here are yours. The *Devastator* will shortly enter lightspeed on the final leg of its journey to the Laspan system. At the same moment, our fleet warships currently in Pioneer orbit will muster and prepare for a coordinated lightspeed jump towards Laspan itself, their arrival timed to coincide with that of the *Devastator*. From then on, we will do everything we can to draw *Ix-Gastiol* away from the sun in order that we can detonate Falsehood without risk."

Everything was as Blake expected so far, however, he detected something unspoken and he could tell he wasn't going to like what it was.

"What about the *Ulterior-2*? We are ready to take off immediately and join the attack on *Ix-Gastiol*."

"You won't be joining the attack, Captain Blake."

"What do you mean?" asked Blake, before Duggan could continue.

"Let me finish, damnit. The *Ulterior-2* is the only warship we have capable of transmitting the details of what transpires once the engagement begins. I expect the Vraxar will disable every other ship's comms as soon as the fighting starts. If I can't see what is happening, I can't be sure if the time has come to order the activation of Last Stand. We need eyes, Captain Blake. Your eyes."

Blake suddenly felt stupid. It was obvious now that it was spelled out to him and he realised he should have guessed earlier.

"My apologies, sir. We will do what must be done."

"As soon as you judge the time is right, you will activate the *Ulterior-2*'s stealth modules and you will take off from the Miol-3 base. I expect you to stay within two hundred thousand klicks of the engagement, yet without betraying your presence."

"Why so close, sir?"

"I would prefer you to be near, on the off-chance the situation dictates a change of plan."

"We might be required to fight after all?"

"I don't want to get your hopes up."

The reasons were easy enough to guess. The *Ulterior-2* had a lot of firepower and if, for whatever reason, the Obsidiar bomb on the *Devastator* failed to perform as expected, every available warship would be required to bombard the Vraxar in the hope they could somehow break through its shields and wreck the ship underneath.

"How long until we go?"

"Minutes."

Blake glanced at his tactical screen. There was no deviation in the flight path of the local fleet – they were still trying to give the outward impression they were ignorant of *Ix-Gastiol*'s presence. At the agreed moment, they would simultaneously activate their short-range transits and launch at the sun.

"The *Devastator* has gone to lightspeed, sir," whispered

Cruz. "It's bringing an additional twenty-six major warships with it."

"It's going to get busy soon," said Duggan.

"I can see that, sir."

"You'll have to time your take-off well. We don't want to give the game away."

"I'm not convinced the enemy cares one way or the other."

"Nor am I. This is a variable I *can* control and I'm damned well going to do just that."

"Understood, sir."

Duggan exhaled noisily, giving the first hint he was under pressure. "The time is coming, Captain Blake. This is an opportunity we couldn't have wished for and now it's been dropped in our laps. If we take out *Ix-Gastiol*, we might actually beat these bastards and wouldn't that be something to be proud of?"

"We'll give it our best shot, sir. I will leave a permanent channel available on the comms for you to access whenever you require and I will also assign Lieutenant Cruz to the sole duty of liaison with the *Maximilian*. The live stream of our sensor data will continue until we hear otherwise."

"This has got to be our time," said Duggan.

"We'll make it so." Blake looked across to see Lieutenant Quinn holding four fingers in the air. "The *Devastator* is due in four minutes, sir. We need to go."

"Goodbye and good luck, Captain. Let us end this war we never asked for."

With that, the channel closed, leaving Blake with no choice other than to act.

"Lieutenant Quinn, activate the stealth modules. As soon as we're off the ground, I want the energy shield up and running."

"Yes, sir." Quinn moved an arm across his console. "The stealth modules are now active."

"I'm setting the autopilot to take us straight up at the fastest speed."

Blake touched one of the screens to his left. The *Ulterior-2*'s engine note changed and the power gauges climbed. Less than two seconds later, the warship lifted upwards and away from Trench Five. The thousands of technicians who were still waiting for the order to resume repairs, watched as the battleship climbed. Air rushed in to the gap left behind, ruffling hair and clothing.

The *Ulterior-2* soared into the parched skies of Pioneer, the note of its engines sending flocks of desert bird to the wing. The effortlessness of the climb belied the grumbling of damaged gravity drives, which carried the battleship aloft with incomparable grace and inexorable power. Blake kept his eyes on the sensor feed, unable to tear them away. The blue outside steadily darkened as the warship approached the outer reaches of the planet's atmosphere.

"One hundred klicks and climbing," said Pointer.

"Less than three minutes until the *Devastator* exits light-speed," said Quinn. "We're going to be just in time."

"Programme in our course, Lieutenant. Two hundred thousand klicks from the action."

"I've wound up eight cores and we're ready to jump on your word, sir."

"Lieutenant Hawkins?"

"We've got two missing Havoc cannons, reduced missile availability and two of the overcharged particle beams are offline. Other than that, everything is ready to fire on command."

The *Ulterior-2* had taken a proper beating during its short encounter with *Ix-Gorghal*. To look at the vessel's exterior it would have been easy to imagine the damage was terminal. Luckily, the Hadron was more or less solid Gallenium and besides, the Space Corps built them tough with dozens of layers of redundancy. It had taken only a short period for the remaining Tucson technicians and engineers to get the *Ulterior-2* into a state where it was a match for almost anything else in the fleet.

Blake spared a moment to look over both shoulders. His main officers were a picture of concentration, whilst the two ensigns appeared no more flustered. A sheen of sweat on Ensign Toby Park's face was the only indication he was feeling the pressure. The man had been tested before and come through, leaving Blake with no doubts as to his competence under duress.

"We are now clear of the planet," said Pointer. "There is nothing unexpected on the nears, fars, and the supers look good. *Ix-Gastiol* has completed its blindside circuit of Laspan and is in full view of our sensors."

Everything was going as expected.

"What about the local fleet?"

"There are seven Galactics and nineteen Imposition class cruisers on our sensors, sir. All doing their very best to look innocent."

It was a whole lot of heavy armour and even these ships represented only a fraction of the Space Corps' might.

"Thirty seconds for the *Devastator*," said Quinn. "We have direct sight on the *ES Grant* and the *ES Safe Haven*. Their power output indicates they're ready to press the button and go."

One of the crew had set up a timer and put it into a corner of the main bulkhead screen. The large, red numbers counted down. Blake watched them intently.

Such are our lives – measured in relentless numbers, disappearing before our eyes.

The time was nearly upon them. Not just for the crew of the *Ulterior-2*, nor for the Space Corps fleet. Not even for the 8.3 billion people on Pioneer. The coming minutes could well decide the fate of the entire 600 billion souls living in the combined human Confederation and Ghast Subjocracy.

It isn't just us, Blake's mind tormented him. *It's every single species in the universe who have yet to meet the Vraxar, and revenge for those who have.* He felt a sudden giddiness at the knowledge of what was at stake. Angrily, he shrugged it off, leaving it to one side where it couldn't affect him – locked away but not forgotten.

3...

2...

1...

The *ES Devastator* appeared in local space, 150 million kilometres closer to Laspan. Other warships clustered around it, in a carefully-arranged pattern designed to ensure the Hadron was shielded from anything inbound.

As one, the other 26 warships nearer to Pioneer vanished into lightspeed, reappearing within the blinking of an eye, having crossed the immense distance towards the sun.

"Time for us to go," said Blake. "Activate SRT."

"Aye, sir. Aiming for the chromosphere at an altitude of one thousand klicks."

The Hadron battleship *Ulterior-2* entered lightspeed and hurtled across space to join the fray.

CHAPTER SIX

THE *ULTERIOR-2'S* engines grated with the switchover to gravity drives and Blake felt it through his palms where they rested on the control bars. The battleship entered Laspan's chromosphere and immediately, a series of alerts brought the crew's attention to the blistering external temperature. The alloy plating on a fleet warship melted at around four thousand degrees Centigrade. The temperatures in this part of the chromosphere were seven thousand.

Only a few thousand kilometres above, the heat in the corona was closer to a million degrees, extending outwards for an enormous distance. This made it necessary to engage with the Vraxar at what was little more than a hair's breadth from the surface of the sun. The underside sensors showed a tumultuous, unending sea of yellows and whites.

"We have re-entered local space - altitude and position within ten klicks of intended. A good landing," said Lieutenant Quinn. "Stealth modules and energy shield activated. Our shield is going to absorb a lot of heat – let's hope this isn't a long encounter."

Blake glanced at the Obsidiar power reserves. They were at 100%, but an indicator beneath the gauge showed the core was being slowly drained by the sun's heat.

"I'm running the scans," said Pointer.

On Blake's tactical screen the positions of the other fifty-three warships populated, the computer-generated dots speckling his display like a flurry of snow. Their apparent positions hopped from place to place as the battle computer struggled with interference from the sun's radiation.

"The main fleet is 150,000 klicks away. Get me a lock on *Ix-Gastiol*. I'll bring us ahead at a slow speed."

"I have located the enemy vessel," said Pointer. "Right where we expected."

"Get me a visual and establish a comms feed to the *Devastator* and *Maximilian*."

"Visual on screen now, waiting on comms links."

The Vraxar ship was a quarter of a million kilometres from the *Ulterior-2*, with the rest of the fleet moving rapidly towards the planned engagement distance. The enemy vessel was still on course, maintaining its low-altitude orbit of Laspan, as if completely unaware of the warships closing in. As soon as he laid eyes on the huge enemy ship, Blake felt his heart jump in his chest.

"What the hell?" he said.

Ix-Gastiol looked nothing whatsoever like *Ix-Gorghal*. Where the latter was ovoid, covered in clusters of weaponry and energy amplifiers, the former was an elongated, bulky cuboid. The appearance of its hull initially defied Blake's eyes to make sense of the details. The Vraxar spaceship was comprised of a seemingly infinite array of shapes and forms. There were domes, angles, sharp edges, complex outer arrays of delicate cables, here and there interspersed with comparatively tiny weapons installations of gun barrels and particle beam emitters. There was no rhyme or reason, no discernible pattern.

And then, it all clicked into place and Blake saw what it was. *Ix-Gastiol* was a graveyard for the warships captured by the Vraxar. The entire, visible part of the vessel was comprised of thousands – tens of thousands – of different spaceships, somehow held together to make up a single, monstrous whole. Once he realised, Blake found his eyes tracing the outlines of the original ships – some were little more than a thousand metres in length, whilst others were ten or fifteen thousand metres, each one positioned roughly against the next. Whatever the inner workings and the interconnections, there was no way to be sure at first glance.

Pointer refused to be distracted by the sight and finished establishing the comms links. The voice of Admiral Willard Harvey came onto the bridge, with the rounded syllables of a native Old Earther. Although he tried to keep his voice calm, it was easy to detect the layers of stress and pressure underlying Harvey's words.

"Flight Squad 1, move into position. Open fire immediately. Flight Squad 2, stay back and draw fire. Remember to keep your stealth modules offline – we want those bastards to see us and we want them to come after us. I'm keeping the *Devastator* in position. As soon as the enemy follows, we'll SRT in and deploy the bomb."

That was the last they heard from Admiral Harvey.

"The comms have gone dead," said Pointer. "I can see receptors, but there's no data going between them."

There was no need to ask for confirmation – it was the expected outcome as soon as the engagement began.

"I have informed the *Maximilian*," said Cruz. "They're watching through our sensors and Admiral Talley has repeated the order for us to stay put."

"Acknowledge the order and tell him we're keeping clear as directed."

The engagement started and the *Ulterior-2*'s tactical display began tracking so many individual targets it caused a noticeable spike on the warship's core cluster. The sun's interference added an edge of uncertainty to the data and Blake hoped it wouldn't become a major issue.

"Approximately twelve thousand missiles in flight," said Hawkins. "Staggered waves to reduce vulnerability to counter-measures."

"From the energy readings, the Ghost vessels *Nistrek* and *Voltsun* are charging their Particle Disruptors," said Quinn. "Whoa that's a lot of burn incoming for those Vraxar bastards."

"Galactics *ES Grant, Railer, Eclipse* and *Safe Haven* have executed short-range transits," said Pointer.

The heavy cruisers jumped to within a few thousand kilometres of the enemy warship. The *Ulterior-2*'s battle computer registered the expulsion of high-intensity beam weapons, directed towards *Ix-Gastiol*.

"Eight successful overcharged particle beam strikes at the enemy's nose," said Hawkins.

"They can't stick around," muttered Quinn. "Get out of there."

The four Space Corps warships jumped away, within moments of their attack. In their wake, they left vast patches of *Ix-Gastiol*'s exterior burning hot. Blake's eyes flicked to the zoomed-out image and he saw the reality - how little of the huge enemy ship was affected by the attack. Pin-points of orange and white were visible, hardly significant in comparison to the whole.

"No retaliation from the enemy," said Hawkins.

"Lieutenant Quinn?" asked Blake. "Any readings?"

"Hard to be sure, sir," he said, chewing on his lip. "They've pulled to a standstill right in an area of high solar activity."

Blake didn't like the answer. "If there's something coming, we need to know about it, Lieutenant."

"I'm aware of the urgency, sir," said Quinn.

In a second pre-planned manoeuvre, another four Galactics initiated SRTs, carrying them through the most intense areas of Laspan's corona. This time, they were joined by two Ghast Cadaverons, equipped with high-yield incendiary weapons. The Ghasts discharged their weapons, with immediate and dramatic effect.

"Whoa, crap!" said Ensign Park.

Ix-Gastiol's energy shield was enveloped in ferocious orange flames. The fires began at two separate points and then spread out from the centre at tremendous speed, until the Vraxar ship was completely hidden in the centre. Brighter white patches from overcharged particle beams shone through, forcing the *Ulterior-2*'s sensors to attenuate the image. Even so, Blake squinted and shielded his eyes.

The first wave of missiles crashed into the incendiary fires, showing as countless, overlapping plumes of plasma, each as hot as Laspan's corona. A second wave detonated, followed by a third.

"That's going to put some stress on their shield," said Hawkins.

"Get out of there," repeated Quinn.

"They have to stay in, Lieutenant. We need to piss the Vraxar off enough that they follow us away from Laspan."

"What the hell are the Vraxar playing at?" said Quinn. "Why aren't they doing anything?"

Another squadron executed their SRTs. The warship names came up on the tactical – *Shadows Linger*, *Blackheart*, *Stone Cold*, *Hunter's Moon*, *Deliverance* and more. Each one was capable of wiping out entire planets, yet each one was a mote against the gargantuan enemy they faced. The allied spaceships unloaded thousands of missiles, the tremendous payloads of the Shimmers visible amongst the chaos.

Still the Ghost incendiaries burned, chewing away at *Ix-Gastiol*'s power reserves and still the enemy warship did nothing to retaliate. Not one of the *Ulterior-2*'s crew was foolish enough to believe this represented any sort of capitulation. In fact, Blake's concern turned to outright fear and it grew with each passing second.

Another fifteen allied warships blinked towards *Ix-Gastiol*, leaving the *ES Devastator* accompanied by fewer than twenty of the original fifty-three. These new warships stayed within five thousand kilometres of the enemy, firing their weapons as they circled around the flaming barrier encircling *Ix-Gastiol*. Missiles and particle beams continued their one-way journeys and the Vraxar didn't respond.

"Sir, here's Fleet Admiral Duggan," said Cruz.

"Captain Blake, I would value your opinion," said Duggan. "What is the feeling you get from being there?"

Duggan had access to exactly the same data as Blake, yet to an experienced captain there was no replacement to actually being close to the combat.

"I don't like it, sir," said Blake. "I'm sorry for offering you a hunch."

"What do you think is wrong?" asked Duggan at once.

The reason for the disquiet struck Blake with a jarring blow and he realised exactly what was wrong. "Those warships making up *Ix-Gastiol* - not many of them are damaged."

Duggan understood. "They were taken without a fight." The channel went deathly quiet for a moment. "Damnit, I can't order a withdrawal! We have to see this through!"

The main bulkhead screen brightened again. Blake looked up in time to see the Oblivions *Nistrek* and *Voltsun* fire their Particle Disruptors after the long charge-up period. At the same time, the third Ghast battleship, *Lantstron*, discharged its earlier-generation version of the weapon. Lines of vivid blue lanced into the fading incendiary flames around *Ix-Gastiol*. Blake had never seen three of these weapons fire at once and the effect was awe-inspiring. The flames grew, building upon each other until *Ix-Gastiol* was an elongated sphere of crackling energy, several thousand kilometres across. At their furthest extent, the Particle Disruptor fires met the surface of Laspan, turning the surface blue.

This time when Quinn spoke, there was no uncertainty. "The readings from *Ix-Gastiol* have climbed six million percent. Make that fifteen million."

Whatever the Vraxar planned, Blake was certain it didn't involve waiting meekly to be annihilated by Particle Disruptors and Shimmer missiles.

"Lieutenant Pointer, please send notice to the fleet, just in case anyone missed the obvious."

Pointer clearly had no idea what to transmit and Blake didn't know exactly what was incoming; all he knew was it was better to make sure the other captains had the information rather than not knowing.

"I've sent the message, sir. They can't respond, but hopefully it'll do some good."

There was no change in the fleet's behaviour and in fact another eight of the *Devastator*'s escort performed SRTs, throwing themselves at *Ix-Gastiol* like the tide breaking against the immense walls of a coastal fortress.

"We're in too far, sir," said Blake. "I think everyone knows the enemy aren't going to follow and all we can do is try to break through their shields."

Duggan was still on the open channel. "The Particle Disruptors are probably new to the Vraxar," he replied. "If the enemy are taken by surprise..."

"*Ix-Gastiol*'s power readings have stabilised," said Quinn, loudly as if he thought his words might not carry to the *Maximilian*. "Whatever is coming, it's coming soon."

There was no let-up in the fleet's bombardment of the Vraxar capital ship. The vessel itself was utterly hidden beneath thousands of metres of explosive blasts and incendiaries. Blake could only watch, hoping against hope his hunch was wrong and that the Vraxar were about to succumb to this surprise attack. Deep inside, he knew he was only fooling himself. *The bastards would have run away if they perceived us as a threat. How else could they have lived for so long and defeated so many other species?*

"Here it..." began Quinn.

He stopped himself mid-sentence, stupefied by the data flooding onto his console screen. Blake caught the readings too – a sphere of *something* completely unknown appeared around *Ix-Gastiol*. It was an energy of some kind, carried amongst a darkness which blotted out the light from Laspan and covering a region with a diameter of nearly a quarter of a million kilometres. This energy had precisely zero travel time, or at least it appeared so quickly the sophisticated measuring tools in the *Ulterior-2*'s sensor arrays were unable to register it.

Where the energy contacted the surface of Laspan, it fought with the sun's incredible reserves and for a split second, the Vraxar weapon suppressed the white heat, turning it dark. Within its boundaries, this sphere caught every single one of the allied ships. At the extremes, it touched against the *Ulterior-2*, whispering over the battleship's nose and along its flanks.

Then, the sphere vanished as quickly as it had come and the fusion process on this area of Laspan resumed, flaring up temporarily more brightly than before.

Blake felt his mouth fall open and his mind raced to figure out what was going on. He noticed several things at once – *Ix-Gastiol* still burned from the Particle Disruptors, the allied warships hadn't been destroyed by the unknown weapon and also there were dozens of alerts streaming onto the *Ulterior-2*'s bridge consoles. Blake marshalled his thoughts and demanded updates from his crew.

"Tell me what the hell that was!"

"Weapon type unknown," said Hawkins. "I'm checking for similarities with other Vraxar technology."

"There was enough power in that one burst to power the whole Confederation for a year," said Quinn in disbelief.

"I need something useful, not trivia!" snapped Blake.

"Yes, sir. Sorry."

Blake brought the *Ulterior-2* to a standstill, as if the Vraxar attack had somehow presented him with a warning that he should stay as far away as possible. His eyes roved across the command displays, picking out the pertinent information.

"Our energy shield has dropped to zero and we've lost nine of our Obsidiar processing units." He tapped the screen with his fingers as if this would somehow change the reading into a more favourable one.

"Our secondary Obsidiar core is offline," said Quinn. "I'm attempting to access it...failed. Stealth modules still functioning. There's a leak from our engines. I'm checking it out."

There was far worse news to come.

"Sir?" said Pointer. She resumed before Blake could speak. "Our ships are drifting."

"What? All of them?"

"Yes, sir. Whatever the Vraxar hit us with, it's shut down everything in the fleet apart from the *Ulterior-2*."

"That can't be right," said Blake, dazed.

Most warships were fitted with disruptors which could interfere with an enemy's processing core. With the advent of new processors, the weapons were no longer effective and there was rarely a need to use them. Here, the Vraxar had somehow managed to achieve a similar result, but over an incomprehensively large area of space and with a far more debilitating outcome.

Deprived of power and in the near-frictionless environment of space, the allied warships continued on the same vector as they'd been following before the Vraxar attack. In the space of a few moments, Blake watched numbly as the ES *Safe Haven* and the Cadaveron *Tiben-5* crashed into Laspan. Without the protection of their energy shields, both vessels burned up in moments, their hardened, heat-shielded alloys no match for the wrath of a star.

"Shit," said Hawkins.

"I need answers!"

"The *Eclipse* is slowing!" said Pointer. "The *Nistrek* and *Blackheart* too!"

"Please report – have they recovered from the attack?" Blake looked over his shoulder towards Quinn.

"Negative, sir. I can't tell." Quinn shook his head. "Something else is slowing them."

With so much crap going on, Blake felt in danger of being overwhelmed and he tried to keep focus on the most vital aspects of the situation. The flames surrounding *Ix-Gastiol* were dying away slowly, the blues becoming lighter as their reach decreased. The *Ulterior-2* was the single remaining operational ship on the allied side and apparently the only one capable of offering a response to the enemy actions.

"Have we broken their shields, Lieutenant Quinn?"

"I don't think so, sir."

A new voice cut in. "Captain Blake, do not fire upon *Ix-Gastiol* until we are clear what is going on," said Duggan. "Even if their shields fall, the *Ulterior-2* lacks the firepower to finish off such a large spaceship."

"We might drive them away, sir. Damage them enough..."

"No!" said Duggan. "For the moment you will wait to see if our fleet recovers."

"The *Deliverance*, *Voltsun*, *Stone Cold* and *Devastator* are also slowing," said Pointer. She furrowed her brow. "They're *all* slowing and the *ES Eclipse* has come to a dead stop."

The heavy cruiser *Eclipse* was one of the closest to *Ix-Gastiol* and the tactical screen showed it stationary, five thousand kilometres from the Vraxar ship.

"Not one of our ships has an energy shield anymore," said Hawkins. "They're going to melt soon."

Blake swore. "Lieutenant Quinn? Any more idea what's going on?"

Quinn was working hard and occasionally conferred in a loud whisper with Ensign Charlotte Bailey. "The enemy shield is not fully depleted," he said, the words coming out in a tumble. "On balance of probability and based on what we know about the Ghast Particle Disruptors, there's a reasonable chance the enemy don't have much left in the tank."

"If our warships are still without power, how are they coming to a halt? Is this another stasis beam?"

"It has to be, sir – *Ix-Gastiol* must be equipped with multiple-point stasis emitters."

"I can confirm that to be the case," said Ensign Bailey. "I can't give you a precise location of the emitters through all of the crap still clinging to their shield."

Blake found himself unexpectedly drained, as though the Vraxar weapon affected biological matter as well as warship engines and Obsidiar cores. He gripped the control bars, finding his hands clammy against the coolness. More than anything, he wanted to fly away from here. It wasn't an option – whatever the risks, it was vital they remain to find out what the enemy was up to.

He checked the damage status again. The *Ulterior-2*'s gravity drive was no longer leaking and the engines had stabilised at a level close to their peak. The primary Obsidiar core was fully operational, but the secondary core remained unresponsive and Blake suspected the Vraxar weapon had somehow managed to burn it out.

"Sir, I would value your input," he said.

"This is a time for the sharing of ideas," agreed Duggan. In spite of everything which had happened in the last few minutes, Duggan sounded utterly calm, as though he were no more than a node on a computer given a convincingly human voice.

"I think that's an understatement, sir."

Duggan didn't respond immediately and it was clear he was juggling a conversation with his officers on the *Maximilian* as well as those on the *Ulterior-2*. The voices got heated and it was clear there was a lack of consensus.

Whilst the talking went on, Blake kept an eye on the events unfolding around Laspan. *Ix-Gastiol* was possessed with predictably vast wells of power and its stasis beams brought the allied warships to a standstill in groups of threes, fours and fives. Those vessels which were the furthest distant, it drew towards it at a steady speed, until it was surrounded by a significant portion of the combined Space Corps and Ghast fleets.

"They don't seem interested in blowing up our warships," said Quinn.

"I know what they're going to do," said Blake.

The fear he'd kept in his mind from the earliest moments he'd seen the makeup of *Ix-Gastiol* came true. The stasis beam holding the *ES Railer* rotated the captured vessel and drew it closer and closer. The smaller vessel collided at low speed with the much larger Vraxar warship and the *Railer* partially covered three of the spaceships already attached to the exterior of *Ix-Gastiol*. Next came the *Deliverance* and then the *Lantstron*, each dragged in and clamped to the hull of the capital ship.

Hawkins shook her head slowly, as if she'd just received the most terrible news and hadn't yet come to terms with it. "How many layers of spaceships are there?" she said quietly. "How many civilisations and how many fleets to make that single vessel?"

"It can't be made up entirely of captured spaceships," said Quinn. His jaw worked while his brain tried to calculate the numbers. In the end, he gave up attempting even an educated guess. "There must be fifty thousand or more."

"What's in the middle of it?" asked Cruz in wonder.

There were so many questions, so easily spoken and with their answers completely out of reach. Blake couldn't think of a response and didn't waste his breath trying to come up with one, knowing anything he said would sound as insane as what was going on.

"Sir, can you see this?" he asked.

"Yes, Captain Blake. We can all see it, and we have the same questions as you do."

They continued watching from a distance, hidden by the *Ulterior-2*'s stealth technology. The enemy ship got on with the task of turning each of the captured warships until they were at the correct angle to be clamped to its hull. It was the worst thing Blake had ever seen.

There's only a single option open to us, he thought. The realisation brought a bitterness so strong it almost made him retch.

Duggan spoke, his words already prophesied. "Captain Blake, we have lost this encounter. The enemy outclassed us and our lack of intel has cost us dear. This leaves us with only one realistic chance at saving our species."

"Star Taker," Blake replied. There was no point in making the words into a question. The Vraxar had just forced the Confederation to play the card.

"Yes, Star Taker. Once *Ix-Gastiol* is finished with our fleet, it will inevitably begin whatever it intends for Pioneer. I will speak to the Confederation Council and seek approval to trigger the bomb's detonation."

"What if *Ix-Gastiol* doesn't come near enough?" said Blake. His face felt numb as if he'd drunk two bottles of strong spirits which affected his body, yet left his mind unaffected.

"They will have to leave the safety of Laspan, I have no doubt about that. If they somehow remain outside the expected blast sphere, we'll be out of options."

"Last Stand," said Blake. It felt important that he say the words aloud, as if his speaking them would drive home everything they encompassed.

"I once made a promise, Captain Blake. I promised I would do whatever it took to defeat the Vraxar. This is absolutely not how I wanted it to end."

"No, sir. It's not how any of us wanted it to end."

"Bring the *Ulterior-2* into a high orbit around Pioneer and await further orders."

"Yes, sir. Fly to Pioneer and await."

"This is not a done deal, Captain Blake. Do you understand that?"

Blake did understand. Of everyone he'd met in the Space Corps, Fleet Admiral Duggan was the most human of them all and the triggering of Last Stand would be the hardest, most abhorrent action for him to contemplate. Blake only had to mourn the consequences. It was Duggan's soul which had to carry the weight of eight billion dead for an eternity.

"There has to be another way, sir," he said, his voice cracking with emotion.

"I hope we can find one. Now, be on your way to Pioneer."

On the viewscreen, the stasis beam holding the *ES Devastator* pulled the trapped battleship to its final resting place. Blake couldn't stand to watch any longer.

"Lieutenant Quinn, you have the coordinates – take us to Pioneer."

"Yes, sir."

The *Ulterior-2*'s fission engines spooled up, launched the vessel across 150 million kilometres and then wound down. Blake's mind was elsewhere, but some part of his body knew what was expected and his hands piloted the spaceship into a high orbit and then activated the autopilot.

Far below, the death of billions had already been decided by others living countless light years away. *Better that they don't know.*

CHAPTER SEVEN

WHATEVER CREW WAS in charge of *Ix-Gastiol*, they showed no indication they were in a rush. One-by-one, the capital ship plucked the stricken allied warships out of Laspan's chromosphere. To Blake's relief, the Vraxar prioritised the spaceships whose trajectory would take them into the sun or higher into the corona where the temperatures were unmanageable. It didn't seem likely the aliens had suddenly discovered a sense of compassion and Blake had no doubt their motives were purely selfish.

The crew's attempts to put names to the warships were fruitless and they soon gave up trying. The distance was too great for the *Ulterior-2*'s sensors to gather any meaningful information and with the local Space Fleet network silent, each captured vessel looked like nothing more than a darkened blur on the surface of Laspan, with *Ix-Gastiol* a larger blur in the centre.

"That's them done," said Lieutenant Pointer. "We lost a total of six combined in the sun and the corona."

"An overall total of fifty-three warships gone, just like that," said Quinn.

"Do we even know they're gone?" asked Cruz. "We can

assume the Vraxar have control over their engines or processing clusters but there have been no intrusions through the hulls, so maybe everyone is still alive."

"Alive and awaiting death or conversion. More likely both."

"I think we're aware of the consequences, Lieutenant Quinn," said Blake.

"Sorry, sir."

Whilst the numbness hadn't gone, Blake found his mind had tucked it into a far recess – a recess to which his optimistic spirit did its best to deny him access. This corner of his mind was like a mass grave, filled with twisted, agonised corpses and covered with a thin veneer of dust to conceal the worst of what lay beneath, whilst a grinning clown danced on top, endlessly repeating the words *Nothing to worry about, nothing to see!*

"This can't be the only way," he said for the dozenth time. "I refuse to accept that every avenue leads to the same outcome."

"There *is* a way, sir," said Pointer. "We've simply got to think of it."

He tried to smile at the words and failed. "There's not much time to find that which eludes us, Lieutenant. I won't give up, though."

"Why don't they remote detonate Falsehood and have done with it?" asked Hawkins. "Maybe Laspan won't be affected – it's a whole damned star after all."

"High command seems convinced it's a definite outcome," said Blake. "At the moment, death is only waiting. While the people on Pioneer are still alive I guess there's no need to bring forward the inevitable. Something might show up." He gave a bitter laugh. "Most importantly, they've lost contact with the bomb. The theory is that its Obsidiar control processor got fried by the Vraxar weapon."

"You didn't tell us that!" said Pointer accusingly.

"I shouldn't be telling you it now, Lieutenant. It was a classified communication."

"Surely the crew on the *Devastator* must be able to get it running again?" said Hawkins. "They could swap in a new processing unit from their spares."

"The same theory also projects that the *Devastator* – and indeed all other warships involved – lost every Obsidiar processor, both those installed and those locked up as spares. The *Ulterior-2* was right on the periphery and we lost a bunch of ours."

"So they might have a bomb which they're unable to activate?"

"That's the likelihood. Regardless, Admiral Harvey will continue to follow his orders and won't risk detonating the bomb so close to the sun."

"Every ship will be completely sensor blind if their processing cores are gone," said Pointer. "They don't install viewing lenses for the crew on warships these days, so there's no way to look outside without the sensors. Even if *Ix-Gastiol* went to lightspeed and the *Devastator*'s crew detected the transition, for all they know, the enemy could be sitting off Pioneer at the end of the journey, or any of our other worlds."

"A bad situation," said Hawkins.

"And it's logical to think the Vraxar have a method of clearing away any unwanted crew from the warships they capture," added Blake. "They may already be dead."

They sat glumly for a time. The channel to the *Maximilian* was still open, though they received no updates or changes to their orders. *Ix-Gastiol* remained in place and gave no clue as to what the Vraxar might do next. Blake found his eyes continuously jumping to the bulkhead clock, as if the answers to the future lay within its ever-changing numbers.

"What would *Captain* Duggan have done?" asked Hawkins, trying to lighten the mood. "Maybe you should ask him, sir."

"I think he'd have told us already if he had a plan, Lieutenant," Blake replied, not really paying attention to the words. Then, an idea of sorts came, unearthed by a combination of Hawkins' question and the endless churning of his brain. He sat bolt upright.

"I know what Captain Duggan would have done! I know what he *did* do."

"Sir?"

"During the Estral wars, he performed a lightspeed jump into the centre of a Dreamer mothership and detonated the *ESS Crimson*'s arsenal of nuclear warheads!"

"And then did an SRT to escape from their hold," said Pointer. "I see you've been doing some reading, sir."

"It seemed remiss of me to ignore the lessons of the past," he said. "Get hold of Fleet Admiral Duggan for me!"

"Yes, sir," said Cruz. "I've put in the request."

"What am I missing?" said Quinn, scratching the side of his head.

"In due course, Lieutenant."

Duggan's voice came through the bridge speakers a few seconds later. "Make this brief, please. I have a lot to be getting on with."

"I have an idea, sir – and it's one you might appreciate."

There were the faintest signs of a stirring interest in Duggan's response. "I'm listening."

Blake found his voice climbing in volume as he spoke through the outline of his plan. "If we do an SRT into the centre of *Ix-Gastiol* while carrying the Star Taker bomb from Pioneer, we could use conventional weapons against the interior of the enemy warship in the hope that it drives them away from here. Once they are gone from Laspan, we leave the bomb behind on a short timer and SRT out. The enemy's shields won't do anything to stop an explosion taking place inside their perimeter."

"It won't work," said Duggan immediately. He was not a man who willingly accepted inevitable failure so he quickly corrected himself. "It almost certainly won't work."

"Sir?"

"There are a few reasons I can think of, chief amongst them is your inability to detonate the Star Taker bomb – as you are aware, it requires a series of command codes to activate. If anything were to happen to the *Ulterior-2* and more importantly the bomb you propose to carry, we would lose the chance to destroy *Ix-Gastiol* assuming it comes close enough to Pioneer to be caught in the blast."

"I am aware of the command codes," said Blake. "Can I be provided with sole authority in the same way you had before?"

"Not easily – it would require approval from each of the existing code holders. That should present no obstacle, however, this would be followed by several hours of reprogramming on the bomb itself. It's tied into Last Stand now and there was no expectation it would need to be removed at short notice."

"How many hours, sir? If it's two or three hours, there may still be an opening for us."

"On top of the reprogramming, there is the time overhead of getting a team to the bomb and then there are many security protocols which prevent the release of the device to the surface. After that, we would require a suitable method of transportation to get Falsehood into the *Ulterior-2*'s shuttle bay. This would need to be accomplished under a constant risk that the enemy would arrive at Pioneer while the bomb is in the middle of being reprogrammed."

"I thought it was worth consideration, sir," said Blake, realising he'd been naïve to think something as powerful as an Obsidiar bomb could be reprogrammed and loaded onto a spaceship in the space of an hour or two.

Duggan wasn't finished. "In addition, there is no guarantee your actions will make the enemy run."

"Once they realise what we've done, they probably won't want to stick around to see if we replicate the tactics using a fleet of a hundred warships. They might go to lightspeed and never come back."

"They might," Duggan mused. "The problem is, we don't have a fleet of a hundred anywhere close, since we've stripped the area of our warships. In fact, the *Maximilian* is one of the closest and I promised to stay out of trouble."

"It's a chance, sir."

Duggan sighed loudly. "I appreciate your commitment, Captain Blake. Time and again you have proven your ability to pull a victory from out of nowhere. I have always prided myself on knowing when to take a risk and when to back off. On this occasion, I can't see how I would be doing anything other than approving your suicides."

Blake swallowed. "The loss of the *Ulterior-2* and its crew would be a small price to pay for what we might accomplish."

"We have no idea what lies within the enemy spaceship. What if the *Ulterior-2* simply exited lightspeed in the exact location of an existing solid object, such as *Ix-Gastiol*'s engines? Our research in this field is extremely limited, however there were a few cases from the early days of lightspeed flight where the guidance computers got it wrong and spaceships are thought to have appeared within the centre of planets. I say *thought* because they disappeared and were never found. We may lose our newest Hadron without it firing a shot at the enemy ship."

A surge of fervour gripped Blake and somehow he knew, without a shadow of a doubt that what he was proposing was the only possible way to force a change upon the inevitable. "Let me do this, sir! Let me and my crew take the necessary action."

Duggan recognized Blake's zeal and his tones softened. "What exactly are you proposing, Captain Blake?"

"A shot in the dark, sir. A reach into the absolute unknown to see what comes from it."

"Explain."

"If you remote detonate Star Taker, the people on Pioneer will die. If you remote detonate Falsehood with *Ix-Gastiol* so near to the sun, the people on Pioneer will die. We're in a position where the destruction of the enemy will have a terrible price. With the local fleet out of action, it is no longer so important for the *Ulterior*-2 to be employed as a mobile sensor station. As soon as you detect the failure of Pioneer's surface comms hub, you'll know it's time to detonate the bomb."

"That's not quite the certainty I am looking for before I authorise the use of Star Taker. I would prefer to know exactly what was happening."

"Then bring the *Maximilian* here, sir. Keep a distance and monitor the situation."

"Let me hear more of your plan."

"We take the *Ulterior*-2 back to Laspan and see if our sensors can identify any open spaces within *Ix-Gastiol*. We execute a short-range transit inside the enemy ship and..." Blake closed his eyes. "...we deploy troops before the enemy realise what we've done."

The outburst of shock or surprise didn't come. "Go on," said Duggan.

"Falsehood isn't on the Last Stand network, sir. You provide us with the codes and we take them to the bomb. Assuming the *Ulterior*-2 is not disabled when it emerges from its SRT, I will activate its battle computer and instruct it to cause maximum damage in order to make the Vraxar leave the Laspan system. We will fight our way to the *Devastator* and activate Falsehood."

"As easy as that."

"I'm aware there is little possibility of success, sir. Any chance that is above zero percent is an improvement."

"The fact isn't lost on me."

"If we are without hope of reaching the *Devastator*, we will sabotage whatever we are able to. It may be a drop in the ocean, but there could be unforeseen benefits in the future. Even if our actions give the Vraxar something to think about, it may cause them to hesitate at a crucial moment."

"I am not convinced."

Blake felt disappointment at the words. In these few minutes he'd mentally built himself up to the coming task and it was hard to come down. Words failed him and he couldn't think of a well-constructed response.

"I think we may regret it later, sir."

Duggan gave a snort of laughter. "I said I wasn't convinced and I'm not. Given what we face, I am willing to let you try whatever it takes. As long as your crew are aware of what you have volunteered them for."

Blake realised he'd forged ahead with his idea and given his crew no chance to speak. He turned and raised an eyebrow.

Lieutenant Pointer returned a stern look, as if disappointed he'd even asked. Cruz simply grinned.

"Hell, yeah," said Hawkins a second later, like she wasn't expecting the question.

Quinn shrugged. "Fine with me."

Neither Ensign Bailey or Park offered any disagreement – they'd seen plenty of action during the Vraxar war and were ready for promotion whenever they asked. That left the troops stationed in the cramped quarters of the *Ulterior-2*.

"The crew are with me, sir," said Blake. "We're carrying seventeen hundred soldiers."

"This is their job, Captain. To do what must be done."

"Lieutenant McKinney is going to be happy."

"He knows how to deal with the crap. I've added you to the list of authorised personnel who can activate Falsehood."

Duggan didn't hang around when it came to the big stuff.

"What if I'm killed, sir?"

"Make sure you aren't. It's only because of your existing rank I was able to add you so quickly to the database of personnel approved for access to the highest-level resources. Our security system will automatically refuse a request to add anyone of a lower rank and, as you're aware, it'll take many hours for any field promotions to become active. In other words, I can't make everyone on the *Ulterior-2* an acting captain, if that's what you were thinking."

"In that case, I'll do my best to stay low."

"Do you know what to do in the event Falsehood's activation panel is burned out?"

"We've got working spare Obsidiar processing cores here. They're a standard size and should fit straight into a diagnostic tablet."

"Once the tablet is ready, you'll need to download the control software for the bomb, which you should now have access to do."

"Yes, sir. Then we bring the tablet to Falsehood and if the range is close enough, we should be able to interface even if the bomb's existing control panel is burned out or offline."

"I'm glad you've been keeping up to speed with our technology, Captain Blake. You're quite correct – if you bring the tablet near enough to the bomb, you'll be able to do what needs to be done."

"In which case I am ready to proceed."

"Good luck." The channel went quiet for a time. Duggan wasn't gone. "Thank you for reminding me that there is always a choice, irrespective of how hard it might be to make the most difficult ones."

Blake caught the layers of underlying meaning and he

addressed the important one. "We aren't dead yet, sir. We will never surrender the lives of our people if there is an unexplored avenue open to us."

"Well said."

With the decision made, the conversation was finished. Duggan was always busy, even during peacetime and Blake had to prepare. With the threat of *Ix-Gastiol* hanging over them, there wasn't time to waste.

"Well, folks, here's another shitty job for us."

"One you asked for," said Pointer mildly.

"And one which you agreed to, Lieutenant."

She smiled, up for the challenge. "After the event."

Blake pretended he hadn't heard and cleared his throat. "Lieutenant Quinn, please target an area in Laspan's chromosphere two hundred thousand klicks from the enemy vessel. We will depart as soon as we're ready. Activate the fission suppression and once we arrive, we'll come in closer to *Ix-Gastiol* using our stealth modules."

The order caught Quinn on the hop and he was evidently expecting a rather more detailed planning phase before the operation started.

"Are we going now?" he stammered.

"I was simply advising you of my intentions. We have a few things to deal with before we leave."

"Two hundred thousand klicks is pretty close," said Quinn.

"The closer we get, the better," said Cruz. "If we're intending to launch an entire Hadron into the middle of *Ix-Gastiol* we'll need to locate a big space to aim for. There's a better chance of the sensors finding what we're looking for when we're near."

"What if the enemy detect us?" asked Quinn. "They could use that area-disruptor weapon on us."

"If they get a lock on us, we'll SRT immediately."

"Even without knowledge of where we might end up?"

"We'll have to handle whatever comes, Lieutenant."

Quinn wasn't the only one with questions to unload. "Fleet Admiral Duggan mentioned a diagnostic tablet and software, sir," offered Lieutenant Cruz.

"Yes, let's get this diagnostic tablet sorted out first. Afterwards, I'll have a word with Lieutenant McKinney."

There was a wide locker on the bridge, flush to the wall, which stretched from the floor most of the way to the ceiling. It was haphazardly filled with stacks of expensive military hardware, much of it probably forgotten about and replaced with new in a demonstration of waste sufficient to make a grown tax payer weep. Blake hardly recognized some of the stuff, but the pile of seven diagnostic tablets was easy enough to locate, sitting atop of the partial innards from a last-gen comms panel. In his haste, Blake dragged two diagnostic tablets out, the second of which clattered onto the floor, its screen breaking in the process.

"Oops," he said absently, sweeping it side-footed back into the locker.

"According to our inventory, there are nine spare Obsidiar processors in the central stores section," said Cruz. "That's a long way from the bridge."

Blake sat himself down. "There are only six in the central stores," he said, entering a series of commands into one of his screens. "And I know that because three of them are in a compartment at the bottom of this console."

Cruz watched open-mouthed as Blake reached between his knees into a square opening in the dull metal of the main control panel for the *Ulterior*-2. He located a thick polymer glove, which he dragged on. Then, he fished out a small, square, black object, which seemed to absorb light. Blake held it between his thumb and forefinger so the others could see it.

"Doesn't look like much, does it?"

"I dread to think what that cost," said Cruz. "And it's a

breach of about fifteen rules and directives for it to be somewhere other than in the central stores. How did it get here?"

"I brought it to the bridge while we were in flight towards Pioneer," said Blake. "There's no point in keeping the spares ten minutes away from where they're needed." With a grunt of concentration, he levered out the existing processor from the diagnostic tablet and placed it nearby. Then, he slid the replacement Obsidiar unit into its place, the task made difficult because of the insulated glove he wore.

"I was expecting something a little more impressive," said Ensign Bailey.

"Fifty years ago, that would have been contained within a specially-designed cube weighing about three hundred pounds," said Blake. "The wonders of miniaturisation."

With that, he laid the tablet onto the floor at his feet and leaned forward to access a series of new menus on his console. It didn't take long to find what he was looking for. Each Obsidiar bomb was unique and each had its own command program. Blake read through the list of names, unsurprised to discover there were several more of the devices in production than he was aware of. The code for the Falsehood bomb was a few hundred thousand lines in length and it downloaded into the diagnostic tablet in a fraction of a second. He bent over and picked the device up.

"Done."

"Is it working?"

"Seems to be." He put the tablet down. "Get me through to Lieutenant McKinney on the internal comms. He'll need to make a few preparations and his time is limited."

Blake's impatience was growing and he listed off a series of requirements and recommendations, to which McKinney listened without speaking. Soon, it was done and Blake closed the channel, relieved the commander of the *Ulterior-2*'s troops wasn't the kind of man who asked a lot of pointless questions.

"Get into your spacesuits and keep a visor and rifle close by."

The others crowded around a second locker, this one containing twenty suits on a rack, a box of visors and a variety of light arms. Space Corps personnel were expected to be able to get into a suit in less than two minutes and although Blake didn't keep a check, he was pleased to find everyone ready and back in their seats in an acceptable time. He flexed his arms and the material of his suit squeaked faintly.

"I told Lieutenant McKinney he has twenty minutes to get ready."

"That's going to be tight."

"He didn't complain."

"Lieutenant McKinney isn't a complainer," said Cruz.

It was true – Blake couldn't recall a single word of complaint from McKinney. Even so, he would have definitely spoken up if he felt he needed more time. For once, the minutes passed quicker than Blake would have liked – quickly enough that his creeping trepidation couldn't take hold. As soon as the action began, he knew his fears would be forgotten. At twenty minutes, his hand snapped out and he opened a channel.

"Lieutenant McKinney?"

"Ready whenever you are, sir."

It was all Blake needed to hear. Activate the short-range transit," he said, his voice firm.

No one requested a further delay, each recognizing that this was going to be a mission in which they would respond to circumstances, rather than being permitted the luxury of advance planning. In a way it was for the best, Blake reflected, since it left them with no time to ponder their tenuous grasp on life.

"Activating SRT," said Quinn.

The *Ulterior-2* entered lightspeed, bringing the crew at unimaginable velocity towards their destiny.

CHAPTER EIGHT

THE *ULTERIOR-2'S* processing cluster dumped the battleship out of lightspeed within a few kilometres of its target location. The fission suppression modules, energy shield and stealth modules produced a brief spike on a dozen different gauges and then it was done. There was a tiny interval during which they were visible to sensor sight – arriving so close to the enemy was a risk, albeit a calculated one.

"Please report," said Blake.

"It's hot outside, but there has been no outward change in activity from the enemy vessel," said Cruz. "They are two hundred thousand klicks ahead and have not moved since the engagement with our fleet."

"I'm checking out their hull readings," said Quinn. "There's nothing untoward. Their shield generators have more than likely replenished whatever damage we did to them before."

Pointer brought *Ix-Gastiol* up on the main feed. "Here they are."

"Not doing anything," said Blake. "That's a whole lot of

spaceship to leave sitting around. They've got to do something soon."

"Yep. We need to get moving, sir," Hawkins replied.

"Lieutenants Pointer, Cruz - can you get the data we need from this distance?"

"If there was only pure, empty vacuum between us the answer would be no," said Pointer. "We need to fire some close-range soundings off their hull and with something as dense as a spaceship, it's not going to be anything like as accurate as we want."

"How much closer?"

"Right on top of them close."

"I'll take us in slowly," said Blake.

Although he itched to push the *Ulterior-2* to its maximum velocity, there was a major benefit to a measured approach - at low speeds the reduced output from the gravity engines made it easier for the stealth modules to mask their signature. When it came to the Vraxar it was always better to arrive unnoticed.

"One hundred klicks per second," said Hawkins. "I could run faster than this."

"Fine, let's double it," said Blake.

At two hundred kilometres per second, the spaceship's engines made barely a murmur. It would take sixteen minutes to cross the intervening space at their current velocity, which seemed like a wise investment. The Hadron gradually closed the gap, whilst the heat from Laspan beat against its energy shields. So far, they were holding and Blake marvelled at the capabilities of the single remaining Obsidiar power core deep inside their hull. At the moment, it was defying a star.

Blake knew he had the easy job – all he was required to do was keep the spaceship at a constant speed along a predeter-mined course. Whilst he sat with his hands resting on the control bars, his technical officers threw ideas and possibilities between themselves.

"Attempting a narrow scan of the enemy vessel's forward upper flank," said Pointer. "Too much interference."

"I'm trying to tune out the radiation from our inbound feed," said Quinn. "That might clear things up a little."

"There are too many fluctuations," said Cruz. "Early indications are the rear twenty percent of *Ix-Gastiol* is solid right the way through. I can't be certain."

"I've added the radiation filters – tell me if that improves things."

"Not much – there's still too much background crap."

"In that case, let me see if I can get a few specific readings from their hull."

"Do we have any useful data from previous encounters with Vraxar spaceships?" asked Hawkins. "Maybe they design them the same way."

"I think *Ix-Gastiol* is something completely new, Lieutenant," said Cruz.

"Worth a go, surely?" asked Blake.

"Yes, sir. I'll see what's in our database."

The Space Corps had captured the remains of several Vraxar warships which were defeated earlier in the war. Mostly the wreckage was too badly damaged to extract anything of much use – when you didn't know what an enemy was capable of it was best to keep shooting at them until you were certain they couldn't fire back.

Blake set the *Ulterior-*2 on autopilot and, using his own console, joined Cruz in combing through the reconstructions pieced together by the Space Corps. In truth, he'd seen most of it before and there were no surprises. The Vraxar ships weren't vastly more advanced than their Space Corps equivalents and were largely made from Gallenium, with compact internal areas for their crews.

"No insights from this," said Blake.

"No, sir."

"We're within a hundred thousand klicks of *Ix-Gastiol*. I'm taking us off autopilot."

"Aha - I'm beginning to get some more useful data," said Pointer. "The *Ulterior-2*'s AI is plotting a model for us."

"Let me see."

"It's not complete."

"I appreciate that."

Blake called up the model of *Ix-Gastiol*. It was an intricate 3D representation of the enemy vessel, which updated with every passing second. There was a series of shapes within the model, outlined in blue and representing the best guesses as to where there might be hollow spaces inside the Vraxar ship.

"It's riddled with them," he said.

"That's my belief," said Pointer. "The trouble is, there aren't many into which the *Ulterior-2* will fit neatly."

"I dread to think what they're keeping in some of these larger spaces," said Blake, remembering what Lieutenant McKinney had discovered within the crashed Neutraliser Ir-Klion-32. There had been a million or more Vraxar, held in an induced sleep and kept pinned against metal posts.

"If we're lucky, it's the entire Vraxar population," said Cruz with venom. "So when we set off Falsehood, it'll knock the bastards out for good."

The *Ulterior-2* continued onwards and the 3D model updated with the new sensor data. The battleship's sensor arrays could pierce most substances, but the denser the object, the less accurate were the results and the closer they needed to be. The ship's core cluster tried to compensate by assigning percentages to each of the assumed open spaces, to indicate the reliability of the data. The ever-changing numbers only confused things and Blake switched off the overlay.

There was something on the model which mystified them all. Running along the centre of Ix-Gastiol was a darker area, two hundred kilometres in length, one hundred high and one hundred in depth.

"Any guesses?" asked Blake.

"They must have additional shielding around that area, sir. Our sensors can't penetrate it at all. I've tried every trick and our soundings are simply bouncing back."

"What could do that? Is there a material dense enough to stop our sensors?"

"It could be a few things, sir. That area could be completely solid – some kind of alloy we aren't familiar with. On the other hand, it could be a charged shielding plate specifically designed to repel attempts to probe through it."

"Seems like a lot of effort."

"We have no idea what the Vraxar have fought against in the past. Five hundred years ago they might have faced a species with advanced scanner technology which could disrupt whatever is in the middle of Ix-Gastiol."

"In other words, there's either something enormously important inside there, or it's little more than a type of solid alloy, most likely used for propulsion."

"Probably," agreed Pointer.

"If it's hollow and it's important, that makes it a good target for our SRT."

"After which there will be a one-hundred-klick run from there to the ES Devastator," said Hawkins.

"And certain death if it's a solid object and we exit lightspeed in the centre of it," added Quinn for good measure.

It was an enigma to which there was currently no answer.

"I'm not planning to come any closer than twenty thousand klicks to *Ix-Gastiol*. Will we know more by that stage?"

"Maybe."

"I was hoping for a little more than probablies and maybes, given what's at stake." He caught the look on Pointer's face. "I am aware this mission hinges on uncertainties, but it doesn't stop me wanting more."

She surprised him with a grin and then dropped her head once more to the comms console.

The next few minutes were tense and Blake had to wipe the sweat from his palms. It was as though the burning heat from Laspan was being transmitted through the energy shield and the battleship's hull, leaving the bridge air conditioning unable to cope. Blake was sure it was his imagination playing tricks, but when he sucked in a lungful of air, there was a definite warmth to it.

This close to the sun, they got an excellent idea of exactly how tempestuous the surface really was. It churned and spat, throwing up occasional plumes, some of which extended for hundreds or thousands of kilometres. For most people, it would have been a vision of hell.

At thirty thousand kilometres from *Ix-Gastiol*, the 3D model reached a stage where it was as close to completion as it was likely to become. There were hundreds of spaces inside the Vraxar ship, the size of most estimated to within a hundred metres. However, the main central area continued to defy their efforts until the very last moment, when Cruz and Pointer made a breakthrough.

"It's hollow," said Cruz.

"How sure are you?"

"Absolutely certain, sir," Pointer replied.

"That's an answer I can work with." No sooner were the words spoken than he realised that the knowing didn't make his coming decision any easier. "Why the hell do they need such a large, open area?"

"Troops or spaceships," said Hawkins promptly.

Those were the logical choices. "Can you work out if the central space is subdivided at all?" asked Blake.

"I can't tell you for definite, sir. Our sensors aren't capable of identifying anything so delicate as a metal floor meant for personnel. We can find large, solid objects and from that we can determine which areas are not solid. There's no subtlety."

"At the moment, the central area is the only space guaranteed to fit the *Ulterior-2*," he mused. "Even if it is a long way from our goal."

"There are thirty additional areas where we *might* fit, with seven of them significantly closer to the *ES Devastator*," said Cruz. "If we accept the loss of the *Ulterior-2* as inevitable, we could SRT into one of these other areas."

Blake studied the 3D model again, his finger absently tracing the possible destinations. While several of these spaces were theoretically large enough, there was the additional uncertainty of lightspeed travel to contend with. With enough processing brute force, a warship's brain could do the calculations well enough to exit a short lightspeed transit more or less on the nose. Therein lay the problem – *more or less* could mean a variation of a few hundred metres and the longer the jump, the greater the variation became. It was unlikely, but there was a chance the *Ulterior-2* might not end up dead-centre in one of the smaller compartments. In addition, the more space the battleship was given once it arrived, the more freely it could open up with its weapons, greatly increasing the damage it might inflict upon the interior of *Ix-Gastiol*. If they couldn't force the Vraxar warship into flight, they couldn't set off Falsehood.

"Everything is contingent upon something else," muttered Blake. "If one thing goes wrong, everything fails."

"Since when was that unusual, sir?" asked Hawkins.

"Ever since the damned Vraxar showed up."

Hawkins could always look on the bright side and she laughed. "What are you going to complain about when they're gone, sir?"

"I'll think of something."

The exchange lasted only a few seconds, yet it was enough for the part of Blake's mind which worked independently of his mouth to make a decision. For better or worse, he was set.

"We're going for the centre," he said. "It's a long run from there to the *Devastator*, but I'm not happy there's anywhere else we can safely transit into. If any of the closer areas was larger, I'd aim for one of those. As it is, I believe we may destroy our ship immediately if we make the wrong choice. Without a spaceship, the plan fails from the outset. If the ship is destroyed it is certain we'll die with it."

"Do you think we can cover a hundred klicks inside that thing on foot?" asked Cruz.

It wasn't the time for lies or false promises. "No, I don't think we can make it. That doesn't mean we shouldn't try."

Cruz shrugged in acceptance. "I have no desire to fly away from here and leave the people of Pioneer to whatever the Vraxar have planned. I'll die one day and it might as well happen in a worthwhile cause."

"That's how I see it, Lieutenant."

"If the Vraxar transport their troops in the same way as they did on the Ir-Klion-32, there could easily be fifty billion of them on *Ix-Gastiol*, whilst leaving huge areas of the interior nearly deserted," said Quinn. "You can fit a lot of bodies into a tight space if you don't care about comfort."

"Maybe that's what these smaller open spaces represent," said Blake. "Vraxar holding facilities, filled with enough of their troops to overrun the entire Confederation."

"I've been downloading the model to the visor computers as it updates," said Cruz. "It may not be a perfect representation of the interior, but it'll allow us to avoid these areas if we wish."

"Good thinking, Lieutenant Cruz, thank you."

"No problem, sir."

The time was rapidly approaching. Blake spoke to Lieutenant McKinney again and was pleased to find the *Ulterior-2*'s troops were in position. There was one last choice hanging over him and he was undecided which way to play it. The plan had always been to leave the *Ulterior-2*'s battle computer in charge, while the crew fought their way to the *Devastator*. After giving the matter a lot of thought, he was beginning to think the best course of action was to leave most of the battleship's crew on the bridge to oversee its operation. He'd initially convinced himself that the interior space of *Ix-Gastiol* was somehow heavily defended and that the *Ulterior-2* wouldn't survive for long, in which case it was wise to abandon ship quickly and leave the battle computer to the task of inflicting the most damage on the enemy vessel. There was little logical in this – it was unheard of for the interior of a spaceship to be equipped with anything more than a few automated miniguns. Certainly, there shouldn't be anything capable of destroying a fully-shielded Space Corps Hadron battleship.

However, there was still something about *Ix-Gastiol* which made him think the normal rules didn't apply. His worries sapped him of his ability to choose and he remained torn. Blake wasn't usually afraid of making the tough choices and he couldn't understand his difficulty. Then, he knew. There was more than dispassionate logic at play here...there was something else. There was someone he couldn't bear the thought of not seeing again and the possibility of her death was too hard for him to imagine, let alone be the deciding force of it.

Deep down, Blake knew he was the only person out of the

entire crew who was required to leave the ship, since he was the only one with the command codes for the Obsidiar bomb.

"I don't want to leave anyone..." he began, realising how weak it sounded.

"You're thinking about it the wrong way, sir," said Pointer. "You have the mentality which dictates everyone has to live through this or you've failed. That isn't the case – if everyone dies apart from you and you manage to activate the Obsidiar bomb at the right time, then this mission will have been the most successful one in the history of the Confederation."

He couldn't meet her eyes. "I can't allow myself to see it that way, Lieutenant."

Pointer came over and crouched next to him. She put her hand to his cheek. "You have to, sir. We have to win this, whatever the cost."

"The costs are high."

Her eyes glistened. "It's not about us. Everything else is more important. Do you understand that, Charlie?"

It was the first time he could remember her using his first name. "I wish it was otherwise."

"I don't ever want you to back down because of me."

He saw in her expression the truth of those words and he understood the enormity of it. Up until now it had been just a war – a war he hated and one he wanted to win with every fibre of his existence. Now, there was a whole lot more to lose than just his life. He was adrift and he hated it.

"Do what you have to, sir."

"When all roads lead to damnation, you've got to do your duty," he said, the words leaden on his lips. He climbed to his feet, picked up the diagnostic tablet, visor and rifle. "I'll join the others. Once I'm in the shuttle, execute the SRT into the middle area of *Ix-Gastiol* and begin shooting. Stay with the *Ulterior-2* and give those bastards hell."

"Don't you worry about that, sir," said Hawkins, forcing levity into her voice.

With his course chosen, Blake became aware of how much time he'd spent in reflection. He touched the tip of his finger to the end of Lieutenant Pointer's nose.

"Thank you."

She tried to smile at him. "See you around, huh?"

"I'll do everything I can to make this work." He raised his voice, so the others could hear. "Take care of yourselves and don't ever tell yourselves that this is the end."

With that, he strode away from the bridge, trying his best to conceal the depths of his emotions. As soon as the blast door closed behind him, he broke into a run towards the *Ulterior-2*'s main shuttle bay. His final words with Pointer had been the hardest test.

Blake wasn't far from the shuttle bay when he felt the metal floor shuddering beneath his feet. The sensation was familiar, unmistakeable and it could only mean one thing. Lieutenant Quinn had activated the SRT earlier than planned.

With the blood pounding in his ears, Blake sprinted for the shuttle bay.

CHAPTER NINE

SHUTTLE ONE WAS CLAMPED against its docking iris and accessed via a long, narrow room which extended for well over a hundred metres. Luckily, Blake's destination was the closer of the two airlocks and he charged inside. The door whisked closed automatically when he was through. There was a group of four soldiers at the far end of the airlock corridor, nervously shifting from foot to foot. Behind, the shuttle door was open, revealing the brightly-lit crowded interior of the transport craft.

"Get in!" shouted Blake.

The soldiers didn't need to be asked twice. As one, they spun and crowded into the passenger bay. Blake reached the door a split second later, pushing his way through the crush.

"Close up the door!" came a voice from somewhere in the bay.

Those men and women nearest to the entrance pressed deeper inside, so as not to trigger the shuttle door's automatic safety cut-off which would prevent the door shutting if it thought someone was going to be trapped. Blake felt the people around him push inwards, squeezing him tightly.

"That's us closed," yelled the same voice which Blake belatedly realised was that of Sergeant Rod Woods.

The gravity clamps holding the shuttle in place clunked and boomed. Blake found himself some room and craned his neck to see what was happening. The passenger bay of Shuttle One was a big space, but at the moment it was holding close to four hundred of the *Ulterior-2*'s soldiers, with the remainder divided between shuttles two through four. There was a constant exchange of wisecracks and grumbling – the standard fare before a battle.

Blake wasn't comfortable being away from the action, so he did his best to reach the cockpit door. It wasn't easy to make progress, not because the troops were reluctant to move, simply because there was nowhere for them to go. Blake felt something hard crack against his shin. He peered down and saw that he'd taken an accidental knock from a gauss rifle barrel. It might have hurt more if it wasn't for the protective suit he was wearing. The owner turned and Blake didn't recognize the face. The man evidently didn't recognize the *Ulterior-2*'s captain too well either and he simply shrugged in apology.

"I hope you've got the safety activated," said Blake, with a twinge of irritation.

The soldier either didn't hear or wasn't interested in the conversation and he turned away. Blake continued his efforts to push through to the cockpit. The gravity clamps boomed again and he felt a surge of acceleration. It wasn't mere curiosity that made Blake so eager to have a look outside – as the most senior officer in the arena it was imperative he be there to make whatever decisions may be thrust upon them.

He reached the door, to find a broad-shouldered man standing directly in front of the access panel.

"The lieutenant doesn't want anyone pissing about and

distracting him," said Rank 1 Trooper Huey Roldan. "Oh, hello, sir."

"Good day, R1T Roldan."

The soldier stepped to his left, unceremoniously knocking several others out of his way. Blake moved into the gap and pressed his hand to the access panel. At the same moment, he heard Lieutenant McKinney's gravelly voice on the internal comms.

"Time to put your visors on, folks. Do it now and don't take them off until I tell you."

"Or he'll kick the crap out of you!" shouted Sergeant Woods.

There was a stirring of activity within the personnel bay, which Blake ignored. The cockpit door opened and he stepped sideways through it. There were three men sitting here and another two standing. Lieutenant Eric McKinney was easily recognizable even with his visor on. Firstly, because he was sitting in the pilot's seat and secondly because he was bigger than most of the others. He spoke without turning.

"Good afternoon, sir. Bannerman, move your backside and let Captain Blake have a seat."

Corporal Bannerman did as he was asked without a word. Blake took the man's place and at the same time, he pulled his own visor into place. The HUD was logically set out and Blake was automatically connected to the groups and sub-groups McKinney had already prepared. There was no opportunity to study it in detail and instead, Blake kept his attention on the shuttle's sensor feeds.

"Just in time, sir," said McKinney, his tone level. "We're coming out of the shuttle bay now. Shuttles Two, Three and Four are on their way and a few seconds behind. Keep your fingers crossed we find somewhere to land and that it doesn't get too bumpy."

Given the pace of events, Blake hadn't spent any time beyond the most fleeting of moments trying to imagine what the Vraxar might be hiding so deep within their largest ship. When the reality came, he was left with no doubt that guessing would not have stumbled upon the truth.

"Whoa, crap," said Sergeant Johnny Li, the first to give voice to what they were all thinking.

Blake took control of the forward sensor array, increased its viewing arc and panned it from left to right, then up and down. There was so much to take in, his brain didn't know where to start.

"Looks like we came in well front of centre," said McKinney, checking the updates fed from the *Ulterior-2*'s navigational system into the shuttle's much more rudimentary system. He aimed the craft towards the bottom of the vast space. "Please scan for a place to set us down. I've ordered the other three shuttles to keep within a thousand metres and follow."

Blake was fully aware he shouldn't be gawping. Even so, he couldn't help but take in the sights. It was easily the strangest place he'd ever been. However, having taken Bannerman's spot on the comms seat, he needed to perform that man's duties.

"No sign of hostiles," he said. "And no alerts from the *Ulterior-2*. Checking for a landing site."

Although there was no obvious threat, the relief Blake experienced was that of a patient given the all-clear on one debilitating disease only to hear they were afflicted by a second, equally unpleasant ailment. He couldn't quite believe his senses and he continued looking for signs of enemy activity.

"There's some kind of external crap our sensors can't recognize," said Li. "What are those green things? Some kind of emitters?"

"The *Ulterior-2* is now ten klicks above us," said Blake. On the sensor screen, the Hadron looked otherworldly in the erratically flickering, sickly green light of *Ix-Gastiol*'s interior. Shadows jumped and leapt, turning the warship's sleek lines into twisted, ugly parodies of the originals. "We got lucky with that SRT – seems like we came in within a couple of thousand metres of the side wall."

Blake continued working on the scanners. The more he saw, the more he became concerned. The cavernous space within *Ix-Gastiol* wasn't cuboid in shape like the sensor scans had suggested. Rather, it was an oval cylinder, which vanished into the distance towards the front and rear of the huge spaceship. The walls were made from what Blake assumed was the Vraxar's usual near-black alloy, but they weren't flat. Every thousand metres, there were thick bands of a green-glowing substance, two hundred metres thick and with a similar depth. These bands formed a series of rings all along the length of *Ix-Gastiol*. The light wasn't evenly-distributed about their surface - as though the power contained within was irregular - and it seemed to pulse faintly.

"It's like a huge coil," said Blake, wondering what the hell it meant. He opened a channel to the *Ulterior-2* and got Lieutenant Pointer on the other end. "Are you getting all of this?"

Her words were crisp and business-like. "Yes, sir. Our readings are unclear on what those bands are made up from. They're emitting some kind of new particle, which we're analysing for specifics, but we're already sure you don't want to be exposed to it any longer than necessary." Her voice hardened, which he understood to mean she was particularly worried about something. "That means either in your suits or in the shuttle."

He gathered from her voice that they had a theory on the bridge which she was hesitant to divulge. "What do the readings say about those bands?"

"Obsidiar, sir, except those pieces of it aren't generating anything like the same level of power."

"Depleted Obsidiar?" Blake said, not sure where the idea came from.

"That's what Lieutenant Quinn thought. There's something else, sir..."

"That thing at the far end? I've been trying to make it out, but the shuttle's sensors aren't reading it clearly."

As he spoke, he kept his eyes on the feed showing the area in question. There was a roughly circular *something* at the extreme end of the cylinder, one hundred and fifty kilometres away. Whatever it was, it had a diameter of eighty kilometres and seemed to hang in the air, like an area of dense, exceptionally grey cloud. There were things within the cloud – amorphous shapes and lines which, no matter how hard Blake tried to figure out what they were, defeated his efforts.

"Yes, sir. That thing. Anyway, we've detected a possible landing space for you near to it, so you'll need to be heading that way. I'm adding the coordinates to the nav computers for each of the four shuttles. If you turn on the autopilot it'll take you straight there."

Blake detected other words unspoken. "Tell me, damnit!"

"Just look, sir. Once you see, you might want to alter our plans."

Pointer's words left Blake utterly mystified and he was tempted to order her to tell him what was going on. He didn't push it. *Maybe it's for the best if I see it without the preconceptions of others,* he thought.

"Lieutenant McKinney, did you get that?"

"Yes, sir. I understand we need to get out of here as soon as possible."

"Take us to the place Lieutenant Pointer suggested."

"Will do." McKinney didn't switch on the autopilot and he guided the shuttle manually, altering their course and pushing on the control joystick to accelerate. "I'm going to maintain a five-klick distance between us and the walls. If it's as bad as Lieutenant Pointer reckons it is, I don't want to go too close."

"Shuttles Two, Three and Four are following our lead," said Li.

Above the flotilla of smaller spaceships, the *Ulterior-2* swung in the air, rotating with effortless grace until its nose was aimed in the same direction. Against the battleship, the transport craft appeared tiny, whilst the Hadron appeared equally insignificant in comparison to the size of this place within *Ix-Gastiol*. Blake suddenly felt extremely small.

McKinney didn't sound overawed. "One-thirty klicks to the target area. Please confirm it's safe to land."

Blake zoomed the sensors in to the place identified by the *Ulterior-2*. In normal circumstances, the shuttle's arrays would have easily picked out the details. Here, there was a hazy quality to the images, as though the sensor lenses were looking through a thick miasma of filthy Vraxar energy, which interfered with the feed.

"There!" he said. "Midway up the side wall. I think there's an opening."

It was difficult to be sure and the green bands provided a physical barrier in addition to whatever other crap was stopping the sensors working properly.

"It's an opening, not a landing pad," said Li. "I'm not in the mood for jumping."

"Maybe we can get on there," said Blake. "Once we get closer, we'll see."

"One hundred klicks," said McKinney. "Keeping it steady."

While the shuttle flew onwards, Blake did his best to understand what it was at the end of the cylinder. What had first appeared to be a cloud now looked more like a heavily frosted window, covered in grime. Details within were gradually becoming clearer, yet his brain couldn't interpret the data coming from his eyes. Bannerman leaned in, his chest pressing on Blake's shoulder.

"Shit!" he said, a hundred emotions compressed into that single word.

Blake then realised what it was. His mind fitted the pieces together and he knew. He was speechless and when he finally got control of his tongue, he didn't know what to say.

"More crazy readings," said Sergeant Li.

Blake snapped out of it and checked the instrument panel and the external feeds. The bands running around the cylinder began to glow with a far greater intensity and a grating vibration shook the walls of the shuttle. Blake heard a screeching, hollow groan from somewhere outside which made him grimace in pain.

"What the hell?"

"Look!" shouted Bannerman.

One hundred kilometres away, something emerged from the floating circle. A Vraxar warship sailed through with the silent menace of a shark hunting swimmers close to shore. It wasn't travelling at anything like its maximum speed, but the entirety of its three-thousand metre length came through in only a few seconds. Blake recognized it as a similar type of vessel to those he'd combatted above Atlantis what seemed like decades ago – it was a black, tapered cylinder with forward-pointing spines, the purpose of which he'd never learned.

Blake had no idea how the enemy warship had got here. However, one thing was beyond doubt – the arrival of the Vraxar cruiser was not good news, particularly for anyone who happened to be in something as small and defenceless as a shuttle.

"Get us out of here!" said Blake.

The words hadn't even left his mouth when everything started going downhill. Each of the shuttle's viewscreens turned completely white and a moment later, the craft was shaken by the explosive force of sixteen Shimmer missiles. The shockwave gripped the shuttle's hull and McKinney struggled to keep it level. He quickly decided on another method and threw the transport into a steep dive, whilst bringing the engines up to full thrust. The life support modules found it hard to keep up with the sudden change and Blake felt the sharp descent in his stomach and chest.

The sensors adjusted and the whiteness faded to a tolerable level. Blake saw the plasma fires spread across the Vraxar cruiser's energy shield, burning with unimaginable ferocity. Another four Shimmers detonated and a second shockwave rolled through the middle of *Ix-Gastiol*.

A new sound joined the din. Vast slugs of hardened Gallenium plunged through the aftereffects of the Shimmer missiles. The *Ulterior-2*'s Havoc cannons produced an unmistakeable retort – a clank, a hum and a thunderous recoil. The battleship fired twice more, punching the Vraxar ship with the most powerful ballistic weapons available to the Space Corps.

McKinney swore, locked in his own battle with the controls. Each new shockwave came with the strength to knock them from the sky and it felt to McKinney as though he wasn't the pilot at all – that his skills were meaningless in the face of the two warships fighting within the Vraxar coil.

"Come on, overcharge!" shouted Sergeant Li. "Do it!"

The overcharged particle beams were devastating weapons, but they also had their own type of recoil. When fired, they emitted a short-range burst of charged particles which could flatten a small town and turn the remains to white-hot dust. The *Ulterior-2* and its crew were shielded, but the energy had to go somewhere and it was designed to be thrown outwards from the weapon housing.

"We're too close!" said Blake. "If they fire, it'll crush us."

The shuttle was fitted with second-gen and third-gen tech,

which was more than adequate for day-to-day operations. It wasn't particularly well-suited to keeping track of the engagement happening here and Blake found himself hard-pushed to follow events. Much of what happened he was able to guess at through years of experience.

"The *Ulterior-2* is flying backwards," he said. "They're trying to make room."

"How much room do they need?"

"Fifty klicks or more."

A shadow passed over the transport vessel as the Hadron went by above. One of the underside Havoc cannons fired again, so close that Blake saw the enormous barrel thump back into its turret. As he was watching, dozens of Bulwark cannons appeared on the battleship's hull. The heavy gauss guns were fitted to runners which could bring the weapons into their firing position in a tenth of a second, making it seem as though they had come from nowhere.

"They aren't holding back," he said.

The Vraxar cruiser was not a passive recipient of the onslaught. Shuttle Three vanished from the tactical screen, turned into a burning lump of overheated alloy and carbonized bodies by a Vraxar particle beam. Another three particle beams lanced into the *Ulterior-2*'s shield.

In return, another salvo of missiles – Lambdas from the size of the blasts – struck the Vraxar cruiser, along with two more crushing impacts from the Havoc cannons.

McKinney swore at the loss of Shuttle Three, trying not to let it distract him from getting Shuttle One to its destination. He levelled them out three-quarters of the way from the top of the coil and brought them closer than he wanted to the green bands of depleted Obsidiar. The other two transports followed his course as closely as they could.

"Don't bunch up," he said over the comms. "Sixty klicks to go. Get ready for a quick evacuation."

Sergeant Li patched into the sensor feed and studied the area ahead. "I reckon we can land, sir. Looks like some kind of bay."

Meanwhile, the *Ulterior-2* continued flying directly away from the Vraxar cruiser, looking to make room to fire the overcharged particle beams. The front Havoc cannon fired again and its projectile collided with the nose of the enemy ship. The slug produced a crater a few hundred metres across before deflecting away to smash against the interior of the coil.

The Space Corps had taken big strides in warship design and the Vraxar cruiser was completely outmatched by the *Ulterior-2*. With its energy shield gone, it was vulnerable to whatever the Hadron's crew chose to launch.

"Come on, finish the bastards quickly," said Blake, acutely aware of how vulnerable the three remaining shuttles were. His eyes flicked to the distance counter, which informed him the *Ulterior-2* was fifty-five kilometres from Shuttle One.

Two things happened. The Vraxar cruiser accelerated hard along the length of the coil. It raced towards the Hadron, leaving the sound of its stressed gravity engines far behind. At the same time, the *Ulterior-2* fired another salvo of missiles and activated two of its four operational overcharged particle beams. A heavy percussive wave accompanied the incredible expulsion of energy as the twin beams tore through the cruiser's metal plating. The Vraxar warship's superheated metal expanded with such speed the vessel was torn into three separate pieces. The smallest front section, a mixture of blacks and dirty oranges, began tumbling at once and it hurtled over the transports, missing them by less than ten thousand metres. It skimmed the *Ulterior-2*'s shields and vanished into the distance.

The second section was the largest and it followed a divergent course to the front section. Again, it missed the shuttles, this time by a wider margin. This piece was alight and it burned so fiercely that it illuminated the interior of *Ix-Gastiol* like a sun. The crew of the *Ulterior-2* were too late to adjust and the main piece of the Vraxar cruiser hit the battleship's energy shield at an angle. Blake winced when he saw it, but to his relief, the Hadron's shield held and the white-hot wreckage glanced to the side, still travelling at speed. It spun wildly, uncontrollably into the side wall of the coil, where it created a wide furrow through six or seven of the depleted Obsidiar bands, before coming to a rest at the far end.

The third section was something else. The force of the sundering had slowed it, so that it spun lazily in the air – a thousand metres of hot Gallenium with a weight of two billion tonnes. The men in the shuttle's cockpit did their best to work out its course. Even though it was the slowest of the three parts, it was travelling with sufficient speed to fool the human eye. Blake tried to predict the arc. It was going to come off the wall nearby and then it might spin. After that...

"It's going to hit us."

There was no doubt whatsoever. Blake was one of the Space Corps' finest spaceship captains – he was born with something which gave him an edge over other people. It didn't make him proud, rather he was grateful for the gift he'd been blessed with. His mind worked through the variables and then it told him exactly what course the incoming wreckage would follow. After it clipped the wall, the rotation would flatten its trajectory, adding spin and then it would crash directly through the line of transports. Blake's fists clenched, longing to be in control of the vessel.

McKinney saw it too. His best skills lay elsewhere, but he was still an expert pilot. He banked hard, forcing the craft into a sharp dive whilst bringing them further away from the wall. It wasn't going to be enough. The pilots of Shuttles Two and Four also attempted evasive action, trying to get below the flight of the projectile. It was exactly the wrong thing to do and Blake felt total helplessness that he couldn't tell them.

Not nearly enough.

There was something he could do. Blake found himself moving instinctively, a slow-motion lunge across the cockpit.

The other shuttles twisted in flight, their engines incapable of providing sufficient thrust to avoid the inevitable. The final piece of the cruiser struck the wall. It didn't come away cleanly and one of the object's irregular edges altered its trajectory. McKinney grunted when he realised he'd misjudged and anger poured off him.

It's the realisation of what's coming. Only one way.

Blake's left hand grabbed the control stick, whilst the fingers of his right hand tore McKinney's thumb away from the throttle control button. McKinney had a death-grip on the joystick and it required all of Blake's strength to drag the alloy bar hard backwards. His forefinger found the emergency brake and he squeezed it tightly, breaking the restraining clip which was there to prevent an accidental activation.

The effect was immediate – the shuttle tipped backwards, its hull groaning with the sudden, severe braking forces. Beneath Blake's feet, the gravity engine shrieked as it went from maximum forward thrust to full reverse. The piece of wreckage streaked by underneath, missing the shuttle by less than ten metres. The spinning metal carried a blisteringly hot wind in its wake and a strong turbulence gripped the transport, shaking it violently. Blake still had hold of the joystick and the muscles in his forearm strained to keep the controller locked in place.

Just when he thought they'd made it, something crashed against the shuttle's hull with a screeching bang. Blake swore when he realised there'd been a much smaller piece of the cruiser behind the larger section. It knocked the transport violently to the side and into a spin. A series of emergency alerts flashed up, warning him of a breach, whilst the control stick took on a mind of its own and vibrated jarringly against his hands.

Moments after it passed Shuttle One, the wreckage tumbled through the remaining two transports, crushing them and hurling their broken shells to the ground. This final chunk of the Vraxar cruiser was so heavy the impacts didn't produce any deviation in its course. The piece struck the walls of the coil far below, before it skittered and spun to a stop fifty kilometres away.

The buffeting against Shuttle One died away and Blake brought them out of the spin.

"All yours, Lieutenant."

He released his hands from the controls. McKinney took over and wrestled them back on course, increasing their forward speed as high as it would go. The engines were damaged and refused to go above twenty percent.

"We've got a big hole in our side and we're burning up," said Li. "Too much heat from that lump of metal."

"We'll make it – keep focus!" McKinney snapped.

Back in his seat, Blake's eyes were drawn to one of the many status alerts.

> PERSONNEL BAY TEMPERATURE EXCEEDS MAXIMUM THRESHOLD

"We've got to set down!"

"Tell me where!"

Blake frantically adjusted the focus on the front sensors. An inbound comms request from the *Ulterior-2* blinked impatiently for his attention. He didn't need the distraction and he ignored it.

"There!" he said. "A platform! Fifty klicks. No sign of hostile activity."

"I see it," said McKinney. He bent the control stick slightly to the side and the shuttle altered course, juddering badly.

They came ever-closer to the landing area. The shuttle

bounced and creaked, whilst its engines made a high-pitched whine of distress. Blake guessed the damage was terminal and could only hope the craft would hold together for another few minutes. It wasn't travelling at anything near full speed.

"Twenty klicks," announced McKinney.

The heat-smouldering shuttle laboured onwards, greasy smoke pouring from its damaged alloys. They were close enough to the target area for Blake to be sure there was plenty of room to set down – he could see a square, unlit opening between two of the bands, wide enough to fit several shuttles side-by-side.

Except now there's only one shuttle.

On the approach to the landing area, Blake got a much clearer view of the anomaly at the end of the coil. One moment it was a shifting, indistinct smear of colours and blurred outlines. The next, it snapped into sharp focus, driving home the absolute shock Blake had experienced a few minutes before when he first realised what it was.

"Here we go," said McKinney. He opened a channel to the passenger bay. "Get ready for a hard landing, ladies and gentlemen."

Once inside the opening, the shuttle's engines resonated against the side walls, making the central pilot console buzz loudly. With the pride of a man determined to get something out of what had so far been a total disaster, McKinney spent a few extra seconds getting them lined up and then he set the transport down with textbook gentleness.

Sergeant Li swore repeatedly, his words embracing relief, anger and fear. As he unclipped himself from his seat, Blake felt all those things and more. This mission had started out badly and it was going to get far, far worse.

Outside, the bands of depleted Obsidiar glowed brighter and a second Vraxar warship slid through the portal and into the coil.

CHAPTER TEN

LIEUTENANT MCKINNEY SNATCHED his gear from the cockpit footlocker and then surged for the door. "We have to move!"

He thumped the access pad three times in quick succession and the door half-opened, before stopping on its runners. McKinney put his hands on the door's edge and heaved. His augmented arm was many times stronger than a normal arm – strong enough that it was easy to damage the surrounding skin if he exerted it too hard – and he used it to drag the stubborn door into the recess.

There was carnage in the passenger bay, with blackened bodies everywhere. They lay where they had perished, the polymers of their protective suits burned through to expose the vulnerable flesh beneath.

To McKinney's right, the inner walls of the hull were pushed inwards and there was a long, ragged hole through which he could see the sickly green light outside. Not everyone was dead – there were those lucky enough to have been sheltered from the baking air sucked in through the breach in the hull wall. They picked themselves up, their suits mottled with patches of grime and thick Gallenium dust brought in from outside. Most of them appeared dazed, though the more alert ones were picking up their weapons and packs.

The sight of it struck McKinney like a hammer blow and it took all of his strength to witness this and not falter. Mercifully, no one was screaming. If there was one thing the medical computers in the visors could take care of better than anything, it was pain. Some of the drugs could make a man with sixty percent burns feel like he was on top of the world.

McKinney refused to dwell - the time for reflection and mourning would come later. For the moment, he couldn't allow himself to think of anything other than the mission.

Blake entered the bay, along with Corporal Bannerman and Sergeant Li. They didn't hesitate and followed McKinney's lead as he tried to find out who was alive and who was dead. The visor HUDs kept a live record of vital signs, but sometimes you just had to see it for your own eyes.

"I guess we got lucky," said Bannerman.

The words were spoken bitterly, even if there was an element of truth to them. There was nothing positive to take from this.

McKinney tried to bring order to the situation. "Sergeant Woods?"

Woods was a dependable soldier and he rose from where he was crouched over the body of someone, alive or dead, it wasn't clear. "Right here, sir."

"We're in a bad place, Sergeant, and we can't stay," McKinney indicated the soldiers nearby. "Get these organised and get the hell off this shuttle. There no sign of enemy ground troops when we came in to land. Even so, we can't stick around."

"I'll do what I can to secure the exterior, sir."

"Don't stay too close – there's a Vraxar warship out there."

"The good news never stops coming."

Woods began the process of rallying the able-bodied and McKinney moved onto the next job on his list. "Where are the medics?" he asked.

"Sandoval, sir."

"Grover, sir."

"Is that it?"

"Sims, Fletcher and Torres are dead."

"Get me a headcount and do it fast. See what you can do to fix up the worst injured."

There was plenty of activity in the passenger bay, now that the living realised they'd been given a chance. Under the no-nonsense guidance of Sergeant Woods, groups of soldiers recovered their equipment from the floor and the wall lockers. There were a few pointless questions, which McKinney didn't waste time answering.

Woods got a group of ten or twelve to the exit door. The surrounding metal was buckled from the recent impact and McKinney held his breath as the door scraped itself clear of its frame, before lowering to the ground to form an exit ramp. The soldiers ran outside, their packs and weapons clattering.

Just then, the green light outside turned into a pure, shocking white. McKinney heard a series of explosions, impossibly loud and much closer than he wanted. The light faded briefly, before brightening again, this time with an even greater intensity than the last.

"Sergeant Woods?"

"Something just detonated in the space behind us, sir. That Vraxar spaceship is still here. It looks like a big bastard to my untrained eye."

"We can't stay here, Lieutenant McKinney," said Blake in a private channel. "I've had a comms message from the *Ulterior*-2 –

the crew won't be able to use its full arsenal in case the overspill hits this shuttle. It puts them in a difficult position."

"Damnit!" growled McKinney in frustration. There was no right answer, no choice he could make, which would offer everyone the same chance at life. The surviving soldiers had a long way to go in order to reach the *ES Devastator* and there was no way they could manage it if they were bringing the injured along with them.

For once, he got a break. Woods came back on the comms.

"Sir, the Vraxar ship has moved out of sight. It's travelling fast."

"The enemy mustn't have seen us down here and now they're going to regret chasing the *Ulterior-2*," said Blake. He dashed towards the door, trying his best to avoid the bodies strewn on the floor and slumped across the metal seating.

The light and sound of distant explosions reached them again, only this time it was magnified tenfold. The thunder from several hundred high-yield explosive warheads roared along the coil, the plasma illuminating the immense space. Amongst the other sounds, McKinney heard the thump-thump-whine of over-charged particle beams and then the booming echo of Havoc cannons. Even in its damaged state, the *Ulterior-2* was capable of inflicting astounding destruction upon the Space Corps' enemies.

McKinney knew there were choices, but only one of them was viable. This knowing made it easier for him, if only slightly.

"We leave the wounded here," he said in the open channel. "If you can't run and you can't shoot, or you're already boosted so high you've forgotten what your name is, you're staying behind."

"What's going to happen to the injured, sir?" asked Sandoval.

"I need a pilot," said McKinney, not directly answering the question. "Cobb, where are you?"

A figure near the rear bulkhead wall raised its hand. R1T Hannah Cobb's spacesuit looked as if it had been put twice through a wood chipper and then fired out of a cannon, though the woman inside appeared unharmed. "Here, sir."

McKinney pointed vaguely at the walls and ceiling of the shuttle. "You've got the certificates to fly these things, right?"

"This shuttle isn't getting off the ground again, sir. I heard the noises when you brought it in."

"Wrong answer, soldier. This shuttle *will* fly and you'll be the one at the controls."

"What about that Vraxar warship, sir?"

"I didn't say it would be easy. Once the *Ulterior-2* has kicked the shit out of that new cruiser, there may be another and then another after that." A further round of explosions shook the transport. McKinney resumed. "Contact the battleship and they'll come in close when the timing is right. That way you won't have to stay in the air for long."

Cobb didn't like it and McKinney couldn't understand her reluctance. No one was going to have an easy time of it from here, so there was no need for her to stand shaking her head as if she'd been asked to jump into a pit full of slugs and razor blades. Once again, the lack of real battle experience within the Space Corps' ground forces was evident.

With the instructions given, McKinney set about rounding up those soldiers whom he could rely on. To his great relief, the core of his usual squad was intact. During the flight, they'd been gathered near to the shuttle's cockpit door on the opposite side to the hull breach. When the hot air had come in, it was the men and women closest who had borne the brunt of it, their bodies providing a tragic shield for the others.

When it came to living and dying, McKinney's small group of soldiers had defied the odds enough times that it was becoming a habit. There were some people who could flip a coin and call it correctly time and time again, and the proof of it was right here in this shuttle. McKinney connected to their sub-channel and was greeted by the sound of R1T Martin Garcia bitching about something. For once, the man's incessant complaining was a connection with normality and McKinney nearly smiled.

"Sergeant Li, clear this shuttle of the able-bodied. You will get out there and help Sergeant Woods. Medic Sandoval, you stay with the shuttle. Grover, you're coming with us."

"Yes, sir."

Sandoval was probably the better medic, while Grover was better with a rifle in a pinch situation. It made sense to leave Sandoval to keep watch over the worst of the injured.

Within a minute, the uninjured soldiers were all outside. McKinney was the last to leave and he followed Blake, Li and Grover at a fast jog along the exit ramp. His rifle was comforting and the bandolier of grenades across his chest bumped up and down with his stride. The portable number cruncher he carried on his back was the only pisser, since it weighed about forty pounds and carrying it meant there was no room for a repeater. Now he was outside the shuttle, he became more aware of a persistent buzzing noise in the background. The atmosphere wasn't breathable – not that he intended removing his visor – and his HUD advised him there was something unidentified in the air.

That same shit Li picked up on the shuttle's sensors.

Without a choice, McKinney ignored the HUD warning, reasoning that he had enough on his plate already without having to think about the possible effects of extended exposure to whatever was inside *Ix-Gastiol*. He spared a brief glance around, though he already knew what to expect having seen it on the sensor feed.

The shuttle was parked two hundred metres inside a huge recess in the walls of the coil. The floor of the recess was solid black metal, with a faint sheen which reflected the green light coming from the bands lining *Ix-Gastiol*'s central area. The walls were more than one hundred metres apart and the ceiling was similarly high. There was no apparent reason for this recess to exist and it continued for another two hundred metres. Fortunately, it wasn't a dead-end and there were three passages leading away, one of which was fifteen metres high and wide.

There was no cover outside except for the shuttle, and the transport made a good target for the enemy warship. Therefore, Sergeant Woods had instructed the soldiers to spread out and stay prone. He'd sent three away to scout the exits and these soldiers were on their way back with whatever information they'd found.

When he saw how few there were left, McKinney's heart fell. Out of the seventeen hundred on the *Ulterior-2*, the final headcount was seventy-eight, plus another hundred-and-eighteen injured who would remain on the shuttle. It was a terrible result.

Once he was a short distance from the shuttle, McKinney crouched and used his visor to connect with the *Ulterior-2*. There had been no explosions for the last minute or two and he assumed the overcharged particle beams had finished off the second Vraxar warship.

"How are things going, Lieutenant?" asked Cruz.

"Not great, ma'am. Just letting you know we're sending the shuttle back to you. The men and women onboard it would be grateful if you could find an opportunity to come and pick them up."

"We'll do what we can. I see R1T Hannah Cobb has signed into Shuttle One's main console."

"If you could keep an eye on things, that would be appreciated."

"I can bring them home on autopilot if required. How do you plan to escape, Lieutenant?" There was deep concern in the question, which Cruz was unable to hide.

"I'll think of something, ma'am. What about you?"

"We're going to open fire on the interior of the coil, and hope no more of those ships come through the portal. We've destroyed two, but we can't go on forever."

"What happens if *Ix-Gastiol* goes to lightspeed and leaves Pioneer? You could escape."

"We aren't going anywhere, Lieutenant."

It was the answer McKinney had been expecting. "Take care, ma'am. If there's a way, I promise you I'll find it."

"I believe you, Eric."

It was hard to continue, and besides, there was nothing more to say. McKinney closed the channel. He didn't usually make promises.

"And here I am making one that's going to be impossible to keep," he muttered, finding he had no regrets about it.

He crouch-ran towards Sergeant Woods. With everyone connected on the comms, there was no need for proximity. Still, it gave an impression of solidarity and he hunkered down to speak.

"What's along these passages?" asked McKinney.

"More spaceship, sir." Woods lifted his hand and pointed a finger at the largest exit, straight ahead. "You can see along there as well as I can. Looks like it goes fifty klicks towards the flank. It's too dark for the visor sensors to make out what's down there."

"There's got to be something."

"You'd think. If there isn't, we've got no cover at all. Nowhere to run and no place to scatter if we come under fire."

"What about these other two exits?"

"They're identical, as far as our scouts can tell. They run parallel to this big central space for as far as it's possible to see. The difference is, there're what might be side passages leading deeper into the ship."

Another figure dropped down next to them and McKinney's HUD identified the arrival as Captain Blake.

"What's the lay of the land?" he asked.

"Black metal corridors and uncertainty," grunted McKinney. "We're going to take the left or right exit and see where it leads."

"We're a hundred klicks from the *Devastator*. It's a shame we have to go a longer route."

"What was that thing back there, sir?" asked McKinney. It was time to move, but he couldn't stop himself asking the question.

"A portal. *Ix-Gastiol* is somehow able to keep it open."

"Like a wormhole?"

"I'm sure the Space Corps' physicists would have more exact terminology. You saw through it, didn't you?"

McKinney nodded. During the final few kilometres of the shuttle flight, he'd been granted an excellent view of what lay on the other side. There was a sphere – what looked like an entire planet clad entirely in black metal and covered in structures – billions of structures of every conceivable design, each of them huge yet too far away to make out their precise details or purpose.

"I saw the Vraxar home world, sir."

"That's what I saw too, Lieutenant. We had theories without evidence and now we have the proof. Wherever the Vraxar came from, it still exists. They aren't adrift in the universe, relying on the conquest of other species to rearm and resupply. They have a base."

"What does it mean for us?"

"I don't know, Lieutenant. It's the most important discovery we've made about our enemy and I'm damned if I can think of a way to put it to use."

"I think we've got a few hurdles to jump before we can start working out how to find and then destroy a Vraxar home world," said McKinney.

"Yes."

McKinney and Blake were different enough that they'd never be firm friends if given the opportunity outside the dictates of a military hierarchy. Even so, McKinney knew the other man well enough to guess he was working on an idea he wasn't yet ready to divulge. He didn't press the matter.

"There are seventy-eight of us in four squads, sir. You're in Squad A with me."

"I'll stick close."

"We'll lose contact with the *Ulterior-2* the moment we enter one of these passages. If there's anything you need to say to the ship's crew, now is the time to do it."

"I spoke with them while you were with Sergeant Woods."

McKinney pushed himself upright, feeling the muscles of his legs protest at the combined weight of the spacesuit and the number cruncher. "In that case, we can leave."

Before he could give the order, the coil was once again flooded with light from a source a long way distant. The thin atmosphere brought the sound a few seconds later.

"Lambdas," said Blake. "A whole lot of them. The *Ulterior-2* has started firing at the insides of *Ix-Gastiol*."

For some reason, McKinney wasn't curious to watch the results. He didn't readily admit it, but there was something frightening about the *Ulterior-2*. Most spaceships made him feel insignificant, but this one scared him far more, as if it rendered humanity's existence redundant. He was glad the Confederation imposed limits on how much a computer was allowed to think for itself. The idea that the whole fleet might suddenly decide to annihilate the species which had built it was chilling.

With a shiver that he put down to the Obsidiar power source keeping the artificial portion of his body operational, McKinney urged the troops to their feet. He selected the left-hand exit passage at random and headed towards it. The soldiers weren't keen to be left behind and they followed smartly. Whatever lay ahead wasn't going to be any better than waiting here, but marching at least gave a soldier the impression of action and control.

McKinney reached the entrance to the passage – it was wide enough for several to walk abreast and the walls tapered slightly towards the ceiling. Everything was as the scouts had described – it was a straight corridor and there were darker patches in the right-hand wall, the closest of which was a few hundred metres along.

He paused briefly. "Listen up everyone. If you want to send anything over the comms, you'll need line-of-sight. There's no way a signal can get through these walls." He banged his fist onto the metal and held it there. "This means if you piss around and wander off, we might never see you again."

"Except as a Vraxar," said Sergeant Li.

"Pretty much," agreed McKinney. "Stay close and don't be tempted to go off exploring."

There wasn't a great deal extra to say and any further words would just slow them down. Before McKinney could lead on, he felt a peculiar sensation running through the metal, something akin to a dentist's drill. He jerked his hand away. The green light from the coil glowed brightly for the third time and *Ix-Gastiol*'s walls groaned as if they were under incredible stress.

"Another Vraxar ship!" said Li.

"Get in!" yelled McKinney, putting his hand on the closest man's back and propelling him through the opening.

The rest of them followed at the double. McKinney pushed his way to the front and led the squads on at a run. The first sounds of explosions reached his ears. He put his head down and kept going, the contact of his feet on the floor making hardly any sound.

They hadn't travelled far when they experienced a feeling of dislocation, accompanied by a crushing sensation. McKinney clenched his teeth and the pain quickly passed.

"Was that what I think it was?" he asked.

"We're at lightspeed," said Blake. "Something's gone right for us."

"What if we're now at Pioneer, sir?"

"I can't allow myself to think that, Lieutenant."

McKinney didn't like to come across as the negative one and he realised he'd done exactly that. In reality, his mind was already preparing him for the hardships which lay ahead – hardships his squad would need to face irrespective of where *Ix-Gastiol* ended up. The next few days were going to be trying, assuming they even lived that long.

CHAPTER ELEVEN

AN HOUR later and McKinney was beginning to wonder if *Ix-Gastiol* was empty except for a tiny crew hidden on the ship's bridge somewhere far away. The squad had travelled four kilometres, along straight, unlit passages, through rooms without apparent purpose and across two expansive areas with high, arched ceilings. There were side passages every so often, none of which appeared to lead anywhere in particular, vanishing as they did into the darkness. The sensors on the spacesuit visors were able to provide enough details for the soldiers to proceed without accidents, but other than that, there was so little light they only provided hints and suggestions as to what lay ahead. Even though the visors had built-in torches, McKinney didn't want to give the game away by using them when it wasn't absolutely necessary.

The worst thing was the noise – *Ix-Gastiol* groaned and creaked like an ancient ship scraping its way over a submerged reef. Occasionally, McKinney heard distant thuds of something inconceivably heavy connecting with another object. There were also pinging noises of alloys strained to breaking point. It was enough to mute the conversation and have everyone looking around constantly in expectation of incoming death.

"While this lack of enemy activity is putting me on edge, I far prefer it to the alternative," said Corporal Bannerman as they entered a third large open area. This place was two hundred metres from side to side and didn't show up on the scans obtained by the *Ulterior-2*.

"There's a long way to go yet," said McKinney. "Ninety-six klicks – that's plenty of time to run into trouble."

"If this map we got from the *Ulterior-2* is remotely accurate, we should be able to avoid the largest of the open spaces simply by going in a straight line to the outer edge of *Ix-Gastiol*. Do you think that's where they keep their troops, Lieutenant?"

"From what we saw on the Neutraliser, I'd bet money on it. For that reason, we're going to do everything possible to stay as far as possible from those areas."

"I thought we might have run into something by now."

Bannerman was looking for reassurance – something McKinney couldn't provide.

"They'll come. This whole ship must be automated, so there's no need for anyone to be down here."

"Maybe we'll get lucky this time around and have a clear run to the outer hull. What do you think?"

"Yeah, maybe it's our turn, Corporal."

Bannerman wasn't fooled. "Except you don't believe it."

"Neither do you."

The two of them fell quiet. McKinney tipped his head back and stared upwards into the darkness. If there was a ceiling above them, he couldn't make it out. There were two side passages at ground level, neither of which led in the direction he wanted to go. The floor of this place was smooth and flat, with no objects or anything else of interest. The Ir-Klion-32 had been one of the more unpleasant experiences in McKinney's career, but *Ix-Gastiol* raised the bar several notches.

While the new soldiers were jumpy, McKinney's usual squad did their best to put on a show of bored disinterest. R1T Dexter Webb walked in a carefree manner with his plasma tube over one shoulder, whistling an irritating tune in the Squad A open channel.

"Piss off with the whistling," said Garcia.

"I don't want to piss off," said Webb and then continued his tune.

In truth, it was annoying to everyone, but now that Garcia had exposed his weakness, no one else could let on.

"I like the whistling," said Ricky Vega, joining in with a tune of his own.

"Yeah, it lights a man's spirit in all this darkness," said Clifton. "I nearly died on Tucson and I need all the happiness I can get."

"It must have only been a flesh wound for you to be back on duty so quickly," laughed Roldan.

Clifton didn't answer and soon, ten or fifteen of Squad A were whistling, each vying to be as tuneless and grating as possible. Garcia managed to hold out for less than a minute before he took himself out of the squad comms channel. McKinney grinned.

His good mood didn't last. His movement sensor highlighted a figure a hundred or so metres ahead along the exit passageway, showing it as an indistinct orange shape emerging from a side corridor. Without thinking, McKinney dropped to one knee and brought his gauss rifle to his shoulder in a single, easy movement. His finger rested naturally on the activation trigger and he squeezed it once. The weapon fizzed and the slug hit the Vraxar in the head, knocking it to the floor.

"Prone!" he shouted into the open channel.

The soldiers did as they were told and they fell flat. McKinney didn't drop to the floor. He grabbed the closest man – Ricky Vega – by his arm and dragged him towards the passage.

"Go right."

Vega responded to the command and pressed himself to the wall on the right side of the entrance to the corridor. McKinney went left and they looked at each other from opposite sides of the opening.

McKinney leaned out carefully. The dead Vraxar was a little way further along, nothing more than a grey shape against black. He listened.

"Clear?"

"Sounds like."

"Wait here."

McKinney entered the passage and ran towards the fallen Vraxar, doing his best to keep the sound of his footfall to a minimum. As he came closer, he was able to discern the branching passage from which it had emerged. He reached it and chanced a look. To his relief, it was deserted.

Before returning to the others, McKinney stooped next to the dead alien. It was a type he'd never seen before – humanoid with yellow skin and thick limbs. It had metal bars stapled to its arms and legs, whilst a single, prosthetic eye stared from its skull. The other eye socket was an empty black circle, into which McKinney didn't wish to look.

With pity and distaste, he lifted one of the alien's arms. It felt light and hollow, as though there was no muscle tissue within.

"Everything okay, Lieutenant?" whispered Vega.

"This one is ancient," McKinney replied. "No clue as to what it was doing down here."

"Let's hope it got lost."

"Yeah."

McKinney rose and jogged towards the room with the other

soldiers. Sergeants Li, Woods and Demarco had been listening in to the comms and now the coast was clear they got the squads back on their feet.

"I don't like it," said McKinney to his officers. "Where's there's one, there could be others."

"Maybe we should pick up the pace," said Li.

"I agree," said Woods. "Like it or not, we're up against time. Sooner or later, they're going to realise we're down here and when that happens, this place will fill up faster than we can pull the trigger on our guns."

Sergeant Demarco was of the same mind. "Speed is good. Once they find us, it's game over."

McKinney nodded slowly. "Let's do what we can to cover some distance, while there's nothing to slow us down."

He didn't like running into the unknown, but felt there was no better way. With the squads organised, McKinney set off quickly, keeping those who were the best shots close to the front. Martin Garcia was one of them – he had excellent reactions and was an expert with the rifle. Even better, the soldier was slowly and steadily learning how to rein in his complaining and he didn't say a word when he was ordered to the fore.

They ran for an hour, along the straight, featureless corridors. To McKinney, a man not known for his fanciful imagination, it felt as though he was inside the dreams of an eternally sleeping god, with endless passages leading onwards, carrying the soldiers ever-further from the familiar until they became lost and made to wander forever, searching for a goal they would never find. He shook away the thoughts, afraid in case they were a symptom of the stress he was under.

They made good time given the circumstances and after the hour had passed, they were a further ten kilometres towards their goal.

McKinney was in a rhythm he felt able to maintain for hours

more and even though his kit weighed heavily on him, his fitness and strength were more than a match. The natural high he felt from his exertions cleared his head and made him feel almost elated. Each stride was another step closer to their goal and once they reached the *ES Devastator*, he was confident Captain Blake would pull something out of the bag. If they managed to take out *Ix-Gastiol*, it would be a devastating blow for the Vraxar.

Then, he saw something in the wall ahead, and his good mood evaporated at once.

"Halt!" he said.

There was a panel on the wall, of a similar type to those he'd seen before. It was made from a material which looked like black glass, though was more likely something different. A number of symbols glowed green on the surface of the panel, and as McKinney watched, they updated to something new. It was the first sign they might be entering a habited area of *Ix-Gastiol*.

"It would be nice if we could understand their language," muttered Garcia. He lifted his leg and kicked petulantly at the panel with the heel of his boot.

"I think there's a door here, Lieutenant," said Jordan Mills, tracing a line along the wall with one finger.

"And there's another panel further ahead," said Rudy Munoz.

They didn't need to find out what was behind the door and McKinney backed away from the panel. He squinted ahead and, sure enough, he could make out a faint green light some way off.

"Just when I was beginning to convince myself we were alone," he said with a short laugh.

"Shouldn't we see if we can get these doors open, Lieutenant?" asked Blake in a private channel. "It might be better if we find out now rather than later."

"Yes, sir. I'll give it a go."

McKinney stepped forward and planted his palm onto the

access panel. The symbols changed briefly and the door remained closed. He tried again, this time using his fingertips, and, when that failed, he tried a couple of sweeping gestures. On each occasion, the Vraxar symbols changed and then returned to their previous state.

"We're locked out," said Blake

"Worth a try," McKinney conceded, lowering his hand from the panel. "I can try the number cruncher if you want. I don't know if it'll work against Vraxar tech."

The number cruncher – known officially as an Internal Security Override Pack or ISOP – was a recent product of the Space Corps labs, designed and manufactured after the Vraxar Neutralisers began shutting down Confederation assets without difficulty. The compact, powerful computer had an Obsidiar processor and a self-recharging energy cell, also made from Obsidiar. In the event of a total failure on a spaceship, it was designed to crack through the security on a self-sealing door and also to provide the necessary short burst of power to allow the door to open. The ISOPs hadn't yet been tested in a combat situation and McKinney hoped the next model would weigh ten pounds instead of forty.

"Let's leave it for the moment."

"Yes, sir."

This time when McKinney set off, it was at a more measured pace. They reached the second panel and found the door it controlled was already open. McKinney looked through and wasn't surprised when he discovered another passage. This time, there were far more of the access panels visible and in the distance, there was another source of light which he couldn't make out.

According to McKinney's HUD map, the side passage headed directly towards one of the bigger open spaces within *Ix-*

Gastiol, albeit fifteen or twenty kilometres away. He had no intention of going that way, so he resumed the original course.

"Some of my guys are getting twitchy," said Sergeant Demarco.

"As long as they don't run when the shooting starts."

"I'll personally strangle anyone who even thinks about running."

Demarco wasn't physically intimidating, but she had a way of getting respect which left McKinney in no doubt about her ability. He left her to do what she would do.

The easy ride so far ended abruptly. The sound of a scuffle caused McKinney to turn and he heard someone shout an alarm over the open channel. He saw the troops behind him falling back towards the right-hand wall and two huge figures towered above them all. Someone fired a gauss rifle three or four times, quickly joined by several more. There was another sound – one which McKinney remembered all too well. It was the sharp crack of a Vraxar hand cannon. Before he could reach the disturbance, the tall shapes fell, scattering the soldiers around them.

McKinney's brain had already built an accurate picture by the time he got there. A side door had opened just as Squad C were walking past. There had been two Vraxar behind it – converted Estral with plates of armour attached to their heads and shoulders. The enemy had been killed, but not before they managed to shoot R1T Debra Barret with one of their blunt-nosed wide-bore guns. Barret was dead and her blood pooled on the floor.

Although McKinney tried his best to suppress the thought, he couldn't help but tell himself it was the smallest of mercies that she'd died so quickly, otherwise she'd have held everyone up trying to save her. That was what he found the hardest – the enemy had reduced humanity to a position where a soldier's life was made as disposable as that of a Vraxar, where a death was to be welcomed, rather than mourned. With a grimace, McKinney told himself he wouldn't succumb. He lifted Barret's visor and let the details of her face burn themselves into his memory. With trembling fingers, he closed her eyes and lowered the visor once more.

There was a cluster of soldiers around the two fallen Vraxar. McKinney pushed his way through – the enemy soldiers had been taken down by gauss fire and they lay unmoving, leaking blood and clear fluids onto the floor.

"I hate them," said one soldier – a man who McKinney hadn't fought with before.

"I don't hate them," he replied. "These were once living, breathing creatures and this is what they've been reduced to. They are no more a willing participant in this war than we are."

"Yeah well, I still hate them. I don't care what anyone says."

There were some things a soldier had to learn for themselves and maybe this man would be lucky enough to live long enough that he got the chance. McKinney didn't waste breath trying to persuade him – hate could serve a purpose when it was used right. *On balance, it's better than fear.*

Ten minutes after this encounter with the Vraxar, McKinney found himself in another unwelcome situation. Up until this moment, he'd been able to lead the squad on a more or less direct route towards their destination. Now, the main passage ended at a T-junction and the intersecting corridor continued into the distance in both directions without any sign of a way to get back on course.

"Shit," he said.

"Maybe there's a way," said Bannerman.

"Can you see one?"

"No."

McKinney checked his HUD again. The navigational computer in the visors was reduced to counting footsteps to estimate their position in a model of *Ix-Gastiol* that was in itself partially based on guesswork. Unfortunately, even if their assumed position was wildly inaccurate, both directions of this intersecting corridor would take them close to one of the vast open areas within the Vraxar capital ship. Bannerman saw it too.

"That's why you're pissed," he said.

"You always had an eye for detail."

"Corporal "Eagle" Bannerman, that's me."

They couldn't turn back, so McKinney picked the left turn and set off along it.

"We might find a way to get on track again," he said.

"I'm guessing it's eight klicks until we get to that big area up ahead, Lieutenant."

"Plenty of time to find an alternative."

McKinney spoke the words with a confidence he didn't feel. This corridor stretched as far as he could see, though he had no idea exactly how far that was, since the visor sensor wasn't nearly good enough to provide clarity.

"You could try that number cruncher on a Vraxar door?"

"It's to get us onto the *Devastator*, Corporal. I have no idea what will happen if I try to make it interface with the Vraxar security system."

"Worst case is the door stays closed."

"I'll think about it."

Bannerman's idea was a good one and - in theory – unlikely to result in any significant harm. With no sign of the corridor's end, McKinney found himself becoming progressively keener to try it out. The trouble was, there were no more access panels in this area of *Ix-Gastiol* and the further they travelled in this direction, the closer they came to what McKinney was convinced was the troop storage area of the Vraxar spaceship. If there was one thing he was absolutely certain about, it was that he didn't want to stumble into an area holding fifty million Vraxar soldiers.

"Movement behind," said Sergeant Woods.

McKinney turned to look. The corridor was wide and the soldiers were in a long line close to one of the walls, which allowed a clear view for his movement sensors to pick out a brief flash of orange, coming from the original passage they'd been following. The orange shape appeared again and then vanished.

"Sergeant Woods?"

"No shots fired, sir."

"Damnit! Were we seen?"

"I don't know, Lieutenant."

It wasn't good. They'd travelled this far without much in the way of resistance, but McKinney had a strong feeling they were no longer going to have such an easy time of it. On a spaceship as large as *Ix-Gastiol* there were certain to be areas which were almost unpopulated. Naturally, there were other areas which would be teeming with the enemy.

"I think we've crossed the threshold," he said to his officers.

The meaning was obvious and no one tried to argue otherwise. McKinney spent another minute watching carefully in case the enemy came into sight. A few of the soldiers crouched around him, their rifles held steadily against their shoulders.

Whether or not they were seen wasn't clear, however McKinney didn't want to hang around here any longer.

"Come on, let's move," he said.

He returned to the front of the line and set off once more. The sounds of the spaceship, which he'd grown accustomed to, suddenly became more ominous to his ears, as if they were a sign that *Ix-Gastiol* was alive and that the Vraxar within were gradually becoming aware of the intruders within the host body.

McKinney shivered, lying to himself that it was down to the chill of his own Obsidiar power source. The soldiers hadn't travelled more than fifty paces when, silently and without warning, the lights came on.

CHAPTER TWELVE

ALTHOUGH THE GREEN light allowed McKinney to see much better than he could in the darkness, he didn't welcome it one bit. Any hope – already unrealistic - that they might make significant progress towards their goal was dashed by this development. Upon reflection, he realised it was a surprise it had taken this long for something so major to go wrong. The stride of his march lengthened until he broke into a jog and the pace of his jog increased until he was running.

As he ran, he kept both hands on his rifle and held it across his chest. Garcia and Vega spread across the corridor, keeping their own guns ready. McKinney could shoot straight, but it was harder to make a clean kill when running and three rifles were better than one.

"Keep watch to the rear," he ordered.

Sergeant Woods was as unflappable as ever. "On it, sir."

"What now, Lieutenant?" asked Li.

"I'll let you know," McKinney replied. He didn't need the interruption when he was trying to think.

The passage went on and on. McKinney zoomed in with his

sensor and still he couldn't see where it ended. There was a darker area in the distance which was caused by either a variation in the light or a side passage. It was something to aim for.

While he continued running, he realised they hadn't come across any steps or lifts so far within the Vraxar ship and their lack struck him as unusual. In a way, it reinforced his idea that they'd landed the shuttle in an area of *Ix-Gastiol* which the Vraxar rarely ventured into.

I wonder if the entire coil was nothing more than a launch pad for the warships we saw them pulling through that wormhole. Bring them in from their home world and send them out to kill and conquer.

"Hostiles behind," said Woods. "Eight, maybe ten."

"Squad D, stop and neutralise."

There was a short volley of gauss fire, the whining hum crushed by the density of the walls.

"Clear?" asked McKinney, slowing down.

"I don't think we got them all, sir. They've taken cover in the side passage."

"Damnit, we can't have them shooting at us from behind."

McKinney stopped, bringing everyone else to a halt with him. The soldiers nearby dropped flat, allowing him a good view of what was happening. The troops of Squad D were thirty metres back, crouched or prone, facing the way they'd come. Two or three of them fired again, though McKinney wasn't able to see any movement on his sensor. He jerked his head around to look ahead – it was clear as far as he could tell.

"I think that's a turning," said Captain Blake, his reflective visor pointed in the direction McKinney was staring. He'd been quiet up until now, content to fade into the background.

"That's what I think too," said Vega.

Squad D fired once again and this time there were many

more shots. A Vraxar toppled into sight from the adjoining corridor.

"They've been reinforced," said Woods.

"Webb, think you can land a shot right on that T-junction?"

"Coming up, Lieutenant."

Webb sprang to his feet as though the heavy plasma tube weighed nothing. The weapon bleeped softly and the missile whooshed over the heads of the soldiers. It was a rare event for Webb to miss and he didn't disappoint.

"Run!" shouted McKinney as soon as he saw the rapidly-expanding cloud of plasma appear exactly where he wanted it. Within the confines of the corridor the blast would travel a good distance, reducing any Vraxar it caught into charcoal.

The soldiers sprinted as hard as they could, panting and cursing into the open comms channel. McKinney was near the front and his hopes lifted now he could see it was definitely a turning up ahead. Vega reached it first and retained enough sense to check out what lay around the corner before committing himself.

"Clear!" he yelled.

The troops dashed into the corridor, with those in front making room for those behind. They came to a halt and remained ready for whatever might come next. McKinney and Garcia waited out in the main corridor for the stragglers to catch up. When the last one entered the side passage, McKinney tapped Garcia on the shoulder and the two of them turned to follow.

"Ah, shit," said Garcia.

McKinney saw it too – there were more Vraxar approaching from the other end of the corridor the squads had just left. The enemy were more than a thousand metres away, but they were coming. There was only one conclusion and McKinney spelled it out to the others.

"They know we're here and they're coming with numbers. That means we've got to keep moving."

"Man, we're screwed," said R1T Matt Summers.

McKinney gritted his teeth. "We're not screwed until I say we're screwed, soldier. Is that clear?"

The tone of McKinney's voice brooked no argument and Summers was wise enough to keep his mouth shut.

They were wasting time and McKinney ushered the closest soldiers on with an impatient wave of his arms. He was keen to be at the front and he forged a way through. The green light exuded by the walls of *Ix-Gastiol* cast misshapen, ugly shadows and reinforced McKinney's feelings that he'd prefer to be anywhere other than here.

Once he reached the front, he was afforded a better view of what lay ahead. It was another long corridor, only this time with more access panels than the last one. He made out cross-passages and, for the first time, what looked like steps a few hundred metres away.

"Do we even want to go up?" asked Vega.

"Those steps are heading in the right direction, so yes, we go up."

The squad's feet pounded against the unyielding floor and they made it to the steps without incident. McKinney paused to make sure everyone was with him and then he started up. The steps climbed steeply, with their high risers and narrow treads making it treacherous to go too fast. They cut in a straight line directly through dark alloys, the exit a square opening far ahead. McKinney cursed when he realised how far they needed to climb and his muscles complained before he was halfway to the top. It was tempting to boost, but he held off. Once fatigue started to slow him down, that would be the time.

"At least we're making progress," said Bannerman, evidently with breath to spare.

McKinney was trying not to watch the estimated distance counting down metre by metre and he only grunted in response. By the time he was close to the top, the number cruncher felt as if it weighed a hundred pounds instead of forty, and the light alloy tube of his gauss rifle felt more like an iron bar. It was a strange sensation – he kept himself fit and while this should have been a tiring run, he felt exhausted. Not only that, the parts of his body he wasn't using had developed a faint bone-deep ache. He used his spare hand to rub at his bicep. The aching didn't go away.

"Steep," said Garcia.

"No shit," said Huey Roldan, his breath coming in harsh, shuddering gasps. "Feels as if I've run five hundred klicks, not fifteen."

Taking care not to fall, McKinney twisted so he could see those following. The steps were as wide as the corridor and from here, he could see the men and women toiling upwards, some of them a long way behind the others.

There was something wrong, though he couldn't put his finger on what it was.

"Come on!" he urged, still twenty metres from the top.

McKinney's call was met by the expected grumbling and he watched for a moment longer, to reassure himself that the soldiers were trying as hard as they could.

"I feel like crap," said R1 T Ramsey.

"Don't wait until you fall down from exhaustion – boost now."

"I did, Lieutenant. The adrenaline hasn't done much."

"I know what she means," said one of the others.

This revelation left McKinney confused – the suit drugs could make a wooden puppet dance without its master. He wasn't allowed time to give the matter any thought.

"You need to get up here, Lieutenant," said Ricky Vega.

A few of the soldiers had reached the top ahead of him and they stood framed in the opening, like green-tinted silhouettes.

"What is it?" asked McKinney, using the words to fill in the gap while he ascended the remaining steps.

"Damned if I know."

Captain Blake was with them. "Looks like..."

He didn't finish the sentence and McKinney reached the top. The steps ended at a short corridor a few metres long. At the end of the corridor was a large open area, lit in the same green. There were no Vraxar in sight and the movement sensors in McKinney's visor showed nothing. His legs still ached and he dug his knuckles into the muscles, watching as Garcia and Vega rolled their shoulders.

A few paces took him into the room. The left and right walls were a hundred or more metres apart and there were wide, solid-looking doors in each, just visible around the central object. An enormous black cylinder rose from the floor, going up for three or four hundred metres until it joined with the ceiling above. A thick band of metal curled around the cylinder all the way to the ceiling, not coming into direct contact and with no visible means of support. The band was black with a near-imperceptible green to it. Other than that, the room was empty, though the far wall was hidden from sight.

"Captain Blake?" prompted McKinney, suddenly eager to hear the conclusion to his earlier sentence.

"It's an amplifier of some kind, probably for a beam weapon or similar."

"I thought it would be bigger," said Clifton.

"I'd expect there to be thousands of these on *Ix-Gastiol*," said Blake. He put his hands on his knees and took a deep breath.

"Is this what's making us all feel like crap?" asked McKinney.

"It's not only me, then? I don't know, Lieutenant, since I've never stood so close to one before."

"We need to get out of here." McKinney summoned up some of his reserves and set off into the room. He felt weak as a kitten and he ordered his suit to give him a shot of battlefield adrenaline. The microneedles jabbed into his flesh and he experienced a surge which lasted for a few seconds before it faded away, leaving him shaky and drained.

The aching in his body increased noticeably with each footstep towards the amplifier cylinder, so he gave it a wide berth. In addition, his visor sensor detected an underlying hum in the air, just at the extent of its detection range. McKinney had no doubt it was coming from the cylinder.

Behind, the others followed him in a ragged group, whilst the last two up the stairs dropped to their haunches and leaned against the wall.

"No time for sleeping!" shouted Sergeant Woods. "Move yourselves!"

Garcia was up near the front. "What if there's no way out, Lieutenant?" he asked. "These side doors look well sealed."

There was no point in guessing, when the answer would be revealed in a few seconds and McKinney broke into a clumsy jog. Soon, he was able to see more of the opposite wall and he experienced a sinking feeling. There *was* another exit, but like the two side ones it was sealed with a large, heavy door.

At that moment, one of the soldiers catching their breath on top of the steps spoke the words McKinney had been dreading.

"Got something coming from behind," said R1T Willis. "Two, maybe three showing up on my movement detectors."

"Do you want us to shoot them, sir?" asked R1T Bass.

There were times when a question was so pointlessly idiotic, it could produce a stunned quiet amongst listeners. McKinney was not so easily silenced.

"Of course I want you to shoot them! Do it now! Sergeant Woods, reinforce the stairwell with Squad D!"

"Yes, sir."

McKinney hurried towards the door he hoped would provide an exit. It was five metres wide and high, a featureless, impassive slab of alloy with an access panel on the side. "Clifton, where are you?"

"About two paces behind you, sir."

"Can you get us through that?"

"I'll tell you shortly, Lieutenant."

The two men reached the door and the first thing Clifton did was thump the palm of his hand against it. The action produced an unsurprising lack of sound.

"Well?"

There was a note of hesitancy in the response, not usually found when Clifton was being instructed to put his talents to good use. "Yes, sir, I can get us through that door."

"What are you waiting for?"

"It'll take up more than half of my charges, Lieutenant, and we might have more need of them later. Maybe you should try the ISOP?"

Captain Blake was nearby and he listened to the exchange. Without a word, he stepped to the panel and pressed it. The door remained closed.

"Second time unlucky," he said.

Sergeant Woods interrupted with an update from the stairs. "There's a shitload of Vraxar coming," he said. "No, make that two shitloads."

"Newton's got a tube. Tell him to use it."

"He is using it, sir. I'm just letting you know we've got half the Vraxar army coming up the stairs."

It was a roundabout way of telling McKinney things weren't going to plan.

"Squad B, go back and help," he ordered.

There was another tube carrier in Squad B and with any

luck, two of the weapons would be enough to wipe out as many Vraxar as could squeeze onto the steps.

Woods had another snippet to impart, the meaning of which wasn't lost on McKinney. "They aren't firing at us, sir. Not one single bullet."

"Not what I wanted to hear, Sergeant, but we'll have to take whatever advantage we can from it."

If the Vraxar weren't shooting, it meant they intended to capture the soldiers and death was likely a preferable outcome to what the aliens had in store for anyone they took alive. McKinney took off his pack and lowered it gently to the ground. It was designed for field use, but he didn't want it to break because of his heavy-handedness.

"How does it work?" asked Vega.

"Watch."

The number cruncher was wrapped in thick, rubbery polymers, designed to withstand the same extremes of heat and cold as a soldier in a spacesuit. The inner workings were hidden away and a mystery to McKinney. A few gauges on top were the only visible indication of what was going on inside the pack. However, the ISOP was as easy to use as any other piece of kit in the Space Corps.

A rectangular screen, four inches by six and with a depth of only a few millimetres, was tucked under a flap of the pack. McKinney pulled it free and checked the display – it was blank except for a flashing cursor in the upper-left corner. There was nothing so crude as a wire in sight and he simply held the screen up to the Vraxar access panel. Immediately, the ISOP display filled with numbers so tiny it was impossible to read them. The digits flew upwards in a blur as the Obsidiar cluster in the pack tried to smash its way through the Vraxar security.

"Look at the panel!" said Garcia.

The green characters had become frozen in the arrangement

which McKinney now recognized as the Vraxar equivalent of *access denied*. For the next few seconds, the ISOP continued its efforts, while McKinney became progressively more agitated.

"What's happening, Sergeant Woods?"

"They're bringing something onto the stairs, sir. I'm not sure what it is yet."

"Mobile gun?"

"Doesn't look much like one."

McKinney's sense of unease grew. "Clifton, plant charges on this door. If the number cruncher doesn't get through in the next sixty seconds, we're going to blow it open."

Clifton had evidently been expecting the order and he had the first shaped charge stuck to the edge of the door before McKinney was finished speaking. The plasma explosive was about the same size as two clenched fists – the heaviest-duty charge a boom man could usually lay his hands on, and Clifton had a pack full.

Sergeant Woods spoke again, still with no sign of tension in his voice. "The enemy have got some kind of floating energy shield, sir. It's blocking our plasma rockets and they're advancing behind it."

The situation was becoming desperate. "Fall back to the far door, Sergeant. Not too close – Clifton is going to blow it open for us."

"Sixty metres would be a safe distance," said Clifton. He gave it some more thought. "Minimum."

At that moment, everything fell apart for Lieutenant Eric McKinney.

"Shit, Lieutenant, that side door has just opened," said Whitlock.

"Same with this other side," said Munoz. "Oh, crap."

McKinney turned first to one side and then the other to confirm it with his own eyes. The doors were open and through them came Vraxar. The aliens poured into the room at full-pelt, with endless numbers of them queuing in the passages beyond. A few of the men opened fire with their gauss rifles and McKinney heard the sound of a plasma repeater from the far side of the amplifier cylinder. It was joined by a second and a third.

"Blow the door!" he shouted, already certain it was too late.

"It's not ready, Lieutenant. I've got to activate four more of these charges."

McKinney's gaze fell onto the ISOP's portable display, just as the numbers changed to letters. *Access granted.*

The door in front of him rose upwards into a recess in the frame. McKinney saw the booted feet through the gap, then the grey, alien flesh visible through torn and shredded clothing. The door disappeared into the frame revealing Vraxar, packed so tightly into the corridor they would have suffocated if they were anything similar to humans. These ones had once been Estral – some of them were eight feet tall - and they towered over the soldiers.

Without a visible signal to start them moving, the Vraxar came.

CHAPTER THIRTEEN

MCKINNEY'S RIFLE was in his hand. He wasn't sure how it had got there so quickly, but he fired it into the chest of the closest Vraxar. A second alien appeared, and, for a moment, the two of them locked eyes, cold blue against fading grey. McKinney thought he detected something behind the eyes of his enemy – a consciousness suppressed and unable to get out. It was a tenuous link.

This creature once valued its life and its existence, he thought.

He shot the Vraxar, put a gauss slug right through the metal plate covering its forehead. It fell and McKinney fired again and again, focused on bringing as many of them down as he could.

End it now. Put the gun to your throat and put a slug through your brain. Death is better than conversion.

A hulking Vraxar, more metal than flesh, charged past him, knocking him easily to one side. McKinney staggered, his energy drained by the amplifier cylinder in the centre of the room. He almost lost his rifle and he tightened his grip on it, bringing it up for another burst of fire.

Can't drop my rifle. Then there'll be nothing to stop them taking me.

He heard the frightened shouts of the others in his squad, crowding the comms, each begging to be heard. Most of them hadn't seen proper combat before and now they faced this. McKinney felt shame that he couldn't save them.

I won't kill myself. Not now, not ever.

To his left, he heard a plasma rocket detonate. He turned towards the sound, still firing his rifle. A Vraxar struck him in passing and he fought for balance. The explosion of plasma was on the opposite side of the room and the white light contrasted with the green. The blast didn't come anywhere close to McKinney and he wondered who was stupid enough to fire a plasma tube with so many friendlies nearby.

He heard someone scream on the open channel, and someone else called for help, their voice laden with panic. McKinney couldn't blame them for their fear – it was a natural reaction to imminent death. There'd be no help coming this time.

"They've got me!"

"Too many of them!"

"Lieutenant? What do we do?"

The room was filled with Vraxar – thousands upon thousands of them. The heavy repeater fire ended and didn't resume. McKinney could still make out the sounds of sporadic gauss fire, becoming less frequent with each passing moment.

A Vraxar stopped to one side of him and McKinney brought his rifle around to put a bullet into its throat. He saw it looking at him, and then it was gone, back into the scrum.

What the hell?

By this point, there were so many Vraxar in the room that McKinney couldn't fire easily. They pressed against him, buffeting him like an insect caught in a hurricane. An elbow caught him in the shoulder and he fired a slug into the Vraxar's leg. The alien ignored him and it pushed its way through a gap, apparently unaffected by the injury.

A few metres away, a figure was lifted aloft and McKinney's visor identified it as Garcia. The man struggled, but his rifle was gone and his repeater had been torn off before he could get it ready to fire. Garcia was carried away, fighting against the merciless grip of his captors.

Other soldiers were also taken – men and women of McKinney's squad overwhelmed by numbers and hauled towards the same doorway in the left-hand wall. One of them – R1T Marcos Abbott, tried to throw a grenade from his belt. Vraxar hands knocked the explosive to the floor and it detonated, sending up a shower of bodies. The shockwave rippled through the crowd and McKinney was almost crushed by a Vraxar as it stumbled back from the force.

To McKinney, the engagement felt as if it took hours to play out, rather than seconds or minutes. The noise in the open channel increased in volume, while the officer's channel was silent. He spoke words, gave orders, with no idea if there was anyone to hear or act upon them.

Through it all, he fired his rifle, pressing the activation trigger until its ammunition ran dry. When its coils clicked empty, he swung the weapon like a club. The barrel was hard, but too lightweight to cause significant damage to the Vraxar. Even when he beat them, not one of the aliens paid him the slightest notice, nor did they try to harm or capture him.

It's like I'm invisible.

His grenade belt was in place and he reached for one of the explosives, wondering if he should start throwing them just for the hell of it. He could see more of his squad being carried away and he withdrew his hand from the belt, letting his arm fall limply to his side. The Vraxar were no longer pushing against him and the crowd of them was already thinning.

They're leaving.

"Where are you, Lieutenant?" It was Sergeant Li, sounding dazed, like he didn't know what was going on.

Make that two of us.

"They're ignoring me," was the only response McKinney could think to make. Such was his shock, he'd lost the ability to think straight.

"All right for some, huh? Newton killed Sergeant Woods and a load of others. What a stupid bastard."

The words had no time to sink in fully.

"I thought the comms was quiet."

"Yeah, a bunch of us are dead."

A Vraxar stopped directly in front of McKinney and stared at him with its single prosthetic eye. McKinney gave it a sarcastic wave. The Vraxar didn't react, except to step around him and continue on towards the exit doorway closest.

"I can't understand it," he said.

"You'll come get us, won't you, Lieutenant?"

The words, redolent with a hope Li knew was utterly remote, tore at McKinney.

"Yeah, I'll come get you, Sergeant. All of you. I promise."

The channel went dead, suggesting Li had been taken far enough that the comms were blocked by the walls of *Ix-Gastiol*. McKinney had no idea if his final words had got through or not.

There I go, making another promise I've got no chance of keeping.

Instead of making him feel like a failure, the thought made him strong. He checked the open channel for active links, just in time to see Rudy Munoz and Nitro Bannerman's connections drop out.

The Vraxar must have knocked them out. Normally, those two don't know how to stop talking.

There were still three others in the open channel. McKinney picked the first name off the list.

"Vega?"

"I'm here, sir."

"Where's *here*?"

"Along the wall from the door we were going to blow. What's going on?"

"I'll tell you when I figure it out. Stay put."

"What about me?" asked Webb.

"Well shit, that's three of us standing," said Vega.

McKinney got his bearings and realised he'd been jostled halfway over the room. He pushed his way through the Vraxar and headed towards Vega. His body was weak and it was slow going. The Vraxar showed no hostile intent, but they didn't make any effort to give him room. He felt like the smallest child at school, trying to reach his class while every other pupil wanted to go in the opposite direction.

The Vraxar streamed towards the door, but once he crossed the flow, it was easy enough to reach the wall as long as he took care not to trip over the numerous corpses. He saw Vega fifteen or twenty metres further along, standing like a statue, as if he feared movement would give him away.

There was a shape on the floor, half underneath the body of a Vraxar. This shape stirred when McKinney knelt to give it a gentle shake.

"Clifton?"

"What's happening?" The man's words were slurred like he'd been woken up six hours too early on the morning after a drinking session to celebrate a major birthday.

"Ask him what his first name is!" said Vega over a private channel.

Clifton pretended he didn't have a first name and even his Space Corps records showed only $R_I T$ Clifton. Dozens of men

148

had tried and failed to get the truth, until a few of the squad were starting to believe the man was telling the truth.

McKinney could bring himself to stoop so low as to take advantage. His men needed to trust him and he couldn't join in with games like this one.

"Sorry, can't do it," he said to Vega.

Clifton stirred again and McKinney shook him for a second time, with more force.

"Get up, soldier."

With an obvious effort, Clifton brought himself around. "There's something on my legs.

With a grunt, McKinney rolled the dead Vraxar to one side. It felt like it weighed more than three hundred pounds and in his weakened state, it was a real struggle. Clifton helped and finally managed to kick himself free. He got shakily to his feet and had to prop himself against the wall.

"Something caught me on the back of the head...man I feel like shit. Why aren't we dead?"

McKinney was out of patience when it came to this particular question. "I don't damn well know why we aren't dead! Stop asking questions when we have more important things to be getting on with!"

"Okay, okay, I'm sorry."

Further along the wall, Vega snapped out of his frozen state and he inched towards the two men, keeping his back firmly to the metal.

"What's the plan, Lieutenant?"

That was a question McKinney could understand. "I made a promise we'd get our soldiers back."

"You don't go in for half measures, do you?"

"I figure we've been singled out for this. We should be dead or captured along with all the others. Except we aren't and now we owe them."

"I'm not complaining." Vega stopped nearby and checked his plasma repeater. "Nearly full ammo." The repeaters were devastating weapons but, in a crush, they were hard to wield effectively.

Clifton was coming to his senses and McKinney was relieved he wouldn't be bringing dead wood along. Webb arrived, stepping neatly through the crowds like a seasoned weekend shopper. He had a tight grip on his plasma tube and held it vertically in front of him.

McKinney looked warily at the remaining Vraxar. Now that they'd captured the soldiers, the aliens didn't seem in any rush. Even so, the room emptied with efficient speed, like water through a funnel. The aliens strode by, their metal-clad feet clunking on the floor and their armour plates scraping.

"They don't say much," said Vega.

McKinney was certain many of the Vraxar soldiers were treated as slaves and allowed hardly any control over their actions. "They only do what they're told." He raised an arm and pointed. "We have to get out of here – they took the squad through that door."

"Wait up, Lieutenant," said Clifton, his voice stronger than it had been only moments ago. "We should get our things."

McKinney scanned the floor nearby, keen to get on. "We can't afford to lose track of our people."

"There's the number cruncher," said Webb, nodding his head towards an object a few metres away, resting inexplicably on top of a dead Vraxar. "We could get stuck behind a closed door and then we'd be a bit pissed that we didn't bring it."

The men were right and McKinney reined in his impatience. "I'll get the number cruncher."

"I'd like to pick up my explosives, Lieutenant," said Clifton. "You never know when we'll need them."

"I always did want to die accidentally in a catastrophic plasma explosion," said Vega.

"You can thank me next time I break us out of a tight spot."

"Not going to happen, Clifton."

"Enough," said McKinney.

The last of the Vraxar exited through one of the far doorways. What remained wasn't a pretty sight – there were bodies everywhere and not all of them were Vraxar. Near to the amplifier cylinder, a patch of the floor smouldered and McKinney saw the tell-tale signs of a plasma rocket explosion. There were smears of char and pieces of alien armour, along with a badly-burned spacesuit visor.

"Here's one of ours," said Vega, picking his way through the mess. "I've got no idea who."

There were other human bodies – far more than McKinney wanted. The causes of death were varied – most had been crushed in the melee, their necks broken and their ribs smashed. Others had suffered friendly fire injuries from explosives or the plasma repeater McKinney had heard. One man sat with his back to the wall, having killed himself with a slug from his gauss rifle. Fear of conversion was worse than the fear of death for this soldier.

"Want me to do a headcount?" asked Webb.

"Leave it - we owe our time to the living."

McKinney reached for the number cruncher. It had been kicked around, yet somehow it looked intact. He felt a momentary concern when he remembered the portable display – it wasn't anywhere in sight. With a sigh of relief, he found he'd tucked it into a pocket on his suit. Even during an engagement there was a part of his mind which looked after his kit.

A gauss rifle lay on the floor nearby, its previous owner having lost it in the fighting. Remembering that his own was out of ammunition, McKinney picked this one up as a replacement.

He held his thumb tightly against a pressure sensor on one side to get a reading from the magazine: seventy percent. It was enough and he slung the rifle across his back, alongside the ISOP.

Clifton was nearby, scrambling over the Vraxar corpses near to the door he'd been about to blow open. With an exclamation of triumph, he rose, holding a half-empty pack of high-explosives.

"I'll get these ones you already stuck to the doorway," said Vega, reaching up to snap one free from the metal. He threw the device underarm at Clifton, who caught it deftly and dropped it into his pack.

Soon, the four of them were finished. Clifton had lost a couple of his charges, doubtless buried amongst the carnage. He was still carrying plenty.

"Let's go," said McKinney, leading the way towards the left-hand door. It was closed.

The other three hurried after.

"I don't want to stick around in here any longer than I have to," said Vega.

There were no living Vraxar left in the room and McKinney wasn't surprised they made no effort to recover their dead. The aliens' behaviour was truly different to anything which humanity would recognize as understandable or acceptable.

By the time he was in front of the left-hand door access panel, McKinney was beginning to feel the pressure of being in this room. He hated the weakness from the amplifier cylinder and he hated the feeling that he'd somehow got off more lightly than everyone else. Mostly, he hated the deaths of his men.

McKinney brought the ISOP screen up to the panel and it interfaced without a hitch. He was prepared for a wait and was pleased when the number cruncher got the door open in less than ten seconds.

"It must have learned what to do from that last door," said Clifton.

McKinney tucked away the interface. "Yeah."

There was a passage beyond the door, leading away into the depths of *Ix-Gastiol*. It was deserted and although McKinney listened hard, the only sounds were the groans of the spaceship itself.

"We've lost them," said Vega.

"Not yet we haven't," McKinney replied.

He set off into the passage, his long strides making the others hurry to keep up. Less than a hundred metres away from the room, he felt his strength return. Not only that, but the effects of the battlefield adrenaline, suppressed up until this moment, surged through his body, making him giddy with confidence and optimism.

"Whoa," said Clifton, evidently feeling the same thing.

With his face hidden by his visor, McKinney smiled grimly to himself. Out of all the crap he'd waded through since the Vraxar first showed up on Atlantis, this pile was looking like the deepest yet. He wasn't going to let it stop him.

CHAPTER FOURTEEN

LIEUTENANT ERIC MCKINNEY and his three companions were lost. It hadn't taken them long to set off in pursuit of the captured soldiers, but they had evidently been too slow. The first passage branched once, twice and then three times. On each occasion, McKinney chose at random, with nothing other than guesswork to rely on. He kept a close eye on the comms, hoping to catch a signal from the missing members of his squad. Everything was quiet and with each new branch in the path the chance they were heading the wrong way increased.

"Where'd the Vraxar go?" asked Clifton, not expecting an answer.

"To the conversion room," said Vega. "That's the only place they'll be taking our guys."

It was true and the knowledge hurt McKinney. He'd seen the Vraxar conversion rooms before and remembered the blood, the greasy fluids and the sharp tools designed to butcher living flesh. He walked faster, hating the fact that the extra speed might actually be taking them further from their goal.

"You think there'd be a few Vraxar wandering around," said Webb. "Maybe we should stop and ask one for directions."

The words caused McKinney to stop dead in his tracks. "Webb, you're a genius."

"That's the first time anyone ever said that to me, Lieutenant. What did I do?"

"Shhh!"

McKinney waved the other man to silence and paced from one side of the passage to the other. Eventually, he stopped, with his shoulder against the wall.

"Clifton, when you got shot up on Tucson, what did they do to fix you?"

It was only a little more than three days ago and Clifton scratched his head like he couldn't remember. "I don't know exactly, sir. They told me afterwards, but I was looking out of the window thinking about something else."

"You mean you have no idea what they did to sort you out?" asked Vega in disbelief.

Clifton shrugged. "It wasn't all that bad. The surgeon told me they only had to fit some kind of power and control unit to keep everything ticking. Keyhole surgery, they called it. A quick operation and then straight back to frontline duty."

McKinney had no idea if the man was pretending ignorance or not. "I think I know why the Vraxar didn't touch us."

"Spill the beans, Lieutenant," said Webb.

"You, Webb," McKinney patted him affectionately on the shoulder. "You got a new heart, didn't you?"

"An Obsidiar-driven one."

"I got a new arm and some other stuff." McKinney thumped his chest. "Obsidiar-powered and with a control unit."

"You think they fitted something that makes the Vraxar think you're one of them?" asked Vega in disbelief.

McKinney shrugged. "Maybe. Augmentation research has

been blocked for a long time in the Confederation. What if they decided to start it up and what if they decided to get a head start by copying some of the control routines from a dead Vraxar? After all, these aliens probably know a lot more than we do about fitting metal parts to flesh."

"Vega only got a new hand," said Clifton. "And Webb was injured on the Juniper, way back at the beginning of the war. There's no way the research teams would have been able to copy the Vraxar tech so quickly."

"Yeah," said McKinney, disappointed his theory had been easily disproved.

"I had to go back to the hospital," said Webb. "They wanted to make some improvements. It seemed like a good idea to do what they told me."

"My new hand failed after a while," said Vega. "The flesh started rotting and they offered me another one made from alloy with a new type of artificial skin. They told me it would last a lifetime."

"You kept that quiet," said Clifton.

"Yeah, well. I couldn't stand the thought of Garcia going on about it – Metal Hand Vega and all that kind of crap - so I didn't say anything. It seemed easier that way."

"It sounds like we've all got something implanted that stops the Vraxar recognizing us," said McKinney.

"I can't believe this," said Clifton. "I mean, I *want* to believe it, but, you know..."

"We're going to put it to the test," said McKinney. "We just have to find a subject."

Webb laughed. "This is going to be fun."

"Sometimes I wonder about you," said Vega.

Unfortunately for McKinney, it wasn't quite so easy as simply deciding and then having everything fall into place. He believed this level of *Ix-Gastiol* wasn't habited and that the

Vraxar they recently encountered had arrived from a different area within the spaceship. Having captured the human intruders, the aliens had vanished to wherever it was they'd come from in the first place. With a sinking feeling, he knew which way the enemy had taken their prisoners. He called up the HUD map inside his visor.

"We're not too far from one of the big spaces picked up on the *Ulterior-2*'s sensors," he said. "It's about six thousand metres that way."

"Is that where we're going?" There was a note of resignation in Vega's voice.

"I don't think we have a choice."

"We never do, Lieutenant. Let's get on with it."

The current passageway didn't lead directly towards this new destination. At the next branch, they turned and then again at the one after. McKinney found it hard to keep to a measured pace, which he put down to a mixture of battlefield adrenaline and his own eagerness to get this over with.

They encountered no Vraxar and McKinney found himself doing some mental arithmetic as he tried to figure out exactly how many of the enemy were onboard the spaceship, given the large areas which were empty. He quickly gave up the attempt – they'd explored only a tiny fraction of the interior and it was fruitless trying to extrapolate.

After a few hundred metres, they came to a closed door. This time, the ISOP cracked the security lock in five seconds and the door opened.

"Another one of those amplifier cylinders," said Vega. "Great."

"We have to cross it," said McKinney. It wasn't strictly true, but he had no intention of backtracking.

The men skirted the room, keeping close to the walls. The sense of weakness returned and McKinney soon felt drained.

There were four exits, with one of them going in the right direction. The number cruncher got the door open and the soldiers found themselves in a short corridor which ended in a closed door. It was soon opened.

"Another amplifier," said Vega with a shake of his head.

They crossed four more such rooms, each one leaving them progressively more exhausted. McKinney requested another shot of adrenaline, whilst his suit medical computer took matters into its own hands and injected him with a mixture of other drugs designed to combat radiation sickness. The result was far from perfect, but McKinney was able to keep going.

"When these drugs really kick in I'm going to have enough strength to lift a fleet destroyer above my head," said Clifton.

"For ten seconds and then you'll die of an overdose heart attack," said Vega.

"Good job the suits can fix those as well, eh?"

Most soldiers quickly learned that when they got into a spacesuit, their body was no longer entirely their own and it was at the mercy of the medical computer programmed by a team of scientists who'd likely never held a gun outside of basic training. There was no bitterness. *Each to their own.*

The small talk continued and it kept the men distracted. The exit door to the fifth room opened and this time there was no corridor leading to an amplifier room.

"A lift," said Vega.

They were in a confined room, lit in green and with no decoration. The far wall curved inwards like a semi-circle and there was a set of wide, high doors shaped to fit the curve. McKinney bent his neck and found that there was no ceiling. He could see up and up, through bands of green light, and the height of it defied the sensor on his visor to locate the top.

"Maintenance shaft?" said Webb.

"Got to be."

"No sign of a crew."

"Maybe they're sleeping."

McKinney crossed the room to the access panel fixed to one side of the doors. Out of curiosity, he poked it with his fingers. As expected, the *access denied* symbols appeared and then returned to the usual display.

"Let's get this open," he said.

The number cruncher took longer this time, as though the lift ran off a different set of access rules to the doors. As the seconds ticked by, McKinney grew concerned they'd have to find another way. He needn't have worried - the ISOP did the business and the access panel changed to blue.

"Why isn't it opening?" asked Webb.

"The lift must be on another floor."

They waited. McKinney became aware of a humming noise, somewhere far above. The sound came closer and then stopped. With a whine, the lift doors parted along the middle and retracted into opposite sides of the wall, revealing the cylindrical interior.

"In," said McKinney.

The lift was a flat, circular plate of dull grey and there was a gap of a few inches between the floor and the edges of the shaft. When McKinney stepped over the gap, he saw that the shaft continued beneath this level, so they weren't getting on at the bottom. He looked up - there was no ceiling, which made him think the lift was no more complicated than a metal disk which was moved up and down using either its own gravity motor, or by a gravity winch at the top of the shaft.

"Blue light, this time. Change is good," said Clifton sarcastically.

The doors closed after only five or six seconds, sealing the men inside.

"What now?" asked Webb.

McKinney suddenly realised the flaw in his plan. There was an access panel fitted to the inside of the lift shaft and separate to the lift itself. It looked exactly the same as all the others and McKinney had no idea how to use it.

"Why not see what the ISOP makes of it?" asked Vega.

"That won't work. The number cruncher breaks stuff open and that's it. I don't think it has any way of choosing what level we want to get off at."

"Do we even know what level we want?"

"Any level that takes us closer to this central space we're aiming for."

"Give it a try, Lieutenant. The worst thing that happens is the doors open again."

With a snort of laughter, McKinney gave it a go, holding the interface device towards the access panel. The number cruncher spun through trillions upon trillions of permutations and...the lift doors opened again.

"There we have it," said McKinney.

"Yup."

The doors closed again, leaving the four of them wondering what they needed to do.

"We don't need to do anything except wait," said Vega in sudden enlightenment.

"How so?" asked McKinney.

The lift moved upwards with unexpectedly sharp acceleration. McKinney's reactions were good enough to keep him on his feet and he watched as the walls flashed by at increasing speed. His brain caught up and he realised what Vega had been about to explain.

"Someone else called the lift," he said.

"That's what I was thinking, Lieutenant. It was only a matter of time."

The lift reached its fastest speed and it ascended through the shaft. Doors passed by in a blur, each sealed to block out curious eyes.

"What are we going to do when the door opens and we find a few Vraxar waiting on the other side?" asked Clifton.

"Play it by ear," said McKinney. "And be ready for anything."

Vega laughed nervously. "Act confident."

The lift slowed, making McKinney's stomach churn. He gritted his teeth and was glad when the lift came to a halt. He wheeled around, looking for where the door was situated on this level. He held his gauss rifle loosely, with a finger on the trigger, ready for anything.

With McKinney urging them on, the men walked towards the door, as if they were innocent passengers simply exiting the lift. The doors opened onto another of the interminable corridors, except this one wasn't empty.

There were eight Estral-type Vraxar outside, in a two-by-four column. These ones were armed with hand cannons and they were dressed consistently with each other. They wore undamaged grey cloth, with metal shoulder and chest guards.

McKinney couldn't help but meet the eyes of the front two. There was something he couldn't put his finger on about them – an intelligence lay behind their grey eyes, as though the conversion process had left more of the original creature than usual.

The left-hand Vraxar had a human body slung over its shoulder, as if it weighed nothing. McKinney's visor made the connection to the comms of the suit.

R1T Ted Bass. Vital Signs: DECEASED

Anger welled up inside and McKinney fought it down. He led the remains of his squad to the side of the Vraxar and into the corridor. The aliens waited patiently for the men to pass and then they marched into the lift.

Once the Vraxar had entered, McKinney turned to face them.

"Where is the conversion room?" he asked.

The enemy troops stared at him and there was a long moment during which McKinney thought he'd blown it. Then, one of the Vraxar grinned, revealing the whitest of teeth, embedded in dead gums which were turning to black. It was one of the most petrifying sights McKinney could remember from all his time at war and he was left with the absolute certainty the Vraxar wasn't fooled.

"Ahead," said the alien.

McKinney wasn't sure if he should ask for a more precise answer. He wasn't given the chance – the doors closed and the lift went on its way, humming softly.

"Holy crap," said Clifton. "I thought it knew."

McKinney exhaled loudly. "Me too, soldier."

"Where is *ahead*?" asked Vega. "That could be anywhere."

"We'll keep going until we find another one of these bastards and we'll ask it the same question."

McKinney turned and led the squad in the only direction available. He called up the visor HUD map and was pleased to find they were heading in the right direction. The navigational software estimated the lift had taken them fifteen hundred metres higher than before and they were approximately two thousand metres from their destination.

He laughed inwardly at the thought that reaching the open space inside *Ix-Gastiol* would be anything other than the beginning of new difficulties. The *Ulterior-2*'s sensor estimates put the size of the area at slightly more than sixty cubic kilometres. There was a lot of ground to cover and he was sure there would be a whole lot more Vraxar.

They continued. McKinney found it was a struggle to keep a good pace and even pumped full of the Space Corps' finest stimulants, his feet dragged reluctantly. The passage branched several times and, on each occasion, McKinney chose what he hoped was the most efficient route.

They saw no more Vraxar, but the floor became increasingly littered with objects of different shapes and sizes. McKinney stooped to examine the first three or four and discovered they were metal struts or armour plates. He was sure metal could last for an eternity, but he got a feeling of great age when he turned the items over in his hands.

"Must've just fell off a Vraxar," said Webb, nudging a skull plate with the toe of his boot.

McKinney felt a profound sadness at the words, without quite knowing why. Humanity celebrated life and when death happened it was greeted with sorrow. The Vraxar just crumbled and fell apart. There was nothing good in any of it.

"There's no damn reason!" he said in fury.

The others didn't respond, but he could tell they understood the meaning. McKinney kicked at a metal strut and it clattered into the distance. The group set off after it, soon leaving it behind.

The distance counter in McKinney's HUD fell steadily, until it was below five hundred metres. There was no discernible change ahead and he wondered if the *Ulterior-2*'s sensors had obtained a false reading.

"Another T-junction a couple of hundred metres ahead," said Vega. "Left, or right?"

McKinney didn't answer and turned right when they reached the place. The corridor went on for another hundred metres and was joined by another passage. They turned left. The distance estimation fell to single figures and McKinney was concerned to find he wouldn't be given the opportunity to scout out the lay of the land. It appeared as if they might well stumble right into the middle of whatever was in the open space.

The passage ended in a door. It was another slab of metal the same as every other damn slab of metal on every damn warship made anywhere. With a damn access panel.

They stopped before it.

"Looks like the guys on the *Ulterior-2* did a pretty good job," conceded Clifton. "We're only fifty metres from where the open space is depicted on the 3D model."

"Here's where it gets interesting," said McKinney.

"Right about now, I'd settle for boring."

Privately, McKinney was in complete agreement. He pulled out the number cruncher interface pad and stepped towards the access panel. After ninety seconds of resistance to the number cruncher's brute-force attack, the Vraxar access panel succumbed to the inevitable. The lights turned blue and the door slid to one side with a grumbling scrape which hinted at the immense weight of the alloys. A wave of freezing, biting cold washed outwards like the dying breath of a god.

What they saw beyond made them realise why there were so few Vraxar on this level of *Ix-Gastiol*.

CHAPTER FIFTEEN

THE CHAMBER WAS immense – the biggest interior space McKinney could remember seeing anywhere, except for the coil. It was square and lit in pale blue, as if this colour were purposely chosen to exacerbate the chill. The ceiling was far above, flat and unadorned. The far wall was more than four thousand metres away and there was a similar distance between the sides. The air was utterly dry, so no ice had formed, though a gentle breeze came from somewhere.

The four of them stood on a grated walkway which ran around the edges of the room, three or four hundred metres from the floor. There was no railing and the men didn't venture near the edge, not that any of them wanted to come any closer to what lay below.

There were pale bodies, piled haphazardly in their hundreds of millions and frozen in every conceivable position by the sub-zero temperatures. It was as if a giant hand had picked up corpses thousands at a time and simply opened its fingers to drop them wherever they might fall. In places, the tops of the piles came level with the walkway, whilst in others places, the black metal of the floor was visible.

Vega dropped to his knees and wept, while Webb remained motionless, staring outwards.

"This isn't real," whispered Clifton hoarsely. "What the hell is this place?"

McKinney didn't know. He didn't have the faintest idea why there would ever be a need for something like this. He zoomed in his sensor, trying to make sense of it. There were many different species – he counted dozens he didn't recognize before he eventually gave up trying. There was so much loss here, so much appalling tragedy, a part of him wanted to curl up and sleep until his suit power supply ran out and he joined the dead in their eternal slumber.

He couldn't – *wouldn't* let it happen. He tightened his grip on emotion, refusing to accept any thought which wasn't logical and rational. As dispassionately as he could, he took in the details, trying to find anything which might be of use – something which would help the Confederation fight this war.

"These were never converted," he said. "They have no augmentations. There must be other doors we can't see at floor level. It's the only way they could have brought in so many."

"But why?" asked Clifton.

"Replacements? Maybe they don't have need of every species they find, yet keep a hold of them just in case."

"What if every other space in *Ix-Gastiol* is filled like this?"

"I think we have to assume they are. They've accumulated so many bodies, they might never run out."

"And still they want more. Like it's a habit they can't kick."

"Captain Blake once told me that the commander of *Ix-Gorghal* referred to the Vraxar as *children*, as though each new convert is something to be cherished. Like it's a damned *privilege* to become one." He lifted an arm and indicated the scene before them. "Lies. Every single word a lie."

"I don't think I can stay here, Lieutenant," said Vega. "I really can't."

There was a note of panic in the soldier's voice. Ricky Vega had been through all sorts of shit and he'd been as solid as granite, whatever came. He'd had enough.

"We're leaving," said McKinney.

There were faint discolorations in the wall further along the walkway, which might have been other ways out. McKinney wasn't certain and besides, they were too far away to make a quick check. It was cruel to keep the men here a moment longer, so he used the ISOP to open the door through which they'd arrived. It opened much quicker than the first time and they exited the room. The door took an interminable amount of time to close itself and when it did, McKinney closed his eyes tightly, trying to keep himself steady.

I made a promise. I made a promise.

The repetition of the words helped and he found a place in his mind into which he could hide the sights of the room. The time would come when he would confront the memories, but that time wasn't now.

The sound of footsteps reached his ears. The noise began faintly and grew in volume until he was certain it was caused by many different feet.

"Coming this way," said Webb, his head cocked to one side.

"I reckon."

A group of Vraxar came around the corner a hundred metres away. They weren't exactly running, instead they marched quickly and with purpose. McKinney got his rifle ready, but didn't make any threatening movements. He studied the group – there were fifteen of them in total and already too close for Webb to take them out with his launcher.

"Hold," he whispered. "Let me handle this."

These were more of the Estral type and McKinney got a sense of their age. Their grey skin was sunken and thin, the skulls visible underneath. They were fitted here and there with metal parts – eyes, jaws and one had an arm made from dull alloy. The lead Vraxar fixed the men with a look of interest, betraying the vestiges of intelligence it was permitted to retain.

McKinney had already realised that not every Vraxar was equal and up until this moment he'd assumed the Estral were the lowest amongst the hierarchy. Now he could see this wasn't the truth – the conversion process could leave some with more of their abilities than others. These Estral here had been left with the necessary skills to act as soldiers – perhaps they'd been taken early in the Vraxar-Estral war, when there was a need for ground troops. The ones on Tucson had been no more than disposable meat shields, representative of the fact that the Vraxar killed far more than they needed.

Like those bodies in that room...

With his anger rising, McKinney prepared to speak with the enemy. They showed no sign of wanting to speak with him and they walked straight past, changing to single file so as to avoid making physical contact. The lead one reached the access panel and pressed a broad-knuckled hand onto it. The display changed to a red colour and the Vraxar left its hand in place.

"What are you doing?" asked McKinney, projecting his voice through the speaker built in to his visor.

The Vraxar didn't look up, nor did it answer.

McKinney tried again. "Why have you come to this part of *Ix-Gastiol?*"

This time the Vraxar did look. It turned its head slowly to the side and studied McKinney, as though it was sizing him up.

It spoke in a voice deep and gravelly, with a wheezing, rasping edge. "There has been a security breach on this door."

"What are you looking for?"

The question appeared to be beyond the Vraxar's scope and its single real eye blinked. "The Aranol does not tolerate security breaches."

"What do you expect to find?"

The Vraxar's answer wasn't direct, though McKinney was certain it was unintentional. "I will report my findings to the Aranol."

"Does the Aranol command *Ix-Gastiol*?"

The eye blinked again. "No."

McKinney knew he was taking a risk by showing his ignorance. In the end, nothing worthwhile came without taking a chance. "Who commands *Ix-Gastiol*?"

"Tuik-Ra-Dak commands *Ix-Gastiol*."

The Vraxar's pronunciation of the name was guttural and harsh, as though it was difficult to form the sounds.

"Where will I find Tuik-Ra-Dak and the Aranol?"

"I don't know."

"Where will I find the conversion room?"

"Conversion room EM-9 is within Section QH93MM91."

McKinney took a deep breath. "Show me."

The Vraxar wasn't persuaded. "There has been a security breach on this door."

"The Aranol has instructed me to attend conversion room EM-9," McKinney replied.

This was beyond the Vraxar's ability to formulate a response. "We do as the Aranol instructs."

"I cannot find EM-9. You must show me."

The Vraxar caught McKinney on the hop by giving its first example of free thinking so far in the conversation. "Why do you not know?"

McKinney shut off his visor speaker and spoke to his men. "Get ready to shoot if I command it." The Vraxar were crowded nearby and since only Vega had a repeater, combat was a distinctly bad option. He turned the speaker on again and said the first thing that came into his head. "We're new here."

As far as excuses went, it was laughable and McKinney slowly, carefully brought his gauss rifle into a position from which he could fire.

The lead Vraxar was silent for a long, drawn-out moment. "The Aranol has instructed me to find out the reason for the security breach. One of these others will show you."

Without any outward sign of communication between the group of aliens, one of them took a step towards the four soldiers. It had no particularly distinguishing features, beyond its existence as a decaying, long-dead former Estral warrior with a missing eye and a face made up almost entirely of metal.

"Come," it said, striding past.

McKinney didn't say a word and he fell in behind, waving the other men to follow. The alien headed along the passage, its gait stiff, as though its tendons were dry and hard.

"Ugly bastard, isn't it?" whispered Clifton across the comms.

"No uglier than you, soldier."

The Vraxar turned at the branch in the corridor, not once checking to see if the men still followed.

"We're *new* here?" asked Vega, putting heavy stress on the word. "Nice work, Lieutenant."

McKinney was glad Vega had managed to pick himself up after the storage room and he laughed at the comment. "What are you complaining about? It worked, didn't it?"

The Vraxar reached another branch in the passage. It didn't hesitate and took the new turning, inadvertently showing McKinney where he'd chosen wrong earlier.

He tried some light conversation. "How far to the conversion room?"

"It is some distance."

"Where is the Aranol? What does it look like?"

"Which question should I answer?"

"Both."

"The Aranol is not here. I do not know what it looks like."

McKinney was sure the Vraxar wasn't specifically trying to speak in riddles, but the effect was the same. He'd been allowed to read a transcript of the conversation Fleet Admiral Duggan had with the Vraxar captured on the Ir-Klion-32 Neutraliser, and there were distinct similarities here.

"Does the Aranol command Tuik-Ra-Dak?" he asked.

"Yes."

It was a revelation of sorts – the captain of *Ix-Gastiol* wasn't the most senior officer in the field.

"Does anyone command the Aranol?"

"No. The Aranol commands the Vraxar."

"How does the Aranol issue its commands to you?"

They entered another lift station, this one bigger than the previous, with three separate sets of doors.

"The Aranol issues commands to all Vraxar."

McKinney was starting to catch on to how conversation worked with the aliens. Whenever the Vraxar flat out didn't understand something, they said so. Otherwise, they fitted in the closest response they could manage, even if it wasn't relevant or didn't answer the question.

The alien touched the control panel for the lift and the door opened after a short delay. It was identical inside to the previous one, with no ceiling and the shaft vanishing upwards. The lift began its ascent. McKinney and his men found the acceleration hard to deal with, while the Vraxar stood impassively.

"Why are there so few Vraxar active within *Ix-Gastiol*?" asked McKinney, once the lift had reached full speed.

"The Aranol operates *Ix-Gastiol*. There is no requirement for a crew."

Except when there's a security breach on a door.

"What does Tuik-Ra-Dak do if the Aranol operates *Ix-Gastiol*?"

"Tuik-Ra-Dak commands *Ix-Gastiol*."

"Fine, fine," McKinney muttered behind his visor. "What does the Aranol intend to do with the prisoners?"

The Vraxar went silent before it answered. "They will be questioned and then they will become Vraxar."

"Will this be done in the conversion room?" asked McKinney, aware he'd been acting on an assumption, rather than confirmed facts.

"Conversions are usually done in the conversion room."

There was a note of mockery in the response which was so fleeting McKinney wondered if he was imagining things. Perhaps some of the Vraxar retained slivers of their living personality which could manifest themselves under the right circumstances.

The lift slowed and then stopped. There were two double doors at this level – leading from opposite sides of the shaft. Only one set of doors opened and the Vraxar walked through, with the soldiers close behind. McKinney called up the HUD map and, according to the visor's positioning system, they'd entered the huge open area again, only much higher up and from a slightly different direction.

The passage leading from the lift was wide enough for six to walk abreast and the ceiling was several metres high. There was a bank of screens embedded in the wall close by, covered in Vraxar script which the suit language modules were still incapable of translating.

The corridor opened into a long room, dimly lit in grey, with a grated metal floor and ceiling. The room was filled with banks of consoles, which were low, squat hunks of metal with green-text displays. Thick cables ran up the walls and across, while black pipes ran overhead. McKinney was no expert, but the kit in this room looked like it was two or three hundred years old and far cruder than the latest stuff available in the Confederation. Much of the Vraxar war machine remained a mystery and McKinney supposed they might have a mixture of old and new spread throughout their fleet.

It was soon apparent this area of *Ix-Gastiol* was more heavily-populated than the other parts they'd explored so far. A pair of smaller Vraxar entered through a wide doorway at the far end. These ones were a dusky red colour, like the sand of a parched world. When they came closer, McKinney saw metal ribs through paper-thin flesh and one had a fist-sized metal box attached to the side of its neck. There were lights on the box and they flashed on and off in sequence.

"What's that one doing?" asked Webb.

One of the new Vraxar extended a spindly arm and McKinney saw its middle finger was some kind of interface device, which it plugged directly into one of the consoles.

"This place is screwed up," said Vega. "Death and misery."

Their escort didn't slow. The soldiers followed it across the room and along a central aisle which took them past the two new Vraxar. The first paid them no heed, while the second watched the men carefully. McKinney was already on edge and the scrutiny left him with the impression they were being led into a trap of some sort – a trap which every Vraxar was aware of, but not telling.

"I'm glad the visors filter out smells," said Clifton nervously. "Those ones look like they'd stink worse than Garcia's underwear drawer."

The exit led to another corridor and then to another room, this one far larger than the previous. There were more consoles here, all connected by cables to a large metal cube in the middle of the floor. This cube was four metres on each side and it dominated the room. There was a buzzing sound coming from somewhere and the temperature was noticeably colder. Numerous passages continued further into the depths of *Ix-Gastiol*.

"What is this?" asked McKinney.

Their escort stopped as if it were going to provide an answer. What it said wasn't good. "I am going elsewhere."

The answer caught McKinney by surprise. "Where?" he asked.

"Elsewhere."

"How do we locate the conversion room."

"Ask for directions." There was another hint of the mockery from earlier, though it wasn't reflected on the Vraxar's face.

Not that I would know what an Estral looks like when it's taking the piss, thought McKinney wryly.

Their escort didn't speak further and it walked off towards one of the exit corridors.

"Thanks for nothing, you mouldy piece of crap," said Clifton under his breath, raising his middle finger to the retreating back of the Vraxar.

"What do we do now, Lieutenant?" asked Webb.

It was a question McKinney was becoming all-too-familiar with.

"We do what the Vraxar suggested and ask for directions."

"They seem friendly," said Vega.

"Yeah, they're the regular kinds you'd be happy to find moving in next door."

With the soldiers struggling to come up with a smart response, McKinney pointed towards the far wall, where there was a choice of two exits visible on the far side of the cube. His boots clanked on the grating and when he peered downwards, he noticed there were more cables running beneath the flooring. He couldn't recall ever seeing cables on a fleet warship, let alone a pipe. Yet, amongst this ancient technology was the cube. Coldness seeped out, like it was filled with Obsidiar. McKinney was convinced it was an advanced processing cluster and there was something about it which made him think it more than a match for anything in the Confederation.

Webb brushed his fingers against one of the smooth faces of the cube and then came out with one of his infrequent-but-intelligent comments. "I'll bet the Vraxar discovered Obsidiar before any other species," he said. "With all that power, there'd be no need to tweak the hell out of every other material."

"Yeah," said Vega. "It's probably why they've been able to kick the shit out of everyone else."

"Until now, soldier, until now."

The closest passage ended at a T-junction a short distance away. McKinney chose left and marched on, ready to ask the first Vraxar he met for those directions.

CHAPTER SIXTEEN

IT WAS a stroke of luck which eventually led McKinney and his squad to conversion room EM-9.

They wandered for fifteen or twenty minutes without seeing any more Vraxar. It was cold in this area of *Ix-Gastiol* and there was enough moisture in the thin atmosphere to allow a layer of ice to form on the walls. McKinney couldn't help himself and he scraped a series of furrows through it with his fingertips. The ice was powdery and it scattered into white dust which reflected the green light like a thousand tiny fireflies.

"Must be Obsidiar behind these walls," said Vega.

"I reckon they just don't bother keeping it heated," said Clifton. "The Vraxar probably don't care if it's twenty below freezing."

"They keep leaking that clear stuff when we shoot them. Do you think it's some kind of antifreeze?"

McKinney could tell when a seemingly open question was being directed his way. "It's a good idea, Vega. The Space Corps must have plenty of specimens by now – I'm sure they've got the truth written down in a report somewhere."

"A door," said Clifton.

It was the first door they'd come to since exiting the lift with the Vraxar soldier. McKinney brought them to a halt and they looked at the door. It was high and wide, with grey symbols etched into the surface. Not for the first time, McKinney was left wishing the Space Corps language labs would sort out a working prototype of a Vraxar language module. Hell, even a semi-working one would be an improvement. The Vraxar seemed to have a decent grasp of the Confederation common tongue – albeit through the interception of comms data – so it seemed only right that the Space Corps get their act together.

"Looks like an important door," said Webb. He tipped his plasma tube forward and tapped it against the metal. "Knock, knock."

McKinney was increasingly aware of the passing time. The longer they delayed, the greater the chance his missing squad would be dead or worse. He got the ISOP interface out of his pocket in readiness.

"Once I do this, we'll need to move fast before the Aranol sends up another bunch of Estral. If this is the conversion room, there might be hundreds in the next patrol and they might not all be fooled into thinking we're the same as them."

He held the display close to the panel. The ISOP screen filled with numbers, the seconds passed and the might of the portable processing cluster defeated the door security.

"Bingo," said Vega when the access panel changed to blue.

The door split down an imperceptible seam and the two halves slid neatly away with a clunk. There was a red-lit room beyond, which McKinney stepped into with a feeling of trepidation. The others followed and he heard them cursing softly at what they saw.

"This is the place," said Clifton.

Conversion room EM-9 was a vast, square room, many

hundreds of metres to each side. The floor was covered in what were strictly speaking *operating tables*, though McKinney thought of them as *biers*. These biers were uniform in size and able to accommodate creatures larger even than the Estral. They were arranged in neat rows, with less than two metres between each and there were thousands of them – tens of thousands.

Above the biers, the ceiling was a forest of automated robotic arms, which were designed to move from *patient* to *patient* along slots. The functions of the arms were easy enough to guess from the implements they terminated in – there were scalpels and serrated blades, along with every type of cutting and cauterising tool imaginable.

With any surgical treatment there was an element of butchery – flesh had to be cut and reformed in order to enact a cure. In the conversion room, the butchery was celebrated, as if the subjects were no more than sacks of meat to be incised and dissected as efficiently as possible. As he stared in horror, McKinney realised there was more than a simple need for efficiency – the conversion process was designed to be as brutal and degrading as possible.

"It's like being back on the Neutraliser," said Vega. "Except much bigger."

To McKinney's endless relief, there were no conversions taking place. He used his visor sensor to scan the far corners of the room to be sure. There were objects he couldn't quite recognize here and there, and some of the robot arms moved jerkily and without apparent purpose.

Whilst there were no conversions underway, there were Vraxar in the room.

"There, to the right, Lieutenant," said Vega. "Four of them over by those screens."

"I see them," said McKinney walking between two of the biers. The floor underfoot was stained brown, but mercifully it was much cleaner than the one in the Ir-Klion-32's conversion room.

These Vraxar were far smaller than most of the others they'd met and for the first time since coming onto *Ix-Gastiol*, McKinney didn't feel undersized. The aliens didn't look up, nor even acknowledge his presence and they operated separate screens without uttering a word between them.

"Where are the prisoners?" asked McKinney.

One of the Vraxar stopped what it was doing and turned to face him. McKinney knew at once he was speaking to a creature killed and converted centuries before. It was humanoid and it looked as if it had spent a thousand years drying in the harsh sun of a long-forgotten world. Its yellow flesh was split and its brown teeth were embedded in pallid gums. The eyes were something different – they were clear blue orbs without a pupil, beautifully preserved as though the willpower behind them wouldn't permit corruption to touch them.

The creature's lips moved as though they were trying to remember how to form words. "You are the same as them," said the creature, its voice whispering like a breeze through the fallen leaves of autumn. "You are not Vraxar."

McKinney found himself lifting his rifle, in case the creature tried to trigger an alarm. "Where are the prisoners?" he repeated.

"You are too late."

There was no triumph, only sorrow in the words and McKinney felt his stomach clench. "Are they dead?"

"Some of them."

McKinney closed his eyes, the visor hiding his emotion from the Vraxar. "What of the rest?"

"Tuik-Ra-Dak wished to speak with them. They were taken from the conversion room before we could complete our work."

"What does Tuik-Ra-Dak hope to learn?"

"I do not know, human. There is little left of the original creature - now there is only the Aranol. Whatever drove the Vraxar is long since forgotten, corrupted until there is nothing recognizable of their once noble goals."

There was something about this Vraxar which made McKinney believe it had far greater depths of knowledge than the others.

"Noble? There is a room filled with the dead below us. There is nothing noble in this!"

"There are fifteen more rooms like it on *Ix-Gastiol*, human. There were others on *Ix-Gorghal*, before your species destroyed it." The creature shook its head slightly. "Irreplaceable records of life, destroyed by your guns."

McKinney shook his own head in turn. "We cannot be blamed for this."

"No, you cannot. The Vraxar are weak, failing. The Estral was the hardest of wars and the Aranol expected humanity to be an easy opponent – a way to replenish ourselves before we reached the Antaron. Now? We are nearly spent."

The questions swirled around in McKinney's head, fighting to be spoken. "You have a home world," he said. "You will rebuild."

The creature made a rustling sound which may have been laughter. "You have seen the Aranol."

"That...it was an entire world!"

"No, human, not an entire world."

"How do you know this? The other Vraxar give away nothing. Are you one of the first races? Are you a leader?" he asked.

"Not a leader and not the first, nor the second, nor the tenth race. The Vraxar have travelled for longer than anyone remembers. I doubt even the Aranol remembers the beginning."

McKinney wished he could stay here and speak to this creature, to find out everything he could about the alien species which had caused such misery to so many. There wasn't the time

– however *noble* this Vraxar claimed they had once been, there was only baseness remaining. Whatever it took, McKinney was going to try his damnedest to stop them in their tracks right here in Confederation territory.

"Can you tell me how to reach Tuik-Ra-Dak?"

"He won't be difficult to locate." The Vraxar indicated the nearest doorway. "Through there you will find one of *Ix-Gastiol*'s launch areas. If you manage to make your way across it, the widest exit will take you to your goal. You should make haste – you triggered an alarm when you came into this room."

McKinney couldn't stop himself from asking. "How do you know?"

"The Aranol learns of any security breach, wherever it may take place. Please run."

There was an imploring note to the final two words and they filled McKinney with an even greater sense of urgency.

"Come on," he said to the others. He stopped mid-stride and turned his head towards the Vraxar. "Thank you."

"Do what you must do, Lieutenant Eric Douglas McKinney."

McKinney faltered. "How did you...?"

He was interrupted by Clifton. "Aren't you going to talk to them first, sir? To ask them where they took the squad?"

"What do you think I was doing?"

Clifton sounded confused. "You didn't say anything."

McKinney became irritated. "I spent the last five minutes talking..." He glanced at the Vraxar, to find it poking at one of the screens and not paying him even the slightest attention.

"You stopped for two seconds like you were going to scratch your arse or something and then you told us to come on," said Webb.

Something had just happened and McKinney had no idea what it was. There were mysteries in the universe and he wise enough to know he couldn't understand them all. More importantly, he didn't waste time beating himself up over it.

"Keep your mouths shut and follow me," he said.

McKinney ran for the door and the others followed. It was a great relief to leave the conversion room so soon, even though they had been denied the opportunity to rescue the other soldiers.

"Where are we going Lieutenant?"

"This way."

"Yeah, I can see that."

At the exit door, McKinney fumbled the number cruncher interface from his spacesuit pocket. Before he could get it free, the door opened in front of him and he dashed through into the corridor outside. It went to the left and right as well as straight ahead. The interior of *Ix-Gastiol* did an excellent job of muffling sounds, but he thought he could hear footsteps coming from the right.

"Getting busy," said Webb, confirming McKinney's thoughts.

The Vraxar hadn't been precise in its directions to the launch area, yet McKinney felt something tugging him towards the passage leading directly away. He ran into it, trying his best to mask the sound of his feet.

The walls of this passage were rimed with ice and there were doors to either side. If there wasn't such urgency, McKinney would have been tempted to open one or two, in order to see if there was anything he could learn about the Vraxar spaceship.

The passage was intersected by another, much larger one. This new passage was twenty metres high and wide, and to the left it cut through this part of *Ix-Gastiol* as far as McKinney could see. To the right, the passage opened out abruptly into another space of incredible dimensions.

Clifton swore softly under his breath, while the others could only stare. McKinney advanced slowly, keeping an eye out for danger. The launch bay was lit in a brighter green than other parts of *Ix-Gastiol* and the greater illumination helped the visor sensors get a reliable ping off the side walls.

"Two klicks that way, and two that way," said McKinney. "And another two to the ceiling."

His view was obscured by the enormous dropship clamped to the wall above. From its shape and size, McKinney guessed it was the same type the Vraxar had deployed on the Tucson base recently. It was made from mismatched cubes of dark metal, fitted together without any apparent regard for appearance. Even though gravity clamps were as reliable as any other tech, McKinney felt distinctly nervous with the spaceship suspended directly over his head. He walked quickly across the solid metal floor, relieved there was no ice.

"How many dropships?" asked Vega. He started counting under his breath.

"Twenty-five clamped to the walls," said Webb. "Plus those three parked in the middle of the floor."

"Do you think they're already loaded with troops?" asked Clifton.

"What do you think?"

"I think it's very likely they are filled with enough Vraxar to overrun Old Earth five times over."

"There you have it, then."

"With lots of other similar launch areas in this spaceship," added Vega.

"How do they deploy them?" asked Webb. "I can't see any bay doors."

"There must be a launch chute or something," said McKinney.

"I think there's something in the ceiling."

"It doesn't matter, since we won't be flying one of these transports any time soon," McKinney replied.

They gave a collective shrug. "Where to, Lieutenant?"

"The widest exit on the far side of the launch area."

"We have to walk all the way over?"

"Do you want me to carry you?"

"No, sir."

The launch area was huge and it was also deserted. As he walked – cautiously checking for movement all around – McKinney found the strangeness of it weighing down on him. Whatever the Vraxar represented, they were so completely removed from any normal civilisation as to make a mockery of the efforts of other species to evolve and improve. The aliens made him think of an aggressive cancer, forever replicating, mindlessly seeking to grow and expand without any purpose. The difference was, they had the ability to move from host to host, turning each conquered species into a part of the disease.

He remembered the creature in the conversion room and its suggestion that the Vraxar were a spent force. For some reason, he couldn't bring himself to believe it. He couldn't escape the notion that if the Vraxar weren't eradicated, they'd grow from the remains until they eventually became as terrible a threat as before.

The Aranol. The thought came unbidden into his head.

The three parked dropships were lengthways across the hangar bay and they hid much of the far wall, so there was no way to be sure they were heading the quickest way. It seemed logical to simply aim directly across the middle and this they did.

Once he'd assured himself there were no enemy soldiers waiting to shoot any passing humans, McKinney broke into a run. The battlefield adrenaline wasn't close to wearing off and he came steadily closer to the middle one of the three dropships. It was definitely the same type as the one which landed on the Tucson base and he suddenly noticed that three of the side doors were open, forming ramps to the floor.

"Anyone fancy a look inside?" he asked.

"You're joking?"

"Of course he's joking. Lieutenant? Tell me you're joking."

"Don't worry about it, soldier. We're not going inside."

They reached the transport and its flat sides towered over them like a prison wall built from the darkest metal. McKinney tried to see up the nearest ramp, but the angle wasn't good. There was light and the hint of shapes, nothing more.

The men ran beneath the spaceship's hull. The landing legs were thick and fitted with a type of damping system McKinney hadn't seen before. It was darker here and he felt like a mouse scurrying beneath a table, while the owners sat eating.

They got a much better view of the opposite wall from beneath the transport and McKinney began counting the exits.

"Five ways out and we want that middle one," he said.

The centre passage was as large as the one through which they'd entered the hangar area and this one also stretched away into the distance. McKinney grimaced at the thought they might need to run for another twenty kilometres before they reached their destination and he asked himself if the telepathic Vraxar had been playing him for a fool by sending him on what was looking like a wild goose chase.

And then, he saw it. A shape emerged from somewhere to the side of the main exit passage. The details were indistinct, but this Vraxar was ten feet tall and nearly as broad. There were other Vraxar in its wake – fifteen or twenty much smaller shapes followed afterwards.

"Take cover!" hissed McKinney.

The men darted behind one of the landing legs – there was enough room for them without crowding.

"What the hell is that?" asked Vega.

McKinney placed his hand on the freezing surface of the landing leg and leaned carefully around. The Vraxar were two thousand metres distant and they walked away from the hangar. The visor sensor resolved some of the information – the largest Vraxar's head was encased in metal, along with its shoulders and arms. The green light made it difficult to be certain what colour its flesh was and the escort of smaller aliens hid its lower body.

"It's probably what you think it is," McKinney replied.

"Tuik-Ra-Dak," said Webb, his pronunciation nigh on perfect.

"It's got to be," said McKinney. "The captain of *Ix-Gastiol*."

"He's a larger than average gentleman and he comes with friends," said Clifton.

"Wherever he goes, that's where we'll find the rest of our squad, soldier."

"I am aware of the inevitability, Lieutenant."

"I can land a rocket in the middle of them if you want," Webb offered.

It was tempting. "Hold. We need to find out where they're going."

The wait wasn't long. The group of Vraxar turned and vanished into either a side passage or through a door. Once the enemy were out of sight, the soldiers emerged from the cover of the landing leg and sprinted at full speed towards the exit tunnel.

CHAPTER SEVENTEEN

EVEN WITH THE battlefield adrenaline giving his body an artificial boost, McKinney was out of breath by the time he entered the tunnel. The number cruncher hadn't got any lighter and it jarred his spine with every footstep. Luckily, the battlefield adrenaline also masked the effects of such minor discomforts and reassured him that everything was tremendous.

There were access panels along both walls and no visible side corridors. McKinney did his best to work out which door the Vraxar had taken – the visor sensor had given him an estimation of distance, but it was difficult to tally up with what his eyes saw, especially when he was running hard.

"Fourth door," said Clifton.

"You sure?"

"As sure as I can be."

McKinney fixed his eyes on the fourth access panel along – it was further away than he'd expected. There again, nothing within *Ix-Gastiol* was as it should be. He slowed to a walk, panting for breath.

"Movement ahead," said Vega.

Way in the distance, there were signs of activity which appeared on the visor movement sensors as an amorphous blob of orange. It wasn't what any of them wanted to see.

"Coming this way, Lieutenant. Looks like a few of them."

McKinney turned – the hangar was three hundred metres away.

"If they start shooting, we're dead anyway."

With that, he pulled out the ISOP interface and walked rapidly towards the fourth door, doing his best to ignore the Vraxar. He held the device close to the access panel and angled his body so that it shielded what he was doing. The adjacent door didn't look much different to any other door – a little higher and a little wider, but there were otherwise no distinguishing features.

"You'll never make a good thief, Lieutenant," said Clifton.

Vega gave an anxious laugh. "He always looks guilty when he's up to something."

"You need to brazen it, Lieutenant. People are fooled by brazen."

"Yeah, you can tell he's an honest man."

McKinney unconsciously shifted stance in order to give the impression he had every right to be using an advanced decryption tool to break open the door.

"You need to try harder, Lieutenant."

"Piss off."

"What's the plan anyway?"

"Shoot on sight."

"I like it."

"The Vraxar along there don't seem in much of a hurry," said Webb, twirling his plasma tube like a baton.

"There's no sign of a general alarm," said Vega.

"We're too much like small fry for them to wake the entire ship up."

The number cruncher was finding this door a tough nut to

crack and McKinney glanced frequently towards the approaching enemy. He knew he shouldn't be worried – the Vraxar hadn't recognized them as intruders so far and there was no logical reason anything had changed.

Except the Aranol knows we're here. Or at least it knows someone is here.

The ISOP screen became warm to the touch and McKinney wondered if it was about to meet its match, or if the Vraxar had beefed up their door security after the recent breach into the conversion room. If the Aranol was as all-knowing as the Vraxar said, it would surely have a good idea that something was happening in this area of the spaceship.

The number cruncher didn't let them down. The access panel turned orange and the door slid into its recess. McKinney pocketed the interface and held his rifle at his side, still doing his best to appear innocent. There was a room through the door and the men stepped inside.

The room was rectangular, with the longest walls at thirty metres. It was lit in a blue-white that was eerily reminiscent of a Space Corps warship. The far wall was mostly taken up by status screens and there were thick cables from floor to ceiling, many of which had been pinned so that they obscured the text on the displays. It only reinforced the idea that *Ix-Gastiol* had evolved over a long time, with more pieces being added with each passing year.

There were three further exit passages and McKinney could see directly along the opposite one. There was another room at the end.

Two Vraxar stood immobile in the far corner. From the corner of his eye, they looked like shadows created by the cables. When McKinney stared closely, he saw they were humanoid, as were all Vraxar, with so little flesh remaining they might as well have been robots. They didn't make any hostile moves, but he shot them anyway, sending gauss slugs through each metal skull and into whatever lay beneath. The two crumpled without falling and he saw with disgust that they were attached to the wall by silvery wires, which held the bodies in place.

"Shoot on sight," he repeated. "This way and stay quiet."

With determination, McKinney entered the opposite passageway. There were indistinct sounds ahead – a buzzing, a hum and a high-pitched whine. Even though the lights were bright, he stayed close to the wall out of habit. Vega came next, then Webb and Clifton.

McKinney stopped near the end of the passage and listened carefully. He could hear rustling sounds now and something bumping, but nothing which suggested there was any alarm. McKinney forced himself to breathe steadily and advanced. He couldn't see too much of the room yet – the lighting was the same and the far wall was distant enough to make him think it was a large space he approached. Then he heard it. A cry of agony came from the room ahead, and there was no mistaking it as anything other than human.

"That's Garcia," said Webb.

McKinney walked faster, his rifle barrel raised to a firing position. He was sure the cry came from the left, so he turned to that side. There were several details which needed his attention, but none more so than the Vraxar he saw ten metres away. It was another of the type he'd seen in the previous room and it was standing near to the wall, directly in front of a figure in a spacesuit.

With a gentle squeeze on the rifle's activation trigger, McKinney sent three bullets into the alien, catapulting it from its feet. A second was in a straight line behind the first and the gauss slugs retained enough momentum to kill this one at the same time. As it fell, McKinney put another round into its chest to make sure. He lifted his gun once more, hunting the next target.

There were two Estral-type flanking a closed door, both of them already in a slow-motion tumble to the floor.

"Bastards," snarled Vega, still firing at them.

Another Vraxar came into McKinney's sight and he spun towards it, too slowly. Vega and Clifton came to his aid and filled the alien with enough holes to kill six.

"Clear," said McKinney. There was a single exit from this room, guarded by the now-dead Estral. "Webb, Vega, cover that door. Clifton, watch the way we came."

The engagement had been resolved in seconds – enough time for McKinney's visor comms to re-link to the other spacesuits in the room. The occupants of those suits were upright against the wall, trapped in place by tight metal bands around their necks and waists. One of them convulsed – it was Garcia, with the end of a thick syringe protruding from his chest.

"Lieutenant," said Sergeant Li. There were so many layers of relief in that single word.

McKinney strode past several of the soldiers. He grasped the end of the syringe and pulled. It slid free from Garcia's chest, slick with his blood.

There were too many things to deal with and McKinney was close to being overwhelmed by the options. His brain continued to register the details – the complicated-looking console in the centre of the room, a panel on the wall which looked vaguely like a replicator, the pipes, the cables and the screens. At the same time, he tried to figure out the priorities.

The area isn't secure. Everything else will have to wait.

"Clifton, stay where you are. Webb, Vega, we're going through that door."

"That's where the big bastard went," said Sergeant Li. "He took Captain Blake with him."

"Anything I should know?"

"Yeah – I watched him kill five of us just to make a point."

McKinney approached the door carefully, stepping across the hulking body of the dead Estral. "What's through here?"

"I've got no idea, Lieutenant."

"Where are your weapons?"

"Not here. That's all I know."

The number cruncher started working on the door, with McKinney hoping it wouldn't take long.

"Want me to use my repeater?" asked Vega.

"Only if you're sure you won't spray Captain Blake full of holes."

"I'm not an aerosol, Lieutenant," said Vega indignantly.

Once again, the ISOP proved its worth by disabling the locks on the door. The panel changed and the door slid aside. McKinney was on his way before the door was fully open and he strode into the short passageway, with Vega and Webb a single pace behind.

If the next room was meant to be the Vraxar equivalent of officer's quarters, McKinney was left unimpressed by the choice of décor. There were more banks of screens and there were more cables. It was freezing, with another of the huge processing cubes responsible for the sub-zero temperatures.

Captain Blake was fixed upright to the visible face, with bands around his neck, waist and wrists. There was a slender cable plugged into the interface port on Blake's visor and the other end of the cable was attached to the cube by means of a socket. There was no sign of Tuik-Ra-Dak.

"Captain Blake?" said McKinney over a closed channel. He got no response and Blake didn't move. The enemy captain wasn't in sight and there was no sound to give away its position. The cube was easily big enough to hide a ten-feet-tall Vraxar.

"Which way?" asked Vega.

With a flick of his hand, McKinney indicated to the right. "Vega, you go first."

Vega had the best weapon for the job and he didn't complain. He walked across to the cube and then sidled along it. At the edge, he looked around.

"Clear."

"Shit. The bastard better not be waiting for us somewhere."

Vega made his way around the cube, with McKinney following a few paces back and Webb coming last. There was no room to safely fire a plasma tube and the soldier had his gauss rifle in hand. As they made their way carefully towards the rear wall of the room, McKinney found his eye drawn to the screens in the wall, with their ever-changing symbols. He couldn't recall seeing a sensor feed anywhere within *Ix-Gastiol*, as if the Vraxar used only words and numbers to describe their surroundings.

At the end of cube's side face, Vega stopped again. He'd been nearly overcome by what he'd seen in the body storage room, but now he faced action, there was no fear. He looked out.

"Clear. There's another passage."

It wasn't what McKinney wanted. More than anything, he wanted to rescue his troops and get away from here. In a way, the Vraxar captain wasn't an important target.

Except for the fact that its close and it killed some of my men.

"One more side of this cube to check," said Webb.

"Watch that passage as you go past," McKinney warned. It was just another passage, like all the others.

He needn't have wasted his breath – these soldiers were neither stupid nor inexperienced. Vega pressed his back against the wall adjacent to the opening and looked around.

"He's here."

McKinney felt his skin go cold. "Where?"

"Eighty metres. Not moving."

Unable to resist, McKinney took Vega's place and had a look. Tuik-Ra-Dak was in a room at the far end of the corridor, standing in front of a piece of Vraxar tech that looked like every other piece of Vraxar tech.

The details were clearer from here. The Vraxar captain was tall but also squat, and when it was hunched, it looked even broader – as if it could snap the strongest Estral with its bare hands. With a start, McKinney saw that the metal plates on the enemy's neck and back weren't meant as armour – they were actually holding the Vraxar together, along with the bars screwed into the creature's legs.

As McKinney watched, Tuik-Ra-Dak turned on the spot and began walking towards the hidden soldiers. Its face was intact, with broad cheekbones and a wide, cruel mouth. Its eyes were gone and in their place were the glowing green circles of advanced prosthetics. McKinney knew instinctively that Tuik-Ra-Dak was one of the original species of Vraxar. He also knew instinctively as he withdrew his head, that he'd been spotted.

"Webb."

Upon hearing his name, Webb dropped his gauss rifle and swung up his plasma tube. The weapon's coils whined, the soldier stepped to the side and fired. A moment later, the rocket exploded with a muted thump and plasma light filled the corridor.

"I think it's going to need more than one shot, Lieutenant."

Webb's words were prophetic. A thudding sound reached the men, starting slowly and building in speed. McKinney knew exactly what it was.

"Fall back!" he shouted.

The three of them walked backwards as fast as they could. The light in the passage didn't recede and it grew with the sound of Tuik-Ra-Dak's footsteps.

"Hold!"

The Vraxar captain appeared in the entrance to the passage,

still burning ferociously from the plasma clinging to its flesh, and large enough to fill the opening.

Vega opened up with his plasma repeater and thousands of white-hot rounds spilled into the enemy. The weapon's roar filled the room and the light from its barrel reflected off the sullen darkness of the cube. It was far too close for Webb to use the launcher again and the soldier fired his gauss rifle in long bursts, trying to find a weak spot that might finish off the Vraxar.

For McKinney, the experience was unutterably surreal. The enemy captain turned towards the three soldiers and all McKinney could see was a pair of glowing green circle eyes, bright against the plasma. He locked eyes with the Vraxar and felt the waves of hatred washing outwards from it.

Just die.

Tuik-Ra-Dak took a step towards them and then another, the measured pace filled with confidence and menace.

McKinney had his gauss rifle – the weapon which gave him the most comfort in times of need - at his shoulder. He aimed and fired once. The light behind Tuik-Ra-Dak's left eye was extinguished. McKinney adjusted and fired a second time. The Vraxar captain's right eye was destroyed.

Up until this moment, the enemy had been silent. When it fell, it was with a deep, resonating groan, like a bull slaughtered. The soldiers didn't let up and they fired at the corpse until the flames died and all that remained was a blackened, chewed up lump of metal and flesh which should have died thousands of years before.

"Enough," said McKinney, just as he heard Vega's repeater run dry of ammunition.

Vega shrugged out of the pack and let it fall to the floor. "That's for everything."

The words weren't eloquent, though they were an accurate reflection of the mood.

"Yeah," said Webb.

McKinney gave them both a clap on the back. He had no sense of happiness or victory, but it seemed right to have this smallest of celebrations.

"We've got work to do."

As McKinney hurried towards Captain Blake, he was only too aware that the future was no less uncertain than it had been the moment the *Ulterior-2* completed its short-range transit into the coil of *Ix-Gastiol*. McKinney did what he always did, and got on with it.

CHAPTER EIGHTEEN

CAPTAIN CHARLIE BLAKE showed no sign of coming around. His vital signs were stable, yet he didn't answer when McKinney spoke. The cable was still plugged into his visor and McKinney yanked it out, letting it fall against the side of the cube. Blake remained unconscious.

Webb was nearby and he reached across to pull at the metal bindings holding Blake in place.

"Feels pretty solid."

McKinney had already tested the metal straps and come to the same conclusion. He was gripped with a temptation to see if his artificial arm was strong enough to snap the bindings, but he didn't want to injure himself trying it out. Not yet, anyway. The comms open channel was already filled with hopeful chatter from the survivors, so he used a private channel to speak to Sergeant Li.

"Any idea how they locked you in?"

"No, Lieutenant. Some of those Estral bastards held us up against the wall and then the bands closed. I didn't see how."

McKinney grunted – there was no way he was going to figure

out how the Vraxar console worked in the other room, assuming it controlled the locks. He had a flash of inspiration and reached for the ISOP interface. With the tablet in one hand, he searched for anything which might be an access panel. There was nothing.

"Let's just try it," he muttered, holding the ISOP close to the bands.

The effect was immediate – the number cruncher interfaced and began its work. The security locks holding the bands shut weren't strong and the job was finished in a few seconds. The metal straps snapped open and Blake slumped forward. McKinney was fast enough to stop the fall and he lowered Blake to the floor.

"Look after him," he said to Webb.

McKinney hurried into the room where the captured members of his squad waited for him.

"Clifton, any sign of activity?" he asked.

"All's quiet here."

"Keep watching."

McKinney surveyed the room, counting.

"Only eleven?" he asked in despair.

He walked to the closest and held the ISOP towards the bands. This time it only took a couple of seconds for them to click open.

"Hey, Lieutenant," said Corporal Bannerman, stumbling free. "I knew you'd come."

Sergeant Li was next. "Is this everyone?" asked McKinney.

"I don't know." Li recognized the problem – they couldn't abandon anyone left alive, but they also couldn't go searching every corner of *Ix-Gastiol* on the off-chance. "They're dead, Lieutenant. Take my word for it."

Li was solid and he was trying to do his bit, rather than offload every burden onto his superior officer. McKinney shook his head sadly. "Even if you told me they were alive..."

"The mission comes first?"

"It has to."

One-by-one, McKinney freed the others. They were physically capable of action, though there were likely plenty of psychological scars which might need treating later. They were scared and uncertain, but mostly they were pissed off.

The next problem was a big one. "Where're your guns?"

"No idea, Lieutenant," said Li. "They got taken off us when we were captured and we haven't seen them since."

"Search the room – see what you can find."

The squad's weapons weren't here. Huey Roldan picked up a hand cannon from one of the fallen Vraxar, aimed it into a corner and discharged the weapon with a loud crack.

"This one works. I don't know what the range is like."

There was one man still struggling. Garcia was on all fours, coughing and retching from the effects of whatever drugs had been in the syringe.

"I'm getting better, Lieutenant," he wheezed. "I've lost count of how many times the suit has stuck needles in me."

"Can you shoot?" asked McKinney.

"Give me a gun and a minute to recover and I'll put slugs through a thousand of the bastards." Garcia's anger was apparent in his voice. He'd need it to sustain him.

Armand Grover, the squad medic, was alive and looking bereft without his med-box. McKinney beckoned him over and the two of them ran to the room with the processing cube. Blake was sitting up, though it looked like he was having a hard job staying awake.

"Good to see you, Lieutenant," he mumbled.

"Sir, we need to get away from here."

"I know. I feel like crap."

It was no excuse and Blake tried to stand. McKinney reached

out a hand and hauled the other man upright. Blake wobbled unsteadily.

"Think you can make it?"

"I'll make it. Space Corps drugs beat Vraxar drugs any day of the week."

"With the human body caught in the middle," said Grover.

Blake suddenly jerked violently and it looked as if he were about to have a seizure. Instead, he vigorously patted at his space-suit, before breathing a loud sigh of relief.

"They didn't find the activation tablet for the Obsidiar bomb," he said. "We'd have been even more screwed if they'd taken it."

Time was wasting and McKinney had itchy feet. He shouted for Vega to give Blake some assistance. With that done, he turned his attention to how they should proceed from here. They were reduced to sixteen, half without any kind of weapon. Killing Tuik-Ra-Dak was a satisfying result, even if it was completely secondary to the main mission. McKinney checked how far they were from the *ES Devastator*.

"Seventy klicks, give or take," he said under his breath. He swore. It might as well have been a thousand kilometres for all the chance they had of making it.

There was some good news. Whilst McKinney was dealing with Blake, Sergeants Li and Demarco had organised a bit of exploration along the corridor past Clifton.

"Got our weapons," said Li. "Gauss rifles and grenades only. No sign of repeaters."

McKinney was enormously uplifted by the discovery, as if this was an indication that their luck had finally changed.

"Kit everyone out, Sergeant," he said. "Garcia promised me he's going to kill a thousand."

"He can let us know when he's finished, Lieutenant, because I'd prefer to be running in the other direction."

Blake joined them, already looking much stronger. "We've got a long way to go, Lieutenant. Have you learned anything we can use to our advantage?"

"I've learned many things, sir, and I can't see a way out of this. *Ix-Gastiol* is filled with dead bodies and dropships, and I wish more than anything I could just snap my fingers and have the whole lot disappear."

"Dropships?" said Blake. "I was unconscious when they brought me here and I didn't see dropships."

McKinney thumbed in what he thought was the right direction. "They've got a big hangar filled with them, sir. The same kind as what landed at Tucson."

"Flying is a lot quicker than walking, isn't it?"

"That is usually the case in my experience, sir."

"Should we go and take a look at these dropships, do you think, Lieutenant?"

"I am certain they will be loaded with enemy troops, sir."

"Did these troops attack when you entered the hangar?"

"No, sir, they did not." It was clear what the outcome of this discussion would be. "Can you fly a Vraxar dropship?"

"I have absolutely no idea."

McKinney kept his voice neutral. "Perhaps this would be a good time to try."

"Yes, Lieutenant, I think you're right."

The decision was made and once again, McKinney felt uplifted. Up until this moment, the future had seemed pre-ordained: the squad would trudge through the endless corridors of *Ix-Gastiol* until the last of them was whittled away, fifty or sixty kilometres from their destination. Now, there was a wild-card in play, which had the potential to change everything.

Everything or nothing. That's a lot better than it was thirty minutes ago.

McKinney brought the squad together and prepared to give them orders.

Jeb Whitlock got in first. "What're we going to do, Lieutenant?"

"You know I don't go in for speeches, soldier, so here it is in a nutshell: we're going to steal an enemy dropship, fly to the *ES Devastator*, detonate the Obsidiar bomb and then we'll fly off into the sunset. After that, Fleet Admiral Duggan will pin fifty medals to each of our chests. If any Vraxar get in the way of our stated purpose, we're going to shoot the bastards. In fact, Garcia has promised to kill ten thousand with his bare hands."

"It was a thousand, sir. With a gun."

"And another fifty thousand with your breath," said Vega.

McKinney called for silence. "The dropships aren't far, so let's not stop to admire the scenery."

They got moving. It wasn't clear how many other rooms were linked to this area, so they were cautious. Demarco had already searched a couple of rooms over – a calculated risk which had paid off – and she seemed confident there were no more Vraxar close by.

"I think this is an enclosed suite of rooms, Lieutenant," she said. "That's an opinion, not a promise."

They gathered in the entrance room where McKinney had earlier shot the two smaller Vraxar. He held the ISOP to the door panel and, while he waited, he gave Blake an extremely concise description of events since the group had split. It was clear Blake had plenty of questions, but the number cruncher got the door open before he could ask them. McKinney stuck his head into the corridor and looked both ways.

"Clear," he said.

He urged the squad into the corridor before the door shut automatically. To the right, the passage went on and on into the depths of the spaceship. To the left, was the hangar bay. He set off at once, keeping a wary eye out for movement. Everything was the same as the previous visit – the three spaceships arrayed on the bay floor, with the others clamped against the walls.

"The doors on the other side of the middle dropship are open," McKinney said.

"And it's the closest," Blake replied. "We'll try that one."

They emerged into the colossal space of the hangar and McKinney once more felt uncomfortably exposed. He increased his speed to a run and checked over his shoulder to make sure Garcia and Blake were keeping up. The group was spread out for all the illusory safety that provided, but there was no sign anyone was unable to keep up with the pace.

With the target vessel a few hundred metres away, the Vraxar appeared.

"Movement to the rear," said Roldan. "Eight or more, coming from that passage centre-left."

"Kill them," said McKinney, dropping to the floor and bringing his rifle to bear.

The squad were well-trained and experienced. They stopped and turned, before falling prone. Gauss rifles fizzed in extended bursts. McKinney used his visor sensor to zoom and saw that these Vraxar were armed with the standard hand cannons. The enemy returned fire briefly, before they were mown down by the superior range and accuracy of the gauss rifles. McKinney didn't get to his feet immediately and kept a careful watch in case there were any more coming after.

After ten seconds, he jumped up. "Let's go! Move!" he shouted.

McKinney sprinted onwards. It wasn't unexpected to find Vraxar onboard a Vraxar capital ship, but he got the distinct impression that last group was on the lookout for intruders. McKinney was beginning to think there was a delay between a security breach and the Aranol responding to it. He had no idea how much information it had to process, so maybe it wasn't able to react to every single incident in real time.

They reached the landing legs of the centre dropship and the squad used them for additional cover. McKinney pointed to show exactly which of the boarding ramps they should head for. He chose the one closest to what he assumed was the front of the spaceship and they made for it.

A second group of Vraxar came into sight along the wide passage opposite. There were far more than in the first group and the movement sensors showed them as a merged cluster of orange, two thousand metres away. McKinney didn't hesitate.

"Take cover! Kill them!"

The landing legs provided excellent shelter and the squad hunkered down, before firing mercilessly into the approaching group of enemy soldiers. The gauss rifles were accurate over much greater distances than this and the squad was able to kill the enemy in great numbers. A smattering of return fire plinked against the metal of the dropship, none of it causing injury. From the soft noise of the impacts, McKinney could tell that the Vraxar cannons were at the extremes of their range.

The second group fell and behind them was a third. At the same time, Garcia spotted another group coming from the right, which he did his best to take out single-handedly. There was further movement from behind and McKinney realised they were fighting against the tide. It seemed as if this was the beginning of a wide-scale alert on *Ix-Gastiol* and he didn't want to stick around to see exactly how many soldiers the Vraxar could muster. On top of that, he had no idea what they would find inside the dropship itself.

"Up the ramp!" he ordered.

The enemy fire increased in intensity by the second and the squad made a run for it. McKinney paused to ensure everyone was able to make it and when he turned back, he saw a rocket scream out of a side tunnel, two kilometres away. The projectile left a faint trace in the air, which McKinney's visor sensor picked up and drew as an orange line across his vision. The rocket was badly-aimed and it curved upwards, before detonating against the side of the dropship with a grumbling thump. The explosion blossomed outwards fifty metres away, leaving McKinney and the squad unharmed. Plasma dripped hissing and spitting onto the ground.

McKinney's feet carried him the remaining distance to the boarding ramp. The ramp was steep, sixty metres long and grated, with lumps of unknown biological matter wedged here and there in the gaps. This might have only been a dropship, but it was designed to contain sufficient troops to overrun an entire country and compared to the Space Corps' largest dropships, this Vraxar model was definitely a larger example of the type.

Halfway up the ramp, a Vraxar slug ricocheted off something nearby and the flattened disc of metal cracked into his shin. The material of his suit spread the impact, but it was still a painful blow and he limped a few paces. Ricky Vega was behind and he gave McKinney a hard shove onwards, which was only half helpful. Still carrying momentum from the push, McKinney stumbled inside.

At the top of the ramp there was an antechamber. It was high and wide, with an opening in the far wall which was large enough to accommodate a gravity-driven artillery piece. The black walls glistened with ice or moisture, reflecting the dull, grey light coming from numerous sources in the ceiling. Various control panels were fixed to the side walls and steps led upwards through the bulkhead wall towards the front of the spacecraft. The first men inside were already poking their noses around.

"You don't want to see what's through here," said Sergeant Demarco, backing away from the largest exit a hundred metres away.

McKinney didn't particularly want to see, and equally, he didn't want to be in this airlock if the Vraxar outside managed to get one of their rockets through the doorway.

"The steps," said Blake. "That's got to be the way."

McKinney agreed. Before he could give the order for everyone to get up there, the grey interior light abruptly changed to green. It strengthened, before fading and then strengthening once more. A few seconds later, there was a deep, clunking boom, which shook the walls of the dropship. The lights and the sound were unpleasantly familiar to McKinney.

"This is what happened on the Ir-Klion-32 when they woke up the troops from that storage room," he said.

Most of the others had been there and they remembered it too.

"Aw, crap," said Garcia.

They ran for the steps and scrambled up. The stairwell was a couple of metres wide, but there was a bottleneck at the bottom while the squad waited to climb. The five second delay was enough for McKinney to see through the large doorway and he was afforded an excellent view of a bay filled with rows and rows of artillery. He recognized the types – repeaters, wide-bores and missile launchers – from Tucson. The angle wasn't good enough to see the storage bay in its entirety, but there were at least eighty of the weapons and there was a cargo lift set into the far wall, to carry whatever hardware was on the upper levels.

The steps were steep and they switched back upon themselves four times, until McKinney was sure they were getting close to the upper deck of the dropship. There was a hold-up at the top and the soldiers in front of McKinney were blocked from climbing higher.

"Why has everyone stopped?" he shouted.

"A locked door," said Blake.

McKinney pushed through the soldiers clustered on the

stairs. There was a door at the top, with no landing area for the squad to move into. He pulled the number cruncher interface from his pocket and thrust it towards the access panel.

"Get back!" he said impatiently, when he felt someone squashing against him. The soldiers were getting nervous at the hold-up and he couldn't blame them.

A Vraxar rocket exploded in the airlock at the bottom of the stairs. Noise and heat reached the squad and caused them to bunch up further.

"It's going to get hot in here, Lieutenant," said last man Casey McCoy, making no effort to disguise his fear.

"Hold it steady, McCoy," said Li. "The Lieutenant's on it."

"Come on, come on," said McKinney.

A second rocket detonated in the space below and this time, a draught of searing air was forced into the stairwell. The blistering heat tugged at the soldiers, found its match in the advanced polymers of the spacesuits and then receded.

"The next one's going to get us," said Rudy Munoz, trying to pretend he didn't care one way or the other.

The number cruncher finished and McKinney could have kissed the screen. The door blocking their way opened. McKinney put the ISOP away, got out his rifle and advanced onto the bridge of the Vraxar dropship.

CHAPTER NINETEEN

THERE WERE no seats on the bridge and the room itself was a cramped, uneven space, with a high ceiling and walls less than four metres apart. There was a command console in the centre, which was a waist-high block of alloy covered in screens, indentations, buttons and dials. The walls were smooth and there was some kind of instrumentation panel fixed to one of them, trailing several wires into the floor. Although the main console looked like it was probably new, everything else reeked of age.

Blake took charge and he ordered the soldiers out of the way, so they wouldn't disturb his concentration. McKinney ordered them to spread out as much as possible and keep watch on the door. There wasn't much room, so they ended up shoulder-to-shoulder, with their rifles trained towards the single entrance.

"Anything we can do to help, let me know," said McKinney.

"This might take a bit of time, Lieutenant."

"Yes, sir, I understand."

Another booming sound reached their ears and Blake felt the reverberation through his feet. There were other sounds, made indistinct by the walls of the dropship. He did his best to tune them out and kept his attention on the central console. It was completely alien to him and on his first circuit, he didn't recognize anything that he could assign a function to. He pushed a couple of buttons, which caused a series of symbols to appear on an adjacent screen. Using his fingers, he checked if the screen responded to touch. It didn't.

A few minutes later and Blake was reasonably sure he'd worked out which area of the console was used to manoeuvre the spaceship. Nearby, there was a crude five-button comms system, which suggested the dropship wasn't intended to operate with any degree of independence and was only expected to communicate with the mothership. He activated the comms and heard the background fizz which indicated nobody was listening on the other end.

After three more circuits of the console, things were beginning to fall into place. Every spaceship made anywhere by any species, required a certain set of tools. It needed to see, it needed to fly and it usually needed to speak to other spaceships. Occasionally it needed to shoot the crap out of things. Once you reduced the functions to these most basic levels, it became a matter of identifying which control related to which function and then testing to see how it was all joined together.

Naturally it wasn't *quite* as easy as that. Blake had years of training, combined with an aptitude for anything to do with space flight, which allowed him to make sense of the Vraxar methods far quicker than most other officers in the Space Corps would have managed it. Soon, he'd figured out much of what he required, though there were several significant obstacles to be overcome. The most pleasing discovery was that the dropship's engines were already running. Blake would have normally detected this once he boarded a ship, but the transport's engines were small, and, he guessed, situated towards the rear.

Without warning, the bridge door opened. McKinney and his

squad were quick to react and a dozen gauss rifles fired. The shooting stopped and Mills threw a plasma grenade through the opening, just as the door closed itself.

"It's going to get rough, sir," said McKinney. "We're an easy target if the next lot throw grenades or have a launcher."

"I know, Lieutenant. They might not all have clearance to enter the bridge."

"Let's hope."

Blake beckoned McKinney over. "I'm nearly ready," he said. "There's an autopilot option and a very basic manual control system. Over here are weapons – we're carrying front and rear missile clusters, which I assume are only for defence." He pointed at a panel of identical green buttons. "These will activate the hangar doors and if I swipe over these indentations, the autopilot will allow us to exit the ship. At least, that's what I *think* will happen. And look at this – I found the internal sensors."

Blake flicked a switch and a screen on the console lit up. The display was divided into twelve and McKinney couldn't take his eyes from the sight. Each section showed a separate storage area on the dropship and the largest space was enormous, taking up almost one whole level.

"Vraxar soldiers," said McKinney.

The bay was filled with Vraxar, their numbers too high to count. Certainly, there were hundreds of thousands of them and they stood in endless rows, their eyes open and staring at nothing. The other screens showed similar and there was a second bay containing yet more artillery.

"A million former Estral," said Blake.

"I thought they'd be tied to posts like the ones on the Ir-Klion-32."

"As far as I can see, there's nothing stopping them from moving out of those holding bays."

"I don't think the Vraxar can act without orders, sir. These ones must be disposable – pieces of meat which can hold a gun and fire it."

With a couple of button presses, Blake brought up a different feed. "They're not all disposable."

The new display showed six much larger Vraxar, confined to a single room. These ones were humanoids, nearly twelve feet in height, thickset and covered in overlapping plates of alloy armour. McKinney remembered them well...the burnt red skin, the helmets which showed little more than the eyes. The only thing missing was the high-powered chainguns.

The worst part of discovering these unwanted passengers was how each of the monstrous Vraxar stared directly at the sensor feed, as if they were fully aware of the observers on the bridge.

"We saw these on the Juniper. They were hard to bring down."

"And here they are on this transport." Blake switched the screen off. "The sight was stopping me from thinking straight. Them and all of those other poor bastards in there." He sighed, unable to finish the words.

"We're here to take them out of their misery."

"The thought doesn't make it any easier."

"Why don't you try opening the hangar doors, sir? It'll tell us if you're on the right track."

"This *Aranol* you mentioned doesn't seem too efficient when it comes to detecting security breaches on its doors. However, I'm sure the departure of a major transport is higher up the list of alert priorities."

McKinney scratched his head. "There seems to be plenty of activity outside already. Are you sure it doesn't know what we're up to?"

"Think of it this way, Lieutenant - if a soldier went AWOL on a military base after consuming too much alcohol from a malfunctioning replicator, and this soldier decided to enter the alien languages facility, what would happen?"

"The base mainframe would instruct a corporal or sergeant to take three or four men and investigate."

"What would happen if that same soldier tried to enter the ammunition warehouse?"

McKinney knew where this was going. "There'd be a greater response. More men and a senior officer would be alerted."

"And if that same soldier somehow tried to make off with the *ES Ulterior-2*?"

"All hell would break loose."

"Exactly. We have to hope that what we're witnessing around this dropship is nothing more than a localised response to what the Vraxar currently believe is a low-level issue. The numbers involved suggest it's being rapidly escalated, but once we fly this dropship out of *Ix-Gastiol*, we can be sure the Vraxar will respond with much greater force."

"In other words, you don't want to touch anything until you're 100% sure you can fly us out of here?"

Blake nodded. "We're riding our luck on this one, Lieutenant. We have to escape from *Ix-Gastiol* before they realise what we're up to and shoot us down. Then we have to find the *ES Devastator*, get from here onto the battleship and then we have to figure out how to set off the Obsidiar bomb and escape without being reduced to disconnected atoms ourselves."

When it was spelled out so bluntly, McKinney was once again confronted by the reality of the situation. They'd come so far, yet the chance of success remained infinitesimally small.

"We're going to die."

"That's where the smart money is."

"I guess I always knew. It's a price worth paying."

"Any price is worth paying to win this one, Lieutenant. This time, we're the lucky ones having to stump up the loose change."

While he talked, Blake continued checking out the arrangement on the console. He was beginning to think the surface controls were more of an afterthought and not really intended to be the primary method of piloting the transport. There were three circular interface ports on the outer edge of the console, which he'd not paid much attention to up until now. Then, he realised what they were.

"The Vraxar must just plug in to this thing," he said.

"And control it with the power of their mind?" asked McKinney.

"With the power of a computer elsewhere, I think. Perhaps the Vraxar onboard are no more than a conduit for the main navigational system on *Ix-Gastiol*."

The idea sort of fit in with what they'd learned about the enemy so far. Only a few of the Vraxar appeared to have freedom to think for themselves, whilst the others did exactly as they were ordered. There were plenty of unknowns, though Blake would have happily killed every single one of the aliens and remained ignorant.

There were still areas of the console he didn't understand, but he felt sure enough about the important parts. In truth, he was beginning to wonder if it would have been better to attempt the journey on foot. He dismissed the idea – he was the only one capable of setting off the Obsidiar bomb and he wasn't blessed with McKinney's ability to blend in with the other Vraxar. It was also far too late to change his mind. "Let's do it," he said.

"What should I tell the squad?"

"Tell them to be ready for anything, Lieutenant. We'll have to react to whatever comes up."

"Yes, sir."

"And stay close in case I need you."

Now he'd made his mind up, Blake acted swiftly. He ran a test on the dropship's engines and found they responded to his commands. It was a start. There was a keypad next to the comms section and it was this he believed would initiate the process of deployment. He tapped the buttons in sequence and waited.

"Not working," he said.

McKinney watched carefully. "This screen here is showing the same symbols as the door panels. I've been running with the assumption it means *access denied*. Or maybe *piss off*."

Blake was pleased to be reminded that McKinney was a man of initiative. Within moments, he was holding up the ISOP towards the console.

"Let's hope it works, Lieutenant."

"It hasn't let us down yet, sir."

The cockpit door opened and the squad opened fire. This time they weren't quite fast enough – a Vraxar hand cannon boomed and Rudy Munoz toppled over, gasping. There was another brief exchange and the door closed again.

Medic Grover dragged Munoz away from the door, out of the line of fire.

"How is he?" asked McKinney.

Grover pulled no punches. "This one will be touch and go. He's taken a slug right in the guts. His suit's put him in a coma. If I had my damned med-box I'd be able to fix him." He swore at the loss.

The door opened once more and Vraxar slugs cracked off the bulkhead behind the soldiers. A grenade sailed through, which Blake saw as a dark shape tumbling towards the squad. Sergeant Li calmly swung his foot and caught the grenade perfectly. It arced back out through the door and exploded on the steps outside. The door closed and the mouths of a dozen soldiers fell open.

"What did I just see?" asked Bannerman.

Li wasn't modest, but he knew when it was time to pretend. He shrugged as if it were nothing.

"Got it!" said McKinney. The dropship's console screen changed in admittance of its defeat to the number cruncher.

Blake stabbed at the buttons with his fingertip. "Come on, manual override," he muttered.

A series of heavy-duty servos whined and clunked deep inside the dropship. Then, Blake heard several of the booming thumps, similar to the sounds from earlier.

"That's the boarding ramps closing."

Blake took three steps sideways and switched to the external sensors.

"Not the underside ones," he said. He made an alteration and one of the displays switched to the upper sensor array.

"The ceiling is opening," said McKinney.

High above the dropship, two immense, rectangular doors swung downwards, like a cargo hatch on a wooden sailing ship. It was a primitive method which reinforced Blake's suspicion that parts of *Ix-Gastiol* were hundreds of years old, if not more. He adjusted the sensor focus and was astounded at how slowly they updated.

"That's our way out, Lieutenant."

Through the doors was a rectangular shaft, which looked hardly large enough for the dropship to enter. The shaft was lined with bright blue lights, which went on and on for kilometre after kilometre.

"According to my visor HUD, we're more than a hundred klicks within the hull," said McKinney.

"I'm going to get us out of here." Blake ran his fingers over the indentations used to trigger the autopilot. A screen a little way across flashed with the unwanted symbols: *access denied*.

McKinney got there with the ISOP. "I don't think they want us to escape, sir."

"I wasn't expecting so much security on the basic controls," admitted Blake. "The autopilot isn't likely to be a simple on-off system, Lieutenant. I don't think the ISOP is going to work."

"What else do we have?"

"Manual. It's not what I wanted, but I'm going to try."

The dropship's manual controls consisted of analogue buttons, which could be used to adjust its roll, pitch and yaw, with other buttons for thrust. Blake had never seen the like and doubted the Vraxar had ever pressed these buttons, no matter how old the spaceship might be.

With a deep breath, he gave it a go. He increased the power feed into the engines and the dropship remained planted firmly on the ground, reinforcing his belief that it was equipped with the smallest possible engine. Only when the thrust button was pressed almost fully in, did the spaceship move ponderously from the floor of the hangar bay. There were a few hundred Vraxar outside and they watched the dropship lift off as though they had no idea what to do.

"We just exponentially increased our chances of detection by the Aranol," said Blake. "If we're exceptionally lucky, the death of Tuik-Ra-Dak will have severed a major line of communication between the home world and *Ix-Gastiol*."

While the thrust controls were not especially responsive, the roll, pitch and yaw buttons were the opposite. Blake's first attempts at delicate manoeuvring caused the dropship to tilt violently to one side. The spaceship was equipped with life support, but the modules had a fractional delay before they stabilised the interior. It was going to make the ride a bumpy one.

The pressure of time weighed heavily on Blake as he tried to adapt to the controls. The ship itself was theoretically too sluggish to present a challenge. However, the unfamiliarity of it ensured Blake was made to work hard. Even though he thrived on pressure, he felt the sweat beading on his forehead. There was worse to come.

"That exit shaft is too tight," he said. "I wanted to fly vertically through it, but that's not going to work."

He took the dropship higher away from the floor and had a go at altering its pitch. The nose struggled upwards and Blake fed in more power to the engines, cursing the vessel as he did so. With a bit of trial and error, he managed to get it pointing directly upwards, with its tail less than twenty metres from the floor. Unfortunately, the nose wasn't beneath the exit shaft and he was required to make further changes. Slowly, the dropship drifted sideways until it was in position.

"Here we go. Keep your fingers crossed the outer exit is open for us, Lieutenant."

With that, Blake pushed harder on the thrust button. The dropship creaked and he heard the sound of distressed gravity engines far away. He pushed the button all the way in, at which point he discovered that the spaceship had rather more in reserve than he'd anticipated. The lumpy note of the gravity engines cleared, becoming a smooth, metallic howl unlike anything on a Space Corps vessel, reminding Blake that the Vraxar had plenty of knowledge when it came to engine tech.

The dropship gathered speed smoothly, crushingly, making Blake shift stance to stop from losing his footing. It climbed through the open hatch and into the shaft. Behind, the hinged doors swung shut with an unexpected finality. Blake didn't let up and the spaceship accelerated through the seemingly never-ending hull of *Ix-Gastiol*. Ahead, the sensors showed the open exit hatch, coming closer with each passing moment. There was a bright, searing light outside – something Blake hadn't expected.

The dropship emerged into space and Blake saw where they were. *Ix-Gastiol* was close to a star – so close it was as if they could reach out and touch the fiery surface. He had no idea where the external temperature readout was and it didn't matter

– they were near enough that the ship would melt if it ventured outside of *Ix-Gastiol*'s energy shield.

"Is that Laspan?" asked McKinney. "Didn't you say that an Obsidiar bomb would destroy a whole star?"

"*Ix-Gastiol* went to lightspeed, Lieutenant. We all felt it."

"What if it's near another one of our planets? What if we somehow manage to detonate Falsehood and it kills billions of our people?"

"The *Ulterior-2* has forced the Vraxar away from our planets," said Blake firmly. "That was always the plan and now we have to do everything to finish the mission."

"Sir…"

"We have no choice. If I get the chance, I will detonate the bomb."

"Yes, sir."

The short conversation with McKinney caused Blake to falter as the doubts came flooding in. He shook them away. Whatever it took, he would do everything to destroy *Ix-Gastiol*. With his heart beating fast, Blake searched through the sensor feeds to see if he could locate the *ES Devastator*.

CHAPTER TWENTY

WITH HIS FINGERS rapidly learning how to operate the Vraxar dropship, Blake levelled the craft out as close to *Ix-Gastiol* as he dared and guided it towards the starboard side at a low enough speed that he wouldn't miss what he was looking for. His brain struggled with the quantity of information and also with the unfamiliarity of flying an alien craft. It was a stretch to operate the sensors and the controls simultaneously, and doing so made his life much harder than it might have been.

With effort, he got all of the external sensors to show their feed at the same time, though he'd have liked it better if he could control them manually rather than leaving each one static. The upper feeds showed the darkness of space, whilst the side ones displayed a mixture of intense light from the nearby sun, as well as the surface of *Ix-Gastiol*. Blake's eyes darted across the screens, searching for recognizable shapes. What he saw was thousands of spaceships, made by hundreds of different species, with a hundred different levels of technological skill.

The dropship was hardly more than a kilometre from *Ix-Gastiol* and from this distance, Blake could see the extent of the damage some of the captured spaceships had suffered. Their hulls were burned, scoured and heavily pocked from disintegration beams, as well as a few bearing the scars of missile strikes. At first, he experienced a fleeting shame that these other species had put up a greater fight than the Space Corps and Ghasts combined. Then, he realised that these spaceships may well have been damaged in earlier engagements and subsequently captured during their confrontation with *Ix-Gastiol*. He felt a kinship for the lost soldiers.

"Corporal Bannerman, get yourself over here," said McKinney, watching Blake jump from screen to screen. "See if you recognize any of this stuff and if you do, ask if you can help out."

"By all means," Blake agreed.

Bannerman hurried over and stood, rubbing his chin. "Give me a minute, sir."

"Everyone else, keep watch on that door!" barked McKinney, when he caught a few of them taking a greater interest in the activity around the main console. As if to reinforce his point, something began hammering on the other side of the door, with tremendous force. The door was thick, so the Vraxar must have found a tool capable of breaking through metal.

"Sir, can you open the external side doors?" asked McKinney. "It might make things tough for the Vraxar we have onboard."

"Good idea, Lieutenant." Blake couldn't help himself and he chuckled evilly when he pressed his hand onto six red buttons at the same time. "That's the port and starboard doors. They don't even have a safety lock. Life is cheap for the Vraxar and death even cheaper."

The hull mechanisms clunked and Blake watched the side ramps hinge smoothly outwards. Within a few seconds, he saw a number of tiny shapes being sucked out of the middle door. Soon, there were thousands – tens or hundreds of thousands - of Vraxar being sucked outside as the interior of the dropship depressurized. Their bodies left a glittering trail as light from the sun reflected off their metal augmentations. Blake couldn't bring himself to feel sympathy – he no longer thought of the Vraxar as *living*. They were just lumps of flesh and metal to be destroyed in the greatest quantities possible.

"I doubt that'll get them all," said Blake. "It definitely won't get the ones on the upper floors."

"Can they survive in a vacuum?" asked McKinney. "I've never found out."

"They're a lot more resistant to environmental changes than we are, Lieutenant. Still, I can't see them being able to survive for long."

The thumping on the bridge door stopped abruptly.

"Garcia, stick your head outside and take a look," said Sergeant Li.

"Really?"

"Don't be stupid."

The rest of the squad jeered Garcia's naivete. It was a moment of brief levity in the face of the constant uphill battle this mission had been so far.

Blake smiled to himself at the sound of the laughter. The expression quickly faded. "There's no sign of the *Devastator*." He tried to picture where exactly they'd emerged from *Ix-Gastiol* in relation to the Hadron battleship. It was difficult to be sure and he didn't want to rely on guesswork.

They got lucky. Bannerman still hadn't gathered the courage to attempt operation of the dropship sensors, however, he did spot the low profile of the *ES Devastator* on one of the feeds.

"That's it, sir. We're running parallel to it."

"Good spot," said Blake.

The *Devastator* was one of the larger spaceships attached to *Ix-Gastiol*, and it was surrounded by seven or eight other craft which appeared to have been built by the same species. These spaceships were about two thousand metres long, boxy in shape and with silvery hulls which gleamed like they'd been polished. Blake couldn't tell from looking if they came from an advanced race or a relatively primitive one. What he was sure about was the fact the *Devastator* appeared far more dangerous if you could judge it on shape alone.

"I'm bringing us around." He took a stab at the distance between the two. "Twenty klicks, I reckon."

Under Blake's control, the dropship banked towards the battleship. He was starting to get the hang of it – not enough to make him a hotshot, but at least he wasn't worried about crashing into anything.

"How are we getting from this spaceship to that spaceship?" asked McKinney.

"I think I've got these Vraxar missile systems figured out," Blake replied. "I'm going to target the rear shuttle bay doors and see if I can make an opening. The armour is less than three hundred metres thick there, so it's our best chance."

"Three hundred metres is a lot of armour."

"It's a battleship and this is a transport. I very much doubt we're going to get through in ten or fifteen shots, so let's hope we don't run out of ammunition."

Blake was denied the opportunity to test out the dropship's offensive capabilities. Without warning, everything went completely, utterly dead. The console shut down, the sound of the engines faded to nothing and the lights on the bridge went out, leaving the squad in total darkness.

A lone voice intruded upon the silence which followed.

"Crap," said Li.

Blake was certain what had gone wrong. "They've got us in their stasis beam. We managed a couple of minutes outside before they caught us. Perhaps we should be grateful."

He turned on his visor torch and the powerful beam cast

shadows upon the walls. McKinney turned on his own torch and the rest of the squad followed suit, filling the room with so much light it was uncomfortably bright.

Blake thumped the edge of the console angrily and then leaned against it in order to think. He was glad McKinney didn't bother him with the *What now?* question. There again, his lieutenant would have heard it enough times himself that he'd be fully aware of when it was best to keep quiet.

"We can't give up," Blake said. "If we make it to the *Devastator*, we'll have a chance."

"How close are we?" asked McKinney.

"Ten klicks now - maybe less."

"Can we jump to the surface and hike it?"

"There's a strong possibility *Ix-Gastiol*'s life support modules will create a gravity field which extends for a short distance beyond the hull. The first few hundred metres might be in zero gravity, but the final hundred might be completed much quicker."

"Damn."

"It may well come to it anyway, Lieutenant. If the gravity field only extends thirty or forty metres, some of us might survive." He tried to click his fingers, a feat he'd seen Sergeant Demarco accomplish. His effort was a miserable failure, but he was too excited by an idea to care about it. "Those artillery pieces downstairs!" he said.

McKinney caught on. "They're too heavy to get sucked outside by the depressurization and they're equipped with gravity motors."

"And they should be capable of getting us to the surface."

"Assuming the stasis beam hasn't shut them down."

"Only one way to find out."

"I'll get the door," said McKinney, already halfway towards it.

Blake felt a restless energy coursing through his veins and he became invigorated at the notion that human ingenuity and old-fashioned guts had an answer for everything the Vraxar could throw at them. He paced to and fro, while McKinney did the business with the ISOP.

"How will the door open?" asked Roldan. "The power is gone, isn't it?"

The ISOP was little more than a prototype, so it wasn't surprising a few of the soldiers didn't know how it worked.

"That pack Lieutenant McKinney has been lugging around with him contains not only a high-burst processing cluster, but also a heavily-shielded hybrid Obsidiar power supply with enough short-term kick to start up a Crimson class destroyer. It's designed to open doors in the event of a Neutraliser attack," said Blake.

"That little thing could start up a *destroyer*?"

"So I'm told," Blake replied. What he didn't say was that such a discharge of power would likely wreck the device in the process - there were times it was best to focus on the positives.

The number cruncher was a stunning piece of kit and it didn't even require a direct wired connection to get the door open. The ISOP hummed loudly and the bridge door opened like it was trialling for the universe's fastest door competition.

"Clear," said McKinney, peering cautiously down the stairs. The light from his torch highlighted a darker patch on the walls, along with some pieces of metal and a single detached Vraxar foot. "I don't think they liked having that grenade come back at them."

Blake was impatient to be on and he was relieved when McKinney exited the bridge. Sergeant Li organised the squad and Blake found himself in the middle, in front of the two assigned to carry Munoz. He had no complaints at being cosseted, since he was the only one able to set off the Falsehood bomb. They waited for McKinney to scout ahead.

"Clear," said McKinney for the second time. He announced

the same at the third switchback on the stairs and then he reached the bottom. "Come on down."

There was something in McKinney's voice which alarmed Blake and when he reached the airlock at the end of the steps, he saw what it was. The beams from the visor torches danced across the rows of artillery guns, joining with the light from the sun outside which came in through the side opening in the dropship's hull. Not one of the guns floated – each and every one of them had fallen to the floor.

"Dead. The stasis beam must have cut their engines."

Blake gritted his teeth in anger and closed his eyes, letting the faint breeze of ongoing depressurization wash around him. Before he knew it, the anger was gone and replaced with a strange feeling that destiny was guiding him towards something. He began jogging across the airlock floor. On the way, he tapped McKinney on the shoulder and beckoned him to follow.

"We'll use the ISOP."

There was no use in discussing if the number cruncher was capable of powering an artillery gun gravity motor for any length of time. It would either work or it wouldn't and it was the best option available to them.

Blake entered the artillery storage bay. The sun's light was weaker here and it didn't reach into the corners. He swung the beam of his torch to see if there was anything he needed to be aware of. There were no surprises – the bay was almost one hundred metres long and fifty deep, with the cargo lift adding a fifteen-metre recess in the centre of the wall. The artillery was mostly based on the same kind of chassis, which was a nine-metre long cuboid, three high and wide, and with a front shield through which the barrel or barrels protruded. Behind the protective shield were ladders running up the sides and there was plenty of room for troops to sit on top.

The missile launchers looked a little different and they were lined up in the back row. Blake didn't pay them much heed. To the left, there was a wide doorway, leading deeper into the dropship. It was dark through the opening and the distance too great for his light to penetrate.

The rest of the squad fanned out, wary in case the vacuum hadn't cleared the ship of enemy troops. There was plenty of space between each of the weapons and it quickly became apparent that the area was devoid of Vraxar. Blake turned towards McKinney and then pointed at the closest artillery piece, which was a wide-bore gauss gun a few metres away.

"We'll take that one."

"Seems as good as any, sir."

McKinney gave his orders and the troops gathered behind the shield. There were two ladders and they took turns to climb, following McKinney's lead. Blake put his hand against the dark grey metal. It was stone cold and the gravity engine didn't even murmur.

He climbed quickly, finding the rungs too widely spread for comfort. Behind him, Jeb Whitlock, who was taller than McKinney and nearly as wide, slung the unconscious Munoz over his shoulder and began hauling himself upwards. At the end of his climb, Blake found McKinney placing the number cruncher reverently onto the flat top of the wide-bore.

"Thought I'd better wait for everyone to get up here before I start testing it out."

Blake was about to respond, when he was interrupted by a sound. It was a long, drawn-out growl, infinitely deep and filled with menace. He jerked towards the far opening and thought for the briefest of moments there might have been a hint of something – an immense shape hiding in the shadows.

"What the hell?" said Demarco.

The sound came again and this time it was joined by a second. It rose and fell unevenly and Blake knew what it was.

"Laughter," he said.

"But what is it, sir?" asked Li.

McKinney was playing with one of the gauges on the number cruncher. "You remember those *things* from the Juniper?"

"The really big ones?"

"There are six of them on this dropship. Looks like they can survive in a vacuum."

The ISOP hummed and, for a second, Blake thought it wasn't going to work. Then, the artillery gun shook and the left-hand side of it rose from the ground. Many of the soldiers struggled for balance and Roldan nearly fell. Blake grabbed the other man's arm and pulled him from the brink. With a lurch, the right-hand side of the gun rose to match the left and the weapon stabilised.

"How do you control this thing?" asked Jeb Whitlock.

"There's a mini-console up here behind the shield," said McCoy.

"How hard can it be?" asked Li.

Blake had a look. "This is a targeting screen," he said, recognizing it at once. "And these buttons control movement."

"Buttons?" asked Li in disbelief. "Welcome to the stone age."

"Got one coming," said Garcia. He fired his gauss rifle on full-auto and the weapon emitted a continuous whine from its coils. Guzman and Mills joined him and in moments, most of the squad were lined up on the edge of the wide-bore, firing into the opening.

Blake glanced up and saw what it was they faced and this time there were several more torches to illuminate the huge Vraxar. It lurked on the far side of the doorway as if it favoured the darkness. It was almost as wide as it was tall and, when it stepped forward, it seemed to fill the opening. Gauss slugs pinged away from the thick armour plates covering much of its body. There were plenty of unprotected areas, but the creature didn't seem troubled by the bullets thumping into its flesh.

"Mills, look after this ISOP. Guard it with your life," said McKinney. "Webb, what are you waiting for? Everyone else, why am I hearing the sound of bullets hitting armour? You are trained to be expert marksmen, not fire and hope parade ground dropouts!"

Webb took the hint and fired. He scored a direct hit – though it was hard to miss from this range. The plasma blast engulfed the Vraxar, at the same time as it illuminated three more in the room beyond.

"Oh shit," said Clifton. He crouched and started rummaging through his pack.

Meanwhile, Blake tried to get the artillery gun moving. The plan was a simple one – drive it straight through the open door and then drift towards the ES *Devastator*. Unfortunately, when he pressed the *forward* button as far down as it would travel, the wide-bore moved with somewhat less urgency than he required. It wobbled unsteadily towards the airlock.

"Is that the fastest this thing goes?" asked Sergeant Li.

"The gauges on this number cruncher don't look too happy," said Mills. "There're a couple of them into the red zone. I assume that isn't good."

Blake swore – he couldn't risk them getting to the *Devastator* with the pack out of juice. It would recharge over time, but he didn't want to sit around waiting to see how long it took. He glanced across and found the first of the Vraxar clambering over the row of artillery guns on the far side of the room. It stood atop a multi-barrelled repeater, its armour melted away by the plasma rocket, and its flesh cracked, split and weeping. It roared, like a hundred lions.

Webb's tube recharged and he fired another shot into the creature, just as a second Vraxar came through the doorway. Without the protection of its armour, the lead Vraxar was torn to pieces by the blast and chunks of dense flesh and yellow bones were thrown everywhere around the room.

The second Vraxar surged through the flames and it leapt from the furthest row of artillery to the next. The soldiers fired non-stop and this time far fewer rounds hit the armour plates. It didn't stop and the third creature came through, followed by the fourth.

"Clifton!" shouted McKinney.

"Yes, sir!" said Clifton, as if he'd been waiting his entire life to get this chance. He drew back his arm and flicked it forward. The action was casual, as if he were skipping a stone across the surface of a pond. Looks were deceiving and the blue-coloured explosive charge arced fifty metres across the room.

The charge was on a timer and it didn't go off immediately. The wide-bore trundled from the storage bay and into the airlock, preventing Blake from witnessing the detonation.

It was for the best.

A few seconds after the rear of the artillery had exited the bay, the charge went off with such incredible force that Blake thought it might have torn a hole in the floor of the dropship. He looked over his shoulder and flinched at the sight of three or four immensely-heavy guns being tossed across the bay, accompanied by a blue-tinged light so bright it caused the feed on his visor sensor to jump crazily before it stabilised. The shockwave was muffled by the intervening walls, but it was still enough to knock Garcia onto his backside. Somehow, Clifton had judged it so perfectly that the expanding wave of plasma reached the airlock, yet without threatening the soldiers crouched on top of the wide-bore.

"Clifton." said McKinney. One simple word of unabashed admiration.

The wide-bore continued on and Blake did his best to think of anything other than the overstressed ISOP which was the only thing keeping them in the game. He was granted an unwelcome distraction when they heard the sound of more movement in the storage bay. It sounded like a heavy object being thrown to one side and colliding with another heavy object. They heard a snarl from deep in the bay, and then footsteps.

"I don't think we got them all," said Li.

Blake did a mental calculation, to figure out if the wide-bore was travelling fast enough to get them off the dropship before their pursuer reached them. The footsteps increased in frequency and took on a heavier note.

"It's running," said McKinney. "Clifton, have you got another rabbit in your hat?"

"Nothing that won't kill us all at the same time, sir."

"Webb, this one's yours."

"Yes, sir."

"I'm not sure I like the odds," said Blake. He took a gamble and used the controls to rotate the artillery gun, at the same time as he kept its forward momentum going. It was tricky to manage, but the wide-bore began turning as he intended. The exit beckoned, promising escape or death to any who went through.

The Vraxar came into sight, running at such a speed it was unable to stop cleanly. It crashed into the frame of the door and stumbled. The creature gave no sign it was injured by the impact and it twisted its head. Blake saw the malevolence behind its eyes. These were the ideal shock troops – they were strong and tough, and they took pleasure in killing.

Webb fired and the plasma rocket exploded against the creature's chest. The blast was close enough for the waves of heat to buffet the soldiers as they fired into the centre of the flames. The Vraxar showed no indication it felt pain and it took a step towards them.

The wide-bore rotated until it was side-on and slowly the front shield blocked the ability of the soldiers to fire. The Vraxar took another two steps, shrugging off the flames and leaving pieces of burning armour behind it. Then, it broke into a run. With a burst of speed which took the watching troops by surprise, the Vraxar put its head down and charged.

"Come on!" Blake shouted, pushing the control buttons even harder. The wide-bore rotated at its own pace and it seemed like it wasn't going to be enough.

The Vraxar sprang at the artillery gun. It was a stride too early and its flailing arm swept the air in front of the line of soldiers. The creature stumbled and leapt again, this time hooking one of its enormous hands over the top of the protective shield. Blake had time to note that the armour-covered knuckles were about two feet wide and the fingers as thick as his lower legs.

The soldiers fired their rifles into the fingers in a fruitless attempt to dislodge the creature. It wasn't enough – a second hand joined the first and then a head appeared over the top of the shield. To his horror Blake saw that both of the Vraxar's eyes had been put out by rifle fire, yet the injuries weren't enough to kill it.

"Try this," he said.

The firing button for the wide-bore was set to one side and he pushed it with his finger. The effect was dramatic. The artillery gun shook with the recoil and the Vraxar was hurled away like a shit-stained rag. Its body thudded into the wall of the airlock near to the doorway and then fell into a heap.

McKinney stood on tiptoes to look over the top of the shield. "It's not getting up from that one," he said.

The artillery was close to the exit and travelling backwards towards it. Blake checked over his shoulder to keep them moving in a straight line. The sun was bright and his visor sensor struggled with the intensity. The gun reached the top of the exit ramp and Blake could see the vast, dark shape of *Ix-Gastiol*, stretching from horizon to horizon beneath them, the brightness of the sun concealing the details rather than making them clear.

The soldiers heard another growling from inside the storage bay.

There were six. Of course the last one was going to show up, thought Blake.

It didn't matter. The wide-bore sailed down the length of the ramp and dropped into space high above *Ix-Gastiol*. Whatever became of the final Vraxar shock trooper, he neither knew nor cared.

CHAPTER TWENTY-ONE

THE SOLDIERS CLUNG to the artillery gun. There wasn't room for everyone hold onto the lip of the protective shield, so those lucky enough to have a position at the front provided anchorage for those further back. It was eerie – against the backdrop of a star and what was surely one of the largest spaceships in the universe, the men felt insignificant. Underlying it was the knowledge that the Vraxar energy shield was the only thing standing against the heat of the sun and stopping them from burning up in seconds.

The wide-bore fell, its gravity engine so weak it was almost as though the gun drifted without volition. Behind, the outline of the dropship dwindled until it was barely visible against the blackness of space. Blake crouched over the control panel, amongst the press of soldiers, doing his best to steer them in the right direction.

"A little to the right, sir," said McKinney, his head over the top of the shield.

Blake made an adjustment.

"That's taken us well off course. More to the left."

It was difficult – the artillery gun wasn't meant to fly and its gravity engine only had sufficient grunt to provide a certain amount of drift. Blake hated flying blind and wished the gun had some kind of visual display to allow him to see where he was going. He had no idea how the Vraxar targeted the thing if they couldn't see, so he assumed the wide-bore was fully automated. The realisation didn't help.

"We're coming in too low, sir."

Blake increased the amount of boost to try and slow them down.

"Go right."

Although he couldn't see, Blake had good instincts when it came to flying and he was sure he was controlling the gun as well as could be expected. The only reason for the difficulty would be if *Ix-Gastiol* was either changing speed or course, which would mean the wide-bore was no longer matching the larger ship's speed or heading.

"If the Vraxar decide they'd be happier five thousand klicks over that way, we'll be stuffed," said Blake. He swore under his breath when he thought about the potential consequences.

"Left a bit more."

"How far away from the *Devastator* are we, Lieutenant? I would like to land us on the roof, dead-centre."

"It's hard to judge the position, sir. These aren't exactly normal visual cues."

"Guess, please."

"Three klicks."

"What about our altitude?"

"Looking good at our current trajectory."

The wide-bore drifted on, sucking power from the tiny cell in the ISOP pack. Mills held the pack tightly, treating it like an extension of his body. To the left and right, Blake began to see some of *Ix-Gastiol*'s taller outcroppings as they became visible over the sides of the gun.

"This is the strangest thing I have ever done," he said.

"You haven't been drinking with Garcia before, sir," said Li, to a chorus of laughter. "If you want strange, look no further."

"If that's an offer, I'll take you up on it when we get out of here."

"You're on," said Garcia, joining in for a change.

"Two klicks to go, sir. Keep it steady."

Blake experienced a sensation of giddiness at the situation. There was nothing amusing about this mission, but he couldn't stop himself from laughing and he wondered if this was the beginning of madness.

More details became clear on one of the structures to the right and Blake identified the upper sections of a Ghast Oblivion. Its nose pointed upwards at a slight angle and he could see the outline of its particle disruptor. The sight of it brought him the answer to a question – a question he'd resolutely avoided asking himself.

There's nobody to save on those ships. They're all dead and gone.

He shivered at the thought.

How many lost? Thousands. I can't pretend it's a price worth paying.

The worst of it was that he knew he was lying to himself, and his humanity wouldn't allow him to accept even a single death as being acceptable. This was not a war anyone in the Confederation asked for. Then came the next question – one he'd kept buried the deepest.

What about Caz? And the others of my crew? I know McKinney has a thing for Lieutenant Cruz. It's hard for everyone. The Ulterior-2 is a solid ship, maybe it's still in the coil, fighting the Vraxar coming through from the Aranol.

He closed his eyes.

"One klick remaining, give or take. Our angle of approach is good."

Blake dreaded the thought of landing without being able to see where he was setting down. In the end, it went as smoothly as could be expected. The ES *Devastator* lay perpendicular to their approach and the sight of its rear particle beam housing gave Blake the information he needed in order to place them more or less in the centre of the battleship's upper section. The gun hovered for a second and then the gravity engine cut out, dumping them onto the armour plating from a height of two feet. The impact was jarring, but the men were still holding on tightly.

"Mills?" said McKinney.

"I've not touched the ISOP, sir. I'm guarding it with my life like you told me."

Blake grimaced. "It must be drained." He stood up, making room amongst the soldiers. "We have to locate a maintenance hatch and pray there's sufficient charge left to get us inside."

It took a short time to get off the wide-bore. The gravity was fairly low, so most of the soldiers did a hang-and-drop off the sides. Whitlock got the duty of carrying the still-unconscious Rudy Munoz down the ladder. Nobody dared ask about the man's chances, as if the question would somehow put a curse on his chance of living.

Blake didn't come down immediately. The top of the gun provided a decent vantage and he used it to search for the nearest maintenance hatch. The upper midsection of the *Devastator* was wide and long enough to land a light cruiser, so it was a relief to find their destination was only a few hundred metres away.

"Over that way, Lieutenant."

With no desire to snap a leg by showing off, Blake climbed down one of the ladders and then jogged around to the other side of the gun, where the squad gathered. Once again, he was struck by the peculiarity – the visible areas of *Ix-Gastiol* put him in mind of huge city, constructed in metal by an advanced civilisation. Rays from the star shone from below, making each shape into a silhouette, filled with hidden meaning.

They spread out and ran in a group towards their goal. The maintenance hatches were flush to the hull and they weren't easy to spot. It took a few precious minutes of searching to locate the flat panel embedded in the metal. Its display was blank and it refused to come to life when Blake touched it.

"Lieutenant McKinney, please try the ISOP."

"The position of these gauges suggests it's recharging, sir."

"We can't wait."

"I hate to say it, but don't these hatches double up as lifts?" said Roldan. "We're going to need a lot of power to get us to the bottom of the shaft."

"And there are plenty of interior doors within the *Devastator* which may well be closed," said Blake. "We're approaching the end, ladies and gentlemen. Success or failure will be decided in the very near future."

McKinney laid the pack down and the squad gathered around it protectively. Blake reached over and rested his hand on top of the device. It vibrated softly.

The ISOP was already equipped with the encryption keys for any vessel in the Space Corps fleet. Therefore, it didn't take longer than a second to power up the maintenance hatch's security lock and complete the handshake. The panel came to life.

"I never thought I'd be so glad to read Confederation text again," said Clifton.

The others were too anxious to bother with wisecracks and they stared intently at the maintenance hatch.

"Here we go," said Blake.

The hatch sank a few feet into the hull of the battleship and then stopped.

"Everyone on."

"It's a bit tight," said Joy Guzman. "Do I have to get on there with these sweaty bastards, Lieutenant?"

"You're welcome to wait behind."

Guzman was first onto the lift. "Any wandering hands get chopped off. You hear me?"

It wasn't easy to fit Munoz onto the lift, but no one wanted to gamble on a second trip and there was no suggestion of leaving him behind, so they held him aloft.

"I swear he's put on weight since he got hurt," said Roldan.

With everyone on the lift, McKinney found himself a few inches of room in order to activate the ISOP. The open channel went quiet and it seemed as though each man and woman held their breath as they willed the device to bring them safely onto the next stage in the mission.

The lift clunked and sank through the armour plating of the *Devastator*. These maintenance lifts didn't normally move fast, but Blake felt sure it was going slower than usual.

I'm falling prey to pessimism, he thought sourly.

"What if it's full of Vraxar?" whispered Vega.

"How's about we shoot them?"

"This lift is the closest one to the *Devastator*'s shuttle bay," said Blake. "That's where they keep Falsehood."

"What does it look like, sir?" asked Sergeant Demarco.

"Like a metal cube, Sergeant. With a keypad and enough explosive force to reduce *Ix-Gastiol* to pieces so small you'd never know it existed."

"And us with it?"

Demarco was right next to Blake, with her visor aimed straight at him. The mirrored surface hid whatever lay within, but it wasn't hard to guess what she was thinking – what any of them were thinking.

"Unless something unexpected happens in our favour, we're

going to die," Blake said. There was no use in trying to sugar-coat what was coming.

"I appreciate the honesty, sir."

The lift came to a halt, level with a passage leading deeper into the warship. Blake was positioned so he could be first off, along with Lieutenant McKinney. The two men squeezed through – there was no light in the passage except for that coming from the visor torches. Blake detected something at once and it took him entirely by surprise. He stopped, stock-still and McKinney bumped into him.

"Sir?"

"Can you feel that?"

McKinney turned his head to both sides, listening. "The gravity engines?"

"They're running!" said Blake. He touched the wall gently with his fingertips. There was no mistaking the comforting thrum of perfectly-tuned Gallenium.

"I thought the Vraxar disabled the ship?"

"They did. Maybe it was only temporarily until they could get the *Devastator* clamped to the hull of *Ix-Gastiol*."

"I guess the answer might be obvious, sir. I can't think of why they'd do that."

"I believe they're using the *Devastator* – all of these captured spaceships - like giant batteries."

Blake set off, walking fast and McKinney hurried after. "Why not use their own power source?"

"I don't know, Lieutenant. The Vraxar utilise modified versions of both Gallenium and Obsidiar. Maybe *Ix-Gastiol*'s original power source is dried up or burned out. We don't know how old it is or how many battles it's faced. It could be that one of the species they conquered damaged the engines of this ship and this is how the Vraxar have adapted to it."

They passed three side-turnings. Blake knew exactly where

he was going and he ignored each of them, until he reached the end of the tunnel.

"Once the squad have gathered up, please open this door, Lieutenant."

The soldiers weren't far behind, their silence indicative of personal reflection and a readiness to see this mission through to its conclusion.

McKinney leaned across and held the number cruncher interface towards panel. He paused. "You'd better keep back, sir. In case there are Vraxar."

There was nothing to disagree with and Blake made his way towards the back of the line. Whitlock was there, carrying Munoz over his shoulder with a stance which suggested he'd carry his squadmate to the ends of the universe and back.

"Done," said McKinney.

The door leading into the main crew area of the ES *Devastator* opened and McKinney darted into the corridor outside, with three of the squad close behind. The line shuffled forwards, listening out for the sound of gunfire.

"Clear. Move up!"

When Blake got into the corridor, he found that while it was clear of enemy, that didn't mean nothing was wrong. There were two bodies a little way along the corridor. They were human and wearing spacesuits. Medic Grover crouched over them, while the soldiers advanced in both directions in order to secure the area.

"What killed them?" asked Blake.

"Their suits are intact and powered up. Their bodies show no sign of injury," said Grover. "There's plenty of oxygen in the air and no indication of toxins. The long and short is that I don't know what killed them, sir."

"We don't want to get caught in the same way."

Grover spread his hands to show he was aware of the concern. "If we can get some power to the med bay and if I can get there without being killed by Vraxar, I might be able to find you some answers."

Blake left the medic and moved away to locate McKinney.

"You should stay back, sir." McKinney peered into the corridor which eventually led to the main mess hall.

"There are no Vraxar here, Lieutenant. They've killed everyone without even needing to set foot on the ship."

McKinney's shoulders slumped. "Looks like it."

"Falsehood is clamped to the wall in the shuttle bay. We shouldn't delay."

"What about the *Devastator*, sir?" There was hope in McKinney's voice, though it wasn't for himself. "Is there anything you can do with it? If you could get it operational..."

"The bomb has to come first, Lieutenant. The bomb before everything."

"Yes, sir. I understand."

McKinney grouped the soldiers up and they set off towards the shuttle bay. The corridors were dark and empty, quiet like the grave. The beams from the visor torches lit the way, but the accompanying shadows made Blake wonder if the darkness would be preferable. The diagnostic tablet carrying the backup codes for Falsehood suddenly felt heavy in his pocket. He tapped it with his hand – for some reason he needed to touch the device even though he knew it was safe. They entered the familiar, long room from which the airlock tunnels led to shuttles one and two.

"Is the bomb on the main bay floor?" asked McKinney.

"So I've been told."

"How do we reach it? Through one of the airlocks? What if the shuttles are latched and we can't get through?"

"There's another maintenance access tunnel and it's right in the middle of that wall."

Blake led the way, since he knew where the door was. He reached it and waited near the panel.

"I never noticed this before," McKinney confessed.

"No reason you would. Please open it."

The maintenance door was just another slab of metal and it slid aside without complaint, to reveal another corridor, just like the others. The new corridor ended fifty metres later at a second door, which the ISOP opened in moments.

The *ES Devastator*'s shuttle bay took up only a fraction of the battleship's interior. Even so, it was a big space and the light from the torches gave away only hints as to what lay in the darkness. The only clearly-visible objects were the two shuttles clamped to this side of the bay. None of the squad liked being here and they muttered amongst themselves.

"Where is it?" asked McKinney.

"On the opposite side of the bay."

Blake was out of patience and he ran. The shuttle bay floor was clear and he kept his torch beam aimed into the distance. After a few seconds, he saw the outline of a shape. It was a grey cube, dull and anonymous, giving no outward clue as to the enormous destructive potential within. Blake felt as though he was attached to the device by a cord, which would pull him ever closer, even if he wished it otherwise.

Before he knew it, he was there. Falsehood was forty metres along each of its rounded edges, with no seam or blemish. He paused, listening to the footsteps of the squad catching up. They stopped a few metres away and waited, silently and respectfully. Blake walked the few metres to the activation panel, which was offset from the centre and fixed at head height. It was powered up, but the display was blank.

He looked for the nameplate he knew would be there. It gleamed, pristine in the torchlight, as though nothing could be permitted to hide the words.

No. 000016. Falsehood.

Death Is A Lie. Life Is Truth.

"Good job I brought this tablet," he said.

"Is the bomb damaged?" asked McKinney.

"I think the control processor has malfunctioned."

Blake held the diagnostic tablet tentatively closer to the panel. It made an immediate connection and awaited input.

"Sir?" It was Garcia.

"Yes?"

"Can we...you know? Say goodbye to each other and stuff?"

The words could have broken Blake's heart. "I don't know about you, R1T Martin Garcia, but I'm not quite ready to die yet. Are you?"

"Not if I don't have to, sir."

There was still a chance to get everyone out alive, Blake told himself. *Am I being selfish?* For once, he didn't care.

"The *Devastator*'s engines are active. I'm going to set the timer on this bomb so that it detonates in thirty minutes, come what may. That's our window, ladies and gentlemen. Thirty minutes to live victorious or die victorious. If you'd offered me either at the start of this mission I'd have thanked you a hundred thousand times."

McKinney stepped forward. "What would you like us to do, sir?"

"I'll take Corporal Bannerman, Garcia, Clifton and Roldan with me to the bridge as an escort. The rest of you wait here. I've got a plan and there won't be a lot of time to put it in motion." He remembered something else. "I'll take the ISOP with me as well."

A private channel opened on Blake's HUD. "Are we going to rescue Lieutenant Cruz and the others, sir?" asked McKinney.

"That's the idea, Lieutenant. In all likelihood, they're dead and gone, but we'll do what we can."

"I know what we're likely to find. I was raised to never give up, sir, and to keep on trying until there's nothing left to try."

"You and me both, Lieutenant."

With that, McKinney shrugged out of the number cruncher's straps. Blake took the device from the other man's hand, grunted once at the weight, and then lowered it to the floor at his feet.

"One last thing," said Blake.

He entered a series of codes into the diagnostic tablet, which it relayed onto the bomb. The security computer asked for confirmation, which he provided. It was done and the display on Falsehood lit up.

000:000:00:29:59

Blake scooped up the ISOP and ran across the hangar bay floor, with his escort struggling to keep pace. Thirty minutes was all they had and it was the greatest amount of time he'd risk on this venture. It had to be enough.

CHAPTER TWENTY-TWO

BLAKE'S DIDN'T slow on his approach to the bridge. If there were any Vraxar onboard the *Devastator*, he knew he might be killed before he could reach his destination. With the timer on the Obsidiar bomb set, he'd become as expendable as the rest of them and, in a way, he felt much better for it. He didn't enjoy hiding behind others.

The journey to the bridge was not a pleasant one. Whilst the corridors he travelled were empty, the main mess hall was filled with dead soldiers. Most of them were fully-suited. Others had placed their visors on the tables in front of them, or on the floor between their feet. Trays of food sat uneaten, frozen by the coldness of the air. Blake found himself looking into the open eyes of one corpse as he ran by. There was a puzzlement upon the man's face, which, in a way, was worse than an expression of terror. Whatever had killed the people onboard the battleship, it had come suddenly and without warning.

There were more bodies closer to the bridge and it was evident the *Devastator* had been packed full of personnel – far in excess of its usual complement. Blake did his best to tune out the horrors. These people were dead and the only thing he could do for them was to finish the job they'd started.

The bridge was designed to seal shut automatically in the event of almost anything unexpected. Therefore, it came as no surprise to be confronted by several thousand tonnes of hardened Gallenium door at the top of the steps leading to the bridge. Blake pulled out the ISOP interface and held it close to the access panel.

"How long did that run take?" asked Bannerman, catching his breath.

Blake had a timer running on his HUD. "Six minutes. Nearly seven."

The bridge door was almost a step too far for the number cruncher's power pack. With a groan, the slab of metal rolled jerkily to one side. With the door halfway open, the ISOP finally gave up and the movement stopped.

Blake swore, dropped the pack and sprinted through the opening. The blast door was ten metres thick and the last thing he wanted was for it to roll shut again. Clifton was carrying explosives, but it didn't seem likely they'd be able to get through this quantity of metal.

The door didn't close on him and he emerged onto the bridge. The lights were out and the crew remained at their stations. Blake turned his head, so the torch beam illuminated the corners of the room. Each and every seat was occupied by a dead man or woman. They weren't even in their spacesuits, not that it would have done them much good.

Admiral Willard Harvey was in the captain's chair. His body leaned forward with its chin resting in its hand, frozen and unmoved since his death.

Blake put his hands beneath Harvey's shoulders and heaved the body to one side. The corpse was stiff and it retained a semblance of its previous pose when it landed on the floor.

"Sorry, sir."

He jumped into the seat, whilst Garcia, Clifton and Roldan looked around quietly. Corporal Bannerman was the most curious and he approached to within a few feet of Blake.

"What is the plan, sir?" he asked.

Blake didn't answer at once. He tried numerous different methods of getting his console to light up, none of which resulted in success.

"I would like to get this ship operational as quietly as possible," he said eventually. "Beginning with the internal comms, so that I can speak to Lieutenant McKinney."

"Are we going to attack *Ix-Gastiol*?"

"Not this time, Corporal. What I hope to achieve is a short-range lightspeed transit into the central coil. Once we're there, we will rescue the crew of the *Ulterior-2* and the soldiers we left behind. Then, we will depart, leaving a gift for our Vraxar friends."

"It is a good plan," said Roldan, nodding sagely.

"Thank you," said Blake, his mind already elsewhere.

It was a mystery how the Vraxar had managed to disable the Hadron. Doubtless the scientists would figure out the specifics and come up with a solution to prevent it happening again, but for now, Blake had only a few minutes in which to find a way around it. He was fairly sure the Vraxar possessed a weapon which could temporarily turn off Gallenium and Obsidiar power sources, and, once the weapon was switched off, those power supplies would once again return to normal. It was guesswork and based solely on his belief that the enemy relied on using captured spaceships as batteries to keep *Ix-Gastiol* running.

"Do you want me to see if the ISOP has recharged, sir?" asked Bannerman. "It might be the kickstart this console needs."

"No, thank you, Corporal. This is a problem with a different solution."

Bannerman's suggestion gave Blake's mind a nudge and set wheels turning. The console was offline and it lacked the power to restart itself. It would usually get that power from the engines running at tickover, except the link had been severed by the Vraxar weapon. The ISOP wouldn't help because the console wasn't an on-off device in the way that a door was. He racked his brains.

When Blake worked out the answer, he could have kicked himself.

"Residual power," he said, shaking his head at his own stupidity.

"What's that, sir?"

"It's what remains in the system when you think it's all over."

"I see."

"I should be able to tap into it in order to restart this console."

Bannerman knew when he was out of his depth and didn't even pretend to understand. "If it gets us out of here, I'm all for it, sir."

Blake had wasted precious minutes on an answer he should have known immediately. He couldn't allow it to distract him and he reached down to knee level, where there was a red button hidden behind a small, movable panel. He slid the panel to one side and pressed the button. It gave a satisfying click.

Within a second, there were lights on the console. The screens lit up dimly, each with a flashing cursor in the top-left corner. The residual power was unreliable and Blake worked frantically to re-route the console so that it was tapping into its primary power source, which was the warship's engines.

Once the primary source was established, the lights on the console strengthened and the console began its self-test routines.

"You just turned that off and on to fix it," said Clifton accusingly.

"Some people make a living from it, soldier."

The internal comms was one of the basic systems and it was amongst the first to become available. Blake opened a channel to McKinney.

"We have action, Lieutenant. I'm about to force-start the four shuttles and the lights will come on shortly. Please tether the bomb to Shuttle Three and let me know when complete."

"Yes, sir. Tether the bomb and advise."

Blake shut off the channel. There was much to do and, according to his HUD timer, less than twenty minutes in which to accomplish it. He activated the engines in the docked shuttles, turned on the battleship's interior lights and then remotely powered up one of the comms terminals.

"Corporal Bannerman, take a seat. I don't have time to answer any in-depth questions, so do what you can with the sensors and comms. Your first task is to find out where we are. If *Ix-Gastiol* is in a Confederation solar system, everything is screwed before we even begin."

Bannerman wasn't shy and he was excited at the chance. Within moments, he'd pushed the body of the previous occupant onto the floor and was in the seat. With tentative movements, he began tapping at the console.

Blake left the other man to get on with it, since he had enough to sort out for himself. He checked the status of the *Devastator*'s gravity engines and found that, as he'd suspected, something was drawing from them. It was the same with the main Obsidiar power core. The audit log showed a number of fluctuations going back several hours, suggesting *Ix-Gastiol* had wildly varying requirements.

It must take an awful lot of resources to maintain the energy shield in the face of an entire star, he thought.

He left things alone for the time being – if he interfered too much, there was a sizeable chance *Ix-Gastiol* would detect his activity and he didn't want to show his hand until he was ready.

The spaceship couldn't take the occupants anywhere without the life support modules active, so Blake brought them online with his fingers crossed. The life support was a major system and could suck a lot of power. When the ship was stationary, the modules hardly caused a flicker on the needles.

"We have life support," he said over the comms. "It should warm up soon and the atmosphere will become breathable in approximately fifteen minutes. Please don't remove your visors."

The next critical system was the weaponry and Blake discovered the offense and countermeasures were in the exact same state as when the *Devastator* first engaged with *Ix-Gastiol*.

"Weapons are online and available," he said. "However, five of our processing cores are offline and almost certainly in a state of complete failure." Blake sat back and ran his fingers through his hair. "The *ES Devastator* is more than ninety percent operational."

He couldn't believe his luck. During the short moments in which he'd allowed himself to think about the loss of the allied fleet, he'd imagined the captured warships would be completely and permanently disabled. Yet here he was, sitting on the *Devastator* with the battleship ready for combat.

The Vraxar probably weren't expecting us to raid their capital ship. The thought buoyed him.

For the next couple of minutes, Blake did what he could to plan ahead. It was another *play it by ear* situation and he gave up trying to predict the future. He looked at his visor HUD. Time was slipping away and Blake drummed his fingers, waiting for Lieutenant McKinney and Corporal Bannerman to complete their tasks.

000:000:00:12:42

Bannerman reported first, just when Blake was preparing to take over the sensor duties as well.

"We're parked off Anxiar-Rho."

It felt as though a weight had been lifted and Blake smiled. "Not a Confederation solar system."

"No, sir. It's a big old star, though, with a diameter in excess of eighty million klicks. We are five high lightspeed hours from Pioneer."

"We made them run, but they didn't go far," said Roldan.

"Yes, they haven't abandoned their plans for humanity, soldier."

McKinney's voice intruded onto the comms channel.

"The Obsidiar bomb is shackled to Shuttle Three, sir," he said.

"Have you automated the launch?"

"As much as I can. You'll have to open the main external bay doors from the bridge and then I'll send the shuttle on its way."

"Thank you, Lieutenant."

Blake spent a few seconds giving McKinney a brief outline of what he intended. McKinney listened impassively.

"When are we planning to execute the manoeuvre, sir?"

There was little to be accomplished by waiting any longer.

"How does *now* sound to you?"

"It sounds very good, sir."

"Your squad are unlikely to have any further direct involvement in the outcome of this mission. Nevertheless, tell them to prepare themselves for whatever might come. Once I begin winding up the *Devastator*'s cores for lightspeed transit, that's the moment whoever or whatever is running *Ix-Gastiol* will realise we're onboard."

The line went dead and Blake turned in his chair. "How are you getting on, Corporal Bannerman?"

"Super-duper, sir. I should be able to get you a few pictures up on the main screen."

"We'll turn you into a warship comms officer yet, Corporal."

"Yes, sir."

Blake made a final check on the battleship's multitude of systems and then spoke to the soldiers with him on the bridge. "Gentlemen, the next few minutes may well determine the fate of billions. Not only amongst the Confederation, but amongst every other species the Vraxar have yet to discover."

"No pressure, then," said Roldan, deadpan.

"The only pressure is that which you allow yourself to feel."

Having delivered what he imagined was one of the shortest motivational speeches ever, Blake filled his lungs and then slowly exhaled. He was calm. Using his visor's remote interface, he fed its database of coordinates relating to *Ix-Gastiol* into the *Devastator*'s navigational computer. With a steady hand, he set their target destination as the coil area in the middle of the enemy warship.

Don't hesitate.

He initiated lightspeed calculations across nine of the *Devastator*'s remaining processing cores, activated the stealth modules and lastly the energy shield. The power draw was enormous and the Hadron's vast Gallenium engines spooled up to meet the demand.

Preparations for lightspeed, which would have taken forty seconds or longer on an earlier generation warship, were given a time of eight seconds to completion. It was long enough for the Vraxar to interfere.

Blake watched a hundred electronic needles dance wildly on the engine management display. "Damnit, they're sucking more power from us."

"What does that mean?" asked Roldan.

It meant many things, such as the possibility of losing shields, stealth and life support. Here and now, it increased the estimated time for the lightspeed calculations to finish.

> SRT CALCULATION: 14 SECONDS TO COMPLETION.

Blake shut down the shields and diverted the power to the processing cluster. The prediction updated.

"Back to seven seconds. Six."

The Vraxar spaceship increased its demands further, until the main engines were at 120% of maximum and the backup Obsidiar core was at full utilisation. The stealth modules shut down.

> SRT CALCULATION: 12 SECONDS TO COMPLETION.

Blake had no idea what technology the Vraxar were using. Whatever it was, it was leeching so much of the Hadron's output, there was none left to complete the intended short-range transit. An updated notification appeared on the navigation display.

> SRT CALCULATION: *ESTIMATED* TIME UNAVAILABLE.

In a few seconds, the *Devastator* would be totally out of power and after that, failure was inevitable. In desperation, Blake fired two of the front underside Shimmer missiles. The warheads carried a massive payload and they exploded directly beneath the hull with sufficient force to set the bridge walls shaking. Damage alerts rolled upwards on two of Blake's console screens.

The gamble paid off. The Vraxar energy drain ceased and power roared into the *Devastator*'s engines. The shields and stealth modules reactivated and the countdown resumed.

> SRT CALCULATION: 4 SECONDS TO COMPLETION.

"Come on!"

> SRT CALCULATION: 2 SECONDS TO COMPLETION.

The Obsidiar cores finished and the transit light illuminated. Blake activated the SRT and the *ES Devastator* exited local space.

000:000:00:09:03

CHAPTER TWENTY-THREE

THE SHIT HIT THE FAN. The moment the *Devastator* reappeared inside *Ix-Gastiol*'s power coil, the tactical display filled up with red dots. Numerous particle beams lanced into the battleship's energy shield and a thick wave of enemy missiles struck them. The energy shield reserves plummeted.

Without a dedicated crew, Blake didn't even bother trying anything fancy - he handed off weapons control to the battle computer. As soon as he did so, the Hadron's advanced response system prioritised the opposition warships and began the task of reducing them to molten lumps of alloy. Four of the particle beams overcharged simultaneously and the coil filled with Shimmers and Lambdas.

"Corporal Bannerman, a sensor feed would be nice," said Blake.

Bannerman's eyes were wide with realisation of what it meant to be on the bridge of a fleet warship. He rose to the task. "Bringing you one now, sir."

He combined a dozen separate feeds and sent them to the main bulkhead screen. There wasn't time to stare and Blake took in the details at a glance. The coil was significantly changed from the time of their first visit. Many of the depleted Obsidiar bands were wrecked and the walls were heavily cratered as a result of the *Ulterior-2*'s all-out assault. Lieutenant Hawkins had unloaded so much weaponry onto *Ix-Gastiol*'s interior that the ambient temperature of this huge space was several degrees higher than earlier. At the far end, the portal to the Aranol hung in space, shapes and outlines hiding within the obscuring patterns swirling across its surface.

Then, there were the Vraxar warships – a total of seven, according to the readouts, each between two and three thousand metres in length, with a displacement no greater than one-third of the *Devastator*'s. The eighth and ninth ships were already destroyed – their shields no impediment to the overcharged particle beams. Blake watched them both crash into the side walls of the coil, sending smaller pieces in all directions. The debris added to the confusion, swamping the battleship's tactical display with thousands of additional objects.

Several hundred Lambdas exploded, the blasts focused on the same target. Beams of dark energy darted amongst the clouds of plasma, whittling away at the *Devastator*'s shields. The battle computer ejected fifteen thousand shock drones, spewing out its entire payload in a single deployment. The drones bounced away from the walls, the floor and the ceiling.

"Holy crap," said Bannerman.

"Find me the *Ulterior-2*, Corporal."

Blake clutched the control bars tightly, even if there was no point in attempting any evasive action. It was immediately clear this would be an ugly case of duking it out until they reached a conclusion and this was going to be the dirtiest engagement of Blake's time in the Space Corps. Even the training simulators where they picked the craziest and most unlikely situations didn't come close to this. The Vraxar had packed the interior of *Ix-*

Gastiol with their ships and there was every imaginable other variable to consider at the same time.

The part of Blake's mind which operated separately and on a higher level to his normal consciousness, evaluated the details. The Vraxar outnumbered them seven-to-one. The *Devastator* was by far the most capable ship in the arena, but its energy shields were taking a lot of punishment and were already close to fifty percent. The wise money was on the Vraxar ships to come out on top.

Meanwhile, there was no sign of the *Ulterior-2*. The coil was vast, but it was also packed with wreckage, active warships, missiles and drones. One thing was certain – there was no single object that was anything close in size to the *Ulterior-2*.

000:000:00:07:08

"They must have got shot down, sir," said Bannerman.

"Find them. We aren't leaving until I'm certain."

"What if they went to lightspeed?" asked Garcia.

"They didn't."

"Would you like me to instruct Lieutenant McKinney to launch the shuttle?" asked Bannerman.

"Not yet. If we launch the bomb and jump clear, the Vraxar spaceships will have plenty of time to destroy the device." There was one preparation they could make in advance. "I'm opening the bay doors. Tell Lieutenant McKinney to hold fast until I give the order."

"Yes, sir."

The *Devastator*'s particle beams took out another of the enemy ships, igniting five billion tonnes of metal at such speed that the opposing cruiser exploded into a hundred thousand pieces. The overcharge was immensely powerful, but it took a long time to prepare and each second allowed the Vraxar more time to deplete the Hadron's shields.

"The *Ulterior-2* isn't here," said Bannerman.

"Check again."

Bannerman had enough confidence to argue his side. "Sir, it isn't here."

"What about the wreckage?"

"No, sir. None of this is from the *Ulterior-2*."

Blake had no choice other than to accept what he was told. If the *Ulterior-2* was gone, that meant they'd been forced to bail out and escape into lightspeed. Given the quantity of enemy spaceships in the coil, the crew would have been obliged to choose between losing the battleship and waiting around on the off-chance they might save the soldiers deployed on *Ix-Gastiol*. The evidence suggested they'd chosen to run. Part of him was overjoyed at the realisation his crew might still be alive. The feeling was tainted by disappointment that they'd put their own lives first.

I can't judge. I don't know what happened or why they made the choices they did.

With the *Ulterior-2* out of the equation, there was one less thing to worry about.

000:000:00:04:22

"Lieutenant McKinney, it won't be long."

"Yes, sir."

The *Devastator*'s battle computer kept up the barrage against the Vraxar. The fast-reload on the Lambdas hurled the missiles out with only a few seconds interval between each. The Shimmers reloaded more slowly, but each launch delivered a massive blow against the target.

A fourth Vraxar ship crumbled beneath the onslaught of missile and particle beams. Its captain tried to ram the *Devastator* in one last act of defiance. Blake pulled the control rods to the side, bringing the Hadron away from the approaching vessel. It was a close-run thing and the Vraxar cruiser impacted with the wall of the coil at high speed.

"They don't care how much damage they do to *Ix-Gastiol*," said Bannerman.

"What else can they do?" asked Blake. "They have to knock us out, whatever it takes."

The *Devastator*'s Obsidiar cores gave up their last reserves and the energy shield faded. Several Vraxar particle beams struck the battleship's upper section. The armour was designed to spread the heat, but there was no way it could handle so much at once. White-hot slabs of liquid alloy slid away from the Hadron and splashed onto the floor.

With the energy shield gone, there was a chance the enemy would land a particle beam hit on the shuttle bay area. It would need a good angle to get far enough inside to wipe out Shuttle Three, but it was an unwelcome development.

000:000:00:02:38

"I'm going to turn us," said Blake. "I'll try and keep the bay entrance close to the wall."

It was easy enough to pull off, even under fire. He rotated the *Devastator* 180 degrees and flew it sideways until it was less than two hundred metres from the side wall, halfway up and halfway along the coil. More particle beams struck them and a row of amber alerts became red. It was going to be touch and go.

"Bad news, sir," said Bannerman. "Another enemy ship has just come through the portal. This is a big one."

The battle computer was far quicker at evaluating raw data than the human brain. It placed the new arrival at the top of the priorities list and unleashed everything it had.

"They sent a battleship," said Blake.

The new spaceship sailed through the portal. On and on it came. It dwarfed the *ES Devastator* and Blake had no doubt the Hadron was outmatched, with or without the other five cruisers still in the coil. The *Devastator* fired its overcharged particle beams, lighting up four thousand metres of the enemy hull.

000:000:00:01:47

"Lieutenant McKinney, please launch the shuttle. Guide it close to the walls – I'll try and keep the *Devastator* in front of it until we depart."

"Yes, sir. I'm activating the shuttle's autopilot."

The enemy sensed a kill and they fired time and again into the *ES Devastator*. The Hadron's battle computer fired in return, focusing its attacks on the nine-thousand-metre battleship.

"Sir, I don't know if this is significant, but one of our missiles just went through the portal."

Blake jerked around. "Are you sure?"

"Absolutely, sir."

This was enormously significant and Blake was furious he hadn't thought of it earlier. Not for a moment had he imagined it was possible to send objects through the portal from this side.

000:000:00:01:05

"Lieutenant McKinney, has the shuttle launched?"

"It is leaving the bay at this exact moment."

Blake's mind whirled with possibilities and opportunities.

"Damnit, can you give it a new destination?"

McKinney sounded stunned. "It'll need a few seconds. Where to?"

000:000:00:00:51

It was too much to handle this late in the engagement. Blake was confronted by an impossible choice – to go for the ultimate prize or accept what would have seemed an unimaginable victory only a few short hours ago.

There was more – Blake realised where the *Ulterior-2* had gone. The crew hadn't run away to safety. In fact, they'd sacrificed everything in the pursuit of the most valuable resource available – intel on the biggest Vraxar asset. They'd taken the *Ulterior-2* through the portal to gather what they could find on the Aranol.

"Sir? What is the new destination?"

Blake opened his mouth, frozen by indecision.

000:000:00:00:27

The ES *Devastator* was in a bad way. The Vraxar battleship was well-alight, but many of its beam domes still functioned. It also had a front-mounted disintegration turret, from which came a high-powered jet of dark energy. The front end of the Hadron simply crumbled under the attack and a billion tonnes of plating and engines turned to grey dust.

"Lieutenant McKinney, there is no new destination. Shuttle Three will remain in place."

"Yes, sir."

The *Devastator* was built tough and it continued trading blows. Its missile volleys were more sporadic and three of the overcharge domes were burned out by the enemy attacks. Right in the centre of the Hadron, in the place mathematically determined to have the lowest possibility of suffering damage, the Obsidiar processing clusters remained at 100%, with short-range transits loaded up on eight of the cores.

000:000:00:00:12

"I'm keying in new coordinates, Corporal Bannerman. I'm sure you won't mind if I take charge for this particular stage of the mission."

On the side sensor feed, Shuttle Three hovered in the air. The Obsidiar bomb was clamped to the rear and the weight of it was far more than the shuttle was designed to carry. It wobbled unsteadily and Blake imagined its engines would shortly burn out with the stress.

With his heart thumping against the inside of his ribcage, Blake moved his finger closer towards the SRT activation pad.

000:000:00:00:03

He left it until the final second before he sent the ES *Devastator* into lightspeed. In its wake, already several million kilometres distant, Falsehood exploded, expanding until its blast sphere was 700 percent greater than the predicted median. *Ix-Gastiol*'s energy shield resisted the force of the detonation for an amount of time too short to register with any known instrument. It didn't matter either way – the Obsidiar bomb was within, rather than without and the Vraxar warship was completely and utterly unmade, along with the thousands of spaceships clamped to whatever the original shape was beneath.

Blake didn't bear witness – Space Corps sensors didn't function normally during lightspeed travel and they were unable to record the event. Even so, he knew that he and every other participant in the mission had succeeded. When he closed his eyes, he could picture the allied fleet as it had once been, prior to its engagement with the enemy. The obliteration of their bodies by the irresistible power of the Falsehood bomb seemed to him like a fitting end.

Death Is A Lie. Life Is Truth, he thought, remembering the words on the nameplate. There was a meaning there he couldn't entirely understand. Perhaps it wasn't important.

The *ES Devastator* flew on and Blake's mind couldn't let go of the two pieces of unfinished business from this terrible conflict. His crew was missing and somewhere, the Aranol waited.

———

Follow Anthony James on Facebook at
facebook.com/AnthonyJamesAuthor

ALSO BY ANTHONY JAMES

The Survival Wars series

1. Crimson Tempest

2. Bane of Worlds

3. Chains of Duty

4. Fires of Oblivion

5. Terminus Gate

6. Guns of the Valpian

7. Mission: Nemesis

The Obsidiar Fleet series

1. Negation Force

2. Inferno Sphere

3. God Ship

4. Earth's Fury

5. Suns of the Aranol

Printed in Great Britain
by Amazon